P9-BJR-856

Nonfiction Books by
Steven T. Collis

Deep Conviction:
True Stories of Ordinary Americans
Fighting for the Freedom to Live Their Beliefs

The Immortals:
The World War II Story of
Five Fearless Heroes, the Sinking of the Dorchester,
and an Awe-Inspiring Rescue

PRAYING
WITH THE
ENEMY

STEVEN T. COLLIS

SHADOW
MOUNTAIN
PUBLISHING

Illustration on page i: Pngtree.com
Photographs on pages 301, 302, and 303 courtesy Ward Millar Family.

© 2022 Steven T. Collis

All rights reserved. No part of this book may be reproduced in any form or by any means without permission in writing from the publisher, Shadow Mountain Publishing®, at permissions@shadowmountain.com. The views expressed herein are the responsibility of the author and do not necessarily represent the position of Shadow Mountain Publishing.

This is a work of fiction. Characters and events in this book are products of the author's imagination or are represented fictitiously.

Visit us at shadowmountain.com

Library of Congress Cataloging-in-Publication Data
CIP on file
ISBN: 978-1-62972-994-7

Printed in the United States of America
Lake Book Manufacturing Inc., Melrose Park, IL

10   9   8   7   6   5   4   3   2   1

For Reid and Darryle,
who never stop giving

CHAPTER 1

Captain Ward Millar soared 22,000 feet above the Korean War. He was tired of this place.

He was tired of putting his life in danger because the Communists felt the need to invade every free country in the world—if their ideas were so great, why didn't they just let them spread of their own brilliance rather than forcing them down the world's throat like a pathetic bully? He was tired of cramming into the cockpit of his Lockheed F-80 Shooting Star for bombing missions—now for the thirtieth time—and dodging flak and enemy fire. He was tired of knowing he needed to do it seventy more times before military policy would rotate him back to the states (one hundred missions was the magic number). He was tired of his promotion to operations officer, which sounded flattering but meant he had to do more paperwork and fewer missions, which only prolonged how long he had to stay in the war. He was tired of the Korean weather, which was hot and humid as a sauna one minute and producing torrential downpours the next—all of which also slowed down how long it would take him to finish his hundred flights. He was tired of the yessirs and the code words and the intelligence briefings and the boredom trailed by near-death exhilaration, as if military culture were trying to do to him what the Communists couldn't.

Most of all, he was tired of being away from Barbara and their life in Oregon. He was a veteran of the Army Air Forces in World War II, studying nuclear physics at Reed College in Oregon. Life had seemed bright. He and his beautiful, faithful, feisty bride had just welcomed their little girl, Adrian, into the world. Because they had no money, he had joined the Portland Air Force Reserve Unit. And why not? The war to end all wars was behind them. At the time, the Korean peninsula was still one country. Yes, after World War II, the Russians had taken over the North and pushed it toward Communism, and the United States had taken control of the South and turned it toward free markets. But it was still one country. Then the Communists decided to invade their free kin to the south. If they couldn't win the ideological battle with ideas, they would force the capitalists out with brute force.

So, the U.S. military mobilized to defend the South, and Ward got the call to fight in another war. Instead of watching little Adrian toddle around the house, try to form words, or finger whatever piece of discarded food she could find on the floor, he was rocketing over a Florida-sized peninsula of misery. He'd managed to get training as a jet pilot while in theater, which was better than flying cargo planes, but that was hardly a great consolation prize.

He radioed the tower for the all clear.

The response crackled back. "Proceed. Weather over target spotty. Expect worse on return."

Bad weather—that would make the run even more dangerous. Ward was already feeling the familiar tinge of anxiety in his gut. As much as he wanted to get these missions behind him, he still couldn't shake the danger they posed. Memories of his previous twenty-nine runs rumbled inside him—the area they were targeting was under heavy protection; the enemy flak had become increasingly dense. Spotty clouds would make hitting the target and escaping even more dangerous.

He scanned his fuel gauge, then thought of the other three pilots on this run with him. If the weather slowed them down even a little, or made landing difficult, they would need extra fuel to stay in the air. He did the math in his head—barring something unforeseen, they should be fine. Beneath him, the United Nations–controlled territory blurred past, increasingly hidden by clouds.

Ward noted the topography. In minutes, they would soar over Seoul, then across enemy lines.

He clicked on his radio again and called up the Joint Operations Center. By that point in the war, pilots making bombing runs always checked in prior to a run to determine if any troops on the front lines needed emergency assistance. If so, the fighter jets would be rerouted to help.

Joint Operations Center—which went by the codename "Snowflake," something Ward always found ridiculous—responded that no one on the front lines needed support.

Ward breathed out his pent-up relief. Their original mission was straightforward in his mind. Earlier in the day, he and the rest of the squadron had attended an intelligence briefing. They learned that North Korean and Chinese troops had formed a camp due north from Seoul, thirty miles behind enemy lines. Ward and the three other pilots were to cut north to that camp, blast it with napalm, and then fly back to their base at Taegu on the southern tip of the peninsula. It was simple enough. But if they'd been called to assist in a full-blown combat situation, that would have been a game changer.

It was time to proceed. Ward locked in and led the three other pilots into enemy airspace.

In no time, they roared over the front lines. The four jets were so high at this point, Ward didn't worry about any of the North

Korean or Chinese armies attacking them. They were out of range, and, in any event, they were well above the cloud line—the overcast sky gave them plenty of cover. Soon they were over the rugged terrain of the North, and the clouds broke enough to reveal the topography: hills and valleys pocked by various evergreens and shrubs, interrupted occasionally by villages and corn and rice fields. It was a shame; if not for the war, the land could be as beautiful as Ward's native California.

When the jets passed over the bomb line—the designated point at which the pilots could drop their weaponry without worrying about striking their own troops—Ward banked in the direction of their target, knowing the others would follow his lead. He scanned the land beneath them, hoping to spy the confluence of two rivers; the enemy bivouac was right near there.

Finally, as the clouds broke completely, he identified it. It was exactly what he had expected to see: an enemy camp, tents, makeshift buildings, trucks, supplies. Ward didn't hesitate.

"Check armament switches," he radioed the other pilots. They were engaged in massive acts—blowing up bridges and tanks and trains and enemy staging areas—but it was the little details that made all the difference, and Ward knew it. Prior to crossing the bomb line, pilots kept their gun switches off, to ensure they didn't fire on their own men. Sometimes they forgot to rearm them, which would be disastrous. Ward's order served as a reminder, but it also signaled that the time for the attack had come.

In his cockpit, Ward switched the napalm toggle switch from SAFE to DROP. He knew the other fighters were doing the same. That had two effects: it prepared the napalm tanks under each of his wings to drop the moment Ward pressed the "bomb release" button on his control stick, but it also armed a grenade inside the napalm tank so that it would explode when it hit the ground. The combination on the enemy was devastating. The napalm was gasoline in jellied form that would slime everything it touched; when the armed grenade blew, the jelly coating would burst into flames. Ward's napalm tanks were now hot, his guns ready. He began his descent. His wingmen followed suit. The lengthy, steady drop brought the enemy target closer and closer. No one had fired on them yet.

Ward watched his speed. He didn't want to surpass five hundred miles an hour, or the wind resistance would rip the napalm tanks off his wings, and the entire flight would be for nothing. Even worse, the napalm might hit the wrong target: U.S. troops, a village of civilians, potentially even another jet.

At two hundred feet off the ground, Ward felt he was in range for his guns. He pulled the trigger on his stick. The nose of his jet roared fire and metal. The ground in front of him popped with the flashes of his bullets. The attack had been everything he'd hoped for: a total surprise.

Chinese soldiers scurried, running like disturbed ants in search of cover. In another life, Ward would have been troubled about firing on his fellow humans; he didn't enjoy combat or destruction. But this was this life—these men had forced this war, had begged for it by invading their neighbors. Who invades their neighbors? And if they wanted it to end, all they needed to do, in Ward's view, was back off. Go back to their homes, instead of forcing thousands of innocent civilian men, women, and children to flee from Communist attempts to enslave them.

After his initial attack, Ward pulled up on his stick, easing his dive and flattening his path so he would pass over the camp just above the rooftops. So far, the Communist soldiers had yet to gather their wits enough to fire off even one defensive shot. This would be as smooth as any mission Ward could have hoped for. One step closer to Barbara and Adrian. When he was over the camp, he pressed the button on his control stick to release the napalm, then immediately began his ascent. His jet peeled up and away from the earth. He was confident. All four planes would have dropped the fiery jelly. Most likely they had achieved their goal with maximum destruction to enemy supplies but limited casualties among the soldiers. The Chinese camp and its equipment would be burning in fiery goo, and he would be back at his own base in time for dinner.

Just then, his radio crackled. It was his wingman. "Your napalm didn't release! Either tank."

Ward twisted in the cockpit and surveyed his wings. Both tanks, with live grenades in each, still clung to their undersides like stubborn cicadas. Ward snapped quickly to his toggle switch, worried he may have forgotten to flick it to DROP. But he hadn't. The bombs simply hadn't released properly. As often happened for him in tense moments, time seemed to slow, and in less than a few seconds, his mind processed a myriad of possibilities—perhaps the malfunction was in the toggle switch itself, in which case the grenades had never been activated and everything was fine. On the other hand, if the grenades were live, ready to detonate with any sort of impact, he was now flying with two live and very explosive tanks on each of his wings. He could imagine what would happen at landing if either of those tanks bumped loose from their perch; his plane, his hopes of seeing Barbara again, the runway—all would vanish in a ball of fire.

Ward needed to make a quick decision. The three other pilots had climbed alongside him and were now flying in formation. For the time being, the enemy hadn't recovered enough from the confusion to fire back on them.

Ward clicked on his radio. He ordered the other pilots to circle while he made a run at another target. He spied something to the west, another enemy encampment that he knew was far enough away from U.S. troops that he didn't need to worry about hitting his own soldiers. He banked. The other F-80s began to circle. The opportunity for a slow, steady drop had come and gone. Ward needed to act fast. He dove, squeezed the trigger on his Browning .50

calibers to give himself some cover, toggled his tanks to drop, and, as he blazed over the camp, pushed the release button twice. Even as he soared back into the sky, he knew it had been a failure.

The other pilots joined him again. Time was running out. If they didn't return to K-2 soon, they would run out of fuel before they could make it back.

In that moment where time seemed to slow to a crawl, Ward's mind did what it always did: it started calculating, dancing through probabilities. Life was one big mathematical problem, and with enough thought, with enough careful calculations, if he understood all the variables, there wasn't a problem he couldn't solve through rational thought . . . he could always compute the next correct step in the formula. Barbara, he couldn't help but acknowledge, would have taken a different approach. She was certainly capable of all the calculations, and definitely willing to make them as appropriate, but she would have added to the cold-hard science an element of prayer and faith that Ward himself simply couldn't muster. For all they had in common—same taste in movies, music, books, and sports—religion was one gulf they simply couldn't cross. She was devout, for starters, a rose-cheeked Catholic schoolgirl from Portland with a faith so unalloyed that Ward had actually seen her tear up during Mass—a ceremony in Latin she couldn't possibly have understood. In Ward's view, God, if he, she, or it actually existed, had set in motion this beautifully organized world, and the prayers of one insignificant pilot weren't going to cause that deity to change a thing about the grand design. If it was Ward Millar's time to leave this world, so be it.

That meant he had only those options his calculations left him. And by his estimation, he had only one last possibility. He radioed again for the other pilots to keep circling, identified another potential target, then dove. Only one thought consumed him: the prospect that the napalm tanks would explode upon landing. He had to ditch them. Again, he fired his guns to stave off the enemy. Somehow, they had yet to reorganize enough to retaliate.

Then, rather than relying on the release button on his control stick, he reached for the end of a cable that ran along each wing. That cable was the one controlling the bomb release. If he could yank it manually, the bombs should drop. As his plane leveled out over the third target, he jerked and pulled on the cable . . . nothing. It was stuck, barely responding. He pulled up. During his ascent, he continued to wrench on the cable. It wouldn't budge.

High in the air, the other planes joined him. They had no choice at this point; the time had come to return, or all four planes would be at risk of not having enough fuel to make it back. While they banked back toward the south, Ward kept his head down in the cockpit, focused on the manual release cable. It was his only hope; he needed to release the tanks before the squadron passed back across the bomb line.

The details, Ward thought as he cursed the cable. The details matter—someone, somewhere had failed to engineer this right, and now his life was in jeopardy. Suddenly, the cable yanked free. Ward enjoyed less than a second of satisfaction before his world began to spiral. His left napalm tank ripped free from its wing and plummeted to the earth. But the right tank refused to budge. With one side lighter than the other, the plane's aerodynamics fell out of balance. The right wing plunged. Ward was flying sideways. To correct, he forced his control stick to the left, hoping he could stabilize the jet before he lost control completely.

Under normal circumstances the stick was easy to maneuver, just like those new power steering wheels Ward had seen in the fancy cars he and Barbara could never afford. But this time, the stick moved as if Ward were stirring it through a vat of glue. He realized that the hydraulic line for a key component of his wings had failed.

He forced the stick as hard as he could to adjust for the imbalanced wings and managed to stabilize.

Then his radio sputtered again. "There's a long stream of vapor coming from your tail pipe," one of his wingmen yelled.

Ward started to shout that it had to be the hydraulic fluid, and then—

"You're on fire! Get out of that thing!" A second wingman's screaming voice crackled over the radio. "You've got flames thirty to forty feet comin' out the tail!"

Ward's wingmen were seasoned. He'd flown with them before. They weren't ones to panic, Ward thought. They were realists. And that meant he was about to die.

But how long would it take him to glide back to friendly territory? For a brief moment, a flash in time, Ward considered the possibility that he might be able to make it. After all, he could fly from the southern part of the peninsula up to the North in less than thirty minutes. It couldn't take that long to get over his own troops so that ejecting wouldn't subject him to enemy capture.

Ward wiped away the temptation as quickly as it came. Just a week earlier, another pilot had been in similar circumstances. He had opted to shut down his engine and glide until he could safely eject over United Nations troops. His entire plane exploded before he even had a chance to get out. In the debriefing after the incident, the pilots, led by Ward, had all agreed on proper procedures going forward: if a jet caught on fire, the pilot was to eject immediately.

"Roger," Ward called into his radio. "I'm bailing." He reached to his side. Next to his seat was a red T-handle—it would eject the glass canopy off the plane. Ward reached for it.

"Let's get on the emergency channel and get help," one of the other pilots yelled into the radio.

Ward yanked on the handle. Nothing happened. Of course, he thought.

The canopy didn't even budge. With it in place, Ward could do nothing; the ejection seat would launch only after the canopy had been blown free. For the first time, panic started to bubble inside him. It seemed everything that could go wrong on this mission was going wrong. He released his grip on the control stick and grasped the T-handle with both hands. Then he jerked it with all the strength he could muster. It tore away from the sidewall of the plane, and as soon as it did, the canopy ripped away, as if the atmosphere had batted it off the plane.

Ward was four thousand feet above the earth, blazing through the sky at four hundred miles per hour. As soon as the canopy stripped away from the jet, the gushing wind blasted him like a fire hose. It blew his helmet and oxygen mask off his head. Its roar blocked out any other sound, including the radio. Everything not bolted down in the cockpit—maps, papers, pen—hurled out of the plane and into the air. Because Ward had released his grip on the control stick, the jet lurched right again, pulled by the weight of the stubborn napalm tank. It started a lazy roll, the first step before spiraling out of control. Soon, he would be upside down and spinning, and any hope of ejecting would vanish.

Ward, trying to focus against the rush and pressure of the airstream, latched onto the stick and tried to level out. His finger accidentally hit the trigger for his .50 calibers, and bright blasts arced into the distance. Fighting against the stubbornness of the hydraulics-failed stick, he bullied the plane upright again.

As soon as he had the jet stabilized, he folded up the armrests of the seat, positioned his feet in the stirrups designed for ejecting, pushed himself into the backrest, then reached down and hit the trigger. Given all that had happened—all those failed details on this mission—he half assumed it wouldn't work.

A stunning detonation underneath him followed, so powerful it might have blown his legs clean off had anything gone wrong.

He was still strapped to his chair; everything went black. His last thought: a pilot a week earlier had blacked out and failed to get out of his seat after ejecting, which meant he couldn't deploy his parachute. The man had died.

CHAPTER 2

Kim Jae Pil didn't know why God had allowed him to languish in this camp, in this godless army. But he knew it must be for a reason.

As long as Jae Pil could remember, he had been certain that God would turn the suffering of His children to His purposes, and for their good. Now that he thought on it, he realized it wasn't an in-born faith necessarily, but a lesson passed down from his ancestors. He had always seen it in the unlikeliest of places: in his own people, after the Japanese colonized his country and tried to strip from the Koreans all things Korean—their language, names, buildings, religion, women, books, and shrines; in his father, and his grandfather before him, who had converted to Christianity in the late 1800s, and had paid a severe price for using the church to resist Japanese rule; in the growl of his own stomach when the lack of food during the Japanese occupation reduced his family to eating whatever plants and weeds they could grow on the hillside near their family hut. "Grandson," his grandfather had told him when he complained of the hunger. "Grandson. Don't you know? God will turn this to your good; just believe."

And Jae Pil did believe. He kept on believing. When the great world war ended with the United States crushing the Japanese and booting them back across the ocean forever, he believed. When the Americans and the Soviets divided his country in half, north and south, and tried to rebuild it in their images, he believed. When the Communists took over the North and his home province, arguing they had a better vision than the American capitalists, he believed. When those same Communists consolidated power and opened fire with their Russian-made rifles, slaughtering two dozen of Jae Pil's schoolmates in Sinuiju and injuring hundreds more, he believed. When the Communists started coming after Christians—imprisoning and killing them—because they were perceived as a threat to the new socialist order, he believed. When he was severed from his father, mother, and sister and sent to prison because of his alignment with Christians, he believed; and when he was finally forced into the Communist army so they could invade the South, he believed.

God, he told himself, would find a purpose in all of this. And, somehow, God would help him escape this army. *Jae Pil,* a voice in his mind had always whispered, a constant presence. *Jae Pil. Patience. Just wait.*

So he did. He was squatting next to his truck, for his role in the army of Supreme Leader Kim Il-Sung was to drive a truck and ship supplies and weapons and food to soldiers across the battlefronts. He watched the village where his unit was currently stationed, and he waited for an opportunity to slip away. God would provide it. Of course, Jae Pil recognized, God worked in all sorts of mysterious ways, and one way He might save Jae Pil from this forced conscription might be to take him away from earth altogether.

Would that be so bad? When he considered the ache in his stomach and his bones, the fact that his family was likely already dead, the way the war had destroyed vast swaths of his homeland already, he didn't think it would be so devastating to be called home.

But he also felt, deep in the innermost part of his being, that he needed to find his family, that his escape would not just be away from the army but back to his ancestral home, where they would be doing what they had always done: father working in the small field behind their hut, mother and sister drying peppers and preparing kimchi, grandfather squatting by the front door so he could preach to whoever happened to pass by. *Just believe,* the voice said.

He continued to believe even when he heard the whir of distant airplanes. Jets. American fighters. Like everyone else in his unit, he had become accustomed to the sound, trained like an animal who knows to run anytime he hears his abusive master open a gate. He leaped to his feet and scanned the skies.

This place was like so many others scattered across the mountains of Korea: a few huts made of wood, some buildings made from concrete and brick, rice and corn fields nearby. The villagers, now mostly just women, children, the elderly, and the invalid (for the Communists had forced everyone else to fight), seemed almost oblivious to the fire and thunder that might be coming their way.

Jae Pil blocked the blaring sun with his hand and watched the skies. Were they surveillance, or soaring in for an attack? He spun around, as if trying to follow a pesky gnat. All around him the other men in his unit did the same. "Where?" one of them yelled.

"Don't know," another said.

"Hurry! Run!" someone screamed.

Everyone scattered. The other two truck drivers sprung into the driver's seats of their vehicles and fired them to life. A group of men had been gathering supplies in crates next to a small house at the end of the path: food, some clothing, weapons they had salvaged from a battle that had occurred a few days before. Now soldiers scrambled to cover the crates—if this looked like a supply site to the Americans, they would surely attack. If it looked just like a simple village, they would pass over.

Jae Pil jumped into his truck and roared it up. The engine growled and churned. He tried to force it into gear, but it fought him, almost as if it didn't want to be saved. He had seen, on their way into the village, a grove of camphor trees that would hide the truck nicely. If he could get there, the Americans would be less likely to think they'd found a fruitful target. Finally, after a sickening grind, the truck lurched backward. Through the mud-flecked windshield, Jae Pil spied soldiers scurrying in every direction.

Women with babies clutched to their chests or strapped to their backs fled out of the huts and into the hills beyond.

Jae Pil's truck skidded to a stop; he shifted gears again, then punched it forward. It was like driving a giant green tortoise for how fast it moved, but he managed to build speed toward the trees. He was certain he would make it.

Then another truck appeared from the side, from behind a cinderblock wall that had once been part of some building the village had long since stopped using.

Jae Pil had fast reflexes, but all the agility in the world couldn't stop the two trucks from colliding. The other vehicle smashed into Jae Pil's front left fender.

Jae Pil raised his hands to stop his head from crashing into his steering wheel, but he lost control of the truck. His forehead still smacked against his own arms. He would never be able to re-create the sequence of events that happened next. He heard glass shattering and expected to feel the shards slice into his cheeks. They didn't. But something—he couldn't be sure what— knocked against the side of his head, and he toppled across the seats.

A simple accident, he told himself. The trucks would be damaged, but they could keep them operating.

Then he heard it: the boom of American jets unleashing fire and metal. In the cab of his truck, his face now pressed against the upholstery, he couldn't be sure where the bullets were hitting.

Explosions followed, and the smell of burning, choking, jellied gas.

Jae Pil covered his face and ears and clamped his eyes closed; he figured this would be the end. *Thank you, Lord, for finally releasing me from this prison.* Outside his truck, somewhere, another soldier was screaming.

His own truck seemed to lift off the ground. He endured the strange sensation that he was being pushed further into the seat, then pulled from it, then slammed into it again, almost as if someone had grabbed the crown of his head and were bashing his face into the cushion over and over. Yet it was all happening as if God himself had slowed down time.

More fire. He could smell it. Another explosion and, amidst all the chaos, what seemed to Jae Pil like the smell of cooking pork. What a strange thing to smell in the middle of this, he thought. He had been blessed to eat pork only once in his life, when he was a little boy and his grandfather had managed to finagle some from a neighboring farmer in exchange for a pot of kimchi.

The smell and the memories it invoked vanished as soon as Jae Pil realized he couldn't breathe. Smoke was choking him. His truck had rested from whatever grand flight it had decided to take, but an intense heat was creeping over his legs.

Heaven, he thought.

But heaven brought with it a searing pain. It jolted Jae Pil back into his surroundings. He opened his eyes and took stock of things. His ears were ringing. He was on his side.

Most of the windshield was gone. Just a few jagged slivers remained, like the teeth of a horrible beast waiting to chomp him in half. Smoke clouded everything and stung his eyes; his breath felt like a blanket had been stuffed down his throat. He was lying on his side, almost as if he had decided to take a nap, but his legs were sticking out the driver's side window, which they had shattered. As he looked closer he realized they were dangling out over a fire.

No, not over a fire—in it. The truck that had crashed into him was ablaze, hit directly by an American napalm attack.

He scrambled, yanking his legs back into the cab. They were still burning, the flames licking up his uniform toward his knees. He kicked at the driver side door, but it was jammed, lodged against the other truck. His efforts slid him across the bench seat, where he bashed his head into the passenger side door.

He lifted his head. There was the handle, just a centimeter from his eyes. He reached over and yanked on it, and then pushed. It swung open and allowed in a gush of fresh air that opened up his lungs like the breath of God. He sucked in the oxygen and then kicked his legs again.

He slithered out of the truck like a sack of rice and crumpled onto the dirt, then rolled and rolled again before coming to lie on his back.

Above him the clouds and wafts of smoke had parted to reveal the crystalline beauty of the sky at midday and a ray of sunlight burning through a particularly lonely cloud.

Burning, he thought. Then he remembered his legs. He crunched into a sitting position, preparing to bat out the flames. Somehow, the journey out of the truck and toppling into the dirt had snuffed out the flames. From what he could tell, his pants had burned, but not too badly.

The pain, he knew, would come later.

He forced himself to stand and take in the area. Everything burned. The collection of crates the soldiers had been stockpiling had been transformed into a column of black smoke.

His own truck was not burning, but the one behind it was creaking and moaning in a fire so grand the heat forced Jae Pil to back away and block it with his hand. Where was the other driver?

Jae Pil rounded the front of his truck, hoping to save the other man, or to see if he had also escaped the flames. But the heat was so intense, he couldn't get close enough to tell. Most likely he was dead.

Stumbling back to the central road in the village, Jae Pil noted one of the huts was now gone. Not burned. Not smoking. Just vanished, like it had never existed. In its place was a patch of black dirt in a burst pattern of an expanding star.

Jae Pil continued to spin, trying to decide what he should do next. There had been three trucks in their unit. Where was the third? He couldn't see it anywhere. Where was his commanding officer, the red-faced man with a penchant for screaming who had forced Jae Pil into this army in the first place? The man was omnipresent in Jae Pil's life. His shrill voice always there, even when Jae Pil tried to sleep or dream or fantasize of a different world. When Jae Pil thought on it, he realized, that was the man he wanted to escape.

Then he saw the opening. It appeared in an instant that expanded into an eternity.

Through all the smoke and flames, a tunnel appeared like a gift. How it held its form, Jae Pil couldn't say. But there it was, a perfect path of smoke and flame, and on the other end of it, a cornfield—undefiled, quiet, the half-grown stocks fluttering in a cool breeze like children playing.

You know what to do. Was it his grandfather's voice? God's? His own? In the end, he supposed it didn't matter. *I told you to be patient.*

The thought nudged him forward. He scanned behind and around him again. If there were people who needed his help, he couldn't see them. In fact, he was certain the villagers had escaped into the nearby hills. The rest of his unit was likely with them, or dead. He turned back to the tunnel. It was drifting as if to say, *it's now or never, this is the only path back to your family.*

But he knew what fleeing would mean if he were ever caught. He had seen what the Communists could do—the real devout ones who believed in the system with as much fervor as he believed in

God. One time a man he knew had been accused of desertion. Within minutes he was on his knees, and Jae Pil's commanding officer had fired a bullet into his head. The image would never leave Jae Pil. He could hold it at bay, but it would always be a part of him.

As would his family. The last he had seen them, they were in their home together on the side of a hill: his father, mother, sister, and grandfather—all standing stoic as the Communist officers marched Jae Pil away.

Jae Pil took one last glance around. He was alone, not a soul in sight.

Then he sprinted toward the cornfield as fast as he could without looking back, knowing that the smoke would collapse behind him, just like the Red Sea.

CHAPTER 3

At least Ward couldn't see how close he was to hitting the ground.

He had opened his eyes at some point after ejection, and all he knew was that he was still spinning through the air somewhere above the earth. Hills, sky, forests, clouds—all melded into one blurry image as he flew through space. His sense was that he still had time. There would be a moment, he knew, when physics would simply work against him, an invisible line that, once passed, could not be regained.

He focused on getting out of his chair so he could deploy his chute. The centrifugal force of his spinning pulled his arms and legs away from his body. He curled his right arm inward. It trembled as if he were moving it through mud. He managed to get his fingers on the quick release at his belt.

Gripping it seemed impossible. It felt like a legion of fiends pulling on his arms. But he finally snagged the release.

The chair ripped away from him with a tear and twirled into the sky.

He was operating on feel now, not sight. He felt along his chest until his fingers curled around the D-ring for his rip cord. He yanked it as hard as he could. The chute spewed out the back.

Immediately he jerked so hard he bounced in the harness, spun up into the chute's straps, then crashed back down again.

For the first time he had an opportunity to assess his surroundings. His mind was still jumbled, but he immediately took note of his altitude. If he had to guess, he was about five hundred feet off the ground—far too low, since he had likely bailed around four thousand feet, but hopefully the parachute would still slow him enough. Scrub-covered mountains peaked all around him, and he was gliding at a fast clip into a valley with a series of farmers' fields along its bottom. It looked almost pristine.

For just a moment, the world was as quiet as a forest after a snowfall. After all the rush of his escape, it was odd. He could take in the landscape—an endless stretch of mountain after mountain, interrupted by river-carved valleys and villages and fields. In another time, perhaps with Barbara by his side, it would have been beautiful—even breathtaking.

Then the shouting, trailed by gunfire.

And everything about his situation hit him like a slap: his plane was gone, likely already crashed into the ground; he had bailed over enemy territory; Chinese and North Korean soldiers were probably already closing in on this American floating through the sky like a gift; and his fellow pilots could offer him cover for only so long before they ran out of fuel.

The valley floor was rising fast. The shouts and small arms fire were coming from a hill to his left. He couldn't see the men, but their yells had grown more urgent.

The roar of the other jets pulled Ward's eyes to the sky above. Two of his copilots had dropped close to the valley. They were circling, just above the hills, around and around the valley. That would keep the enemy away for a time. The third jet was climbing in altitude—exactly as Ward would have guessed. The protocol was straightforward: when a pilot was shot down, one of the other three jets was to immediately climb high enough to call the Joint Operation Center and give them everything they needed to send help—what went wrong, the coordinates of the downed pilot, and how much longer the other jets could stay before their fuel demanded they leave.

In normal circumstances, it worked. The circling jets would keep the enemy at a distance while the downed pilot stayed hidden until a chopper could pick him up. But these were not normal circumstances. Given the multiple passes it had taken Ward to get rid of his napalm tanks, he knew his pilots were running out of fuel. Their time for departure was soon.

Ward scanned his memories, searching for anything he might have heard over the radio about other missions. He could think of only one, but he didn't know what type of planes they were using. If they were modern jets, they could get to him in less than half an hour and continue to protect him from enemy troops until a helicopter could soar in and rescue him. But if they were the older prop planes, he would have to survive on his own for much longer.

Either way, he would need to hold out on the ground long enough for his people to save him.

It wouldn't be easy. All their training, all the intel, told them that chances of survival if captured were close to zero.

Ordinarily, Ward didn't like to dwell on the negatives in life, on the potential for failure—he found it counterproductive. Perhaps that was one thing he and Barbara did have in common. She approached things with faith, and that allowed her to escape the pessimism that plagued so many. Ward reached the same destination but took a different path; for him, focusing on potential failure was just a waste of time and effort. Still, his mind couldn't help but go there now. This wasn't Europe in World War II—a white American couldn't just blend into the crowd. The only people on the ground were Chinese and Korean soldiers and civilians. He would stick out like a flare in the night sky.

And the Communists did not take prisoners. During the previous winter, they had murdered nearly all the American POWs they had captured. There was another problem for Ward too: he was a pilot. It was one thing to be an infantryman on the ground; you could do only so much damage. But Ward and his fellow pilots had caused most of the harm to the enemy. If there was anyone the other side would summarily execute, it was a pilot.

Ward reached into his survival vest and yanked his M1911 .45 pistol from its shoulder holster. It was covered in plastic. He tore that away and tossed it into the wind.

Then he noticed something—something so strange it almost couldn't have been true. Yet there it was: both of his feet were bent at the strangest angles, askew at the ankles in a way no feet should ever be. The ejection explosion must have broken them. Why wasn't he feeling the pain? Shouldn't they hurt?

He didn't have time to think about it. Twenty feet now—touchdown time. Ten feet.

He clutched the .45 to his chest. Out of instinct, he tucked his legs under him so his broken ankles wouldn't crunch into the ground. Then both his knees crashed into the soil of an empty field with a thud like a rock. He immediately toppled face-first into the dirt and tried to catch himself.

The parachute didn't pause. It shot past him, and he felt the straps yank his body. Then he was tumbling in a blur of dirt and dust. His only thoughts: don't drop the .45, and get the stupid harness off. With one hand clinging to the pistol, he struck the harness's quick release with the other.

The parachute and everything attached to it released from his body. As quickly as he had hit the ground, he was now lying still on his back.

His ears were ringing. Although he knew he had stopped, the earth felt like it was tumbling all around him. Everything seemed to tilt and totter. So he just lay there, looking up into the mostly cloudy sky. It was a perfect place to rest. He saw a cloud that looked a bit like a dog. *Adrian likes dogs—she tries to pant like them,* he thought. He heard the roar of a jet so loud it felt like an earthquake. A second thought followed the first: *I want to see Adrian do that again; I have to get out of here.*

He lifted his head. His parachute had billowed across the field and come to rest among some of the plowed rows a hundred feet away. One of the jets was making another pass, barely off the ground—giving him the cover he needed.

Ward waved. His time was running out. In a manner of minutes, those jets would have to start their return trip.

He scanned the mountainsides. Wherever the enemy soldiers were shouting and shooting, he couldn't see them, but he could hear them. He needed cover. And fast. Not only would they be searching for him as soon as the jets left, but if they were snipers, they might just pick him off from the safety of wherever they were hiding.

He examined the field. With no crops growing and no trees, this wasn't exactly the best place in the world to disappear. About fifty feet away, a small stream meandered through the field. Some meager bushes fought for its water along the banks; they weren't much, but given the probability of successfully hiding anywhere else, it seemed to be his best option.

But . . . his ankles. What in the name of—

Each of his feet were bent backward, like some God-child had been putting him together the wrong way during playtime. They still didn't hurt, and, for just a moment, he thought he might even be able to walk. Shock, he realized a second later. The pain would come soon enough.

He rotated onto his stomach. When he swung his legs over, his feet flopped, as if he were made of nothing more than gel, and he heard a distinct grating sound, particles of bone crunching against one another. He thought of an article he had read some years before where a man in a car wreck had died because a piece of bone had chipped free from his broken legs, floated into his bloodstream, then lodged in his heart.

But the alternative was Chinese snipers.

He'd take his chances with his own body. Staying on his stomach, as low to the ground as possible, he crawled like an inchworm toward the creek and the cover of the bushes. Every time he pushed with his knees, he heard his bones grinding.

The heat and humidity started taking their toll immediately. He hadn't noticed either until now, but within a minute of slithering to the embankment, beads of sweat started pouring down his forehead. He felt like he was breathing with his head submerged in a toilet; the air might as well have been water it was so thick, and the dirt in the field smelled like feces.

Finally, he reached the bank of the stream and slid down its slick sides into the water, which was only about half a foot deep. Though it stunk just as badly as the mud in the field, at least it felt cool on his face and body. He rested for just a second, then a thought came as clearly to his mind as if it were written there. *Get as far away from the parachute as you can.*

He rotated into the center of the creek, where there were enough bushes to swallow him up, or at least not make his location so obvious. He thought he might be able to slink downstream across the stones and pebbles like a fish flopping in shallow water, and the flow would cover his trail. No doubt his path across the field to the stream would be obvious, but from there, he figured he had a fifty-fifty chance the Communists would chase him the wrong direction along the stream. And by the time they realized he'd gone the other way, maybe he would have bought himself enough time. All he had to do was hide long enough for the chopper to get to him. He didn't bother looking up, but he could tell from the sounds that two of the jets had already left. Only one, with perhaps just a bit more fuel than the others, was hanging around as long as it could. But once it left . . .

Ward pushed the thought away. He focused on the banks of the creek. There had to be a bush or pool of water that would hide him until the rescue team arrived.

Ward froze. Since he was crawling downstream, the water flowed away from his face, and he noticed something that made him panic. The liquid all around him had turned a bright yellowish green. He dared a glance over his shoulder. Nothing. Then he realized he was still wearing his Mae West life preserver. It was bright yellow, which was fantastic if he wanted the rescue team to see him, or if he had ditched over the ocean and needed to be spotted amidst the waves and the sharks. Right now, it made him an easy target. And the vest came with a dye packet, which, again, if he were in the ocean, would be extremely helpful—he could have broken it open and the dye would color the saltwater all around him so rescue ships could find him easily. Right now, all it was doing was marking his precise location for the Communists.

He swore under his breath.

As much as he wanted the vest when the chopper came, he couldn't risk being seen now. The bright yellow was just too much. He started to take the vest off, then noticed, just a few yards up the stream, something he never thought he would see again: his brown leather jacket. When he had ejected, it had been blown from the plane. Somehow, it had landed here, right to where he was crawling. He stopped fiddling with his Mae West and instead dragged himself to the jacket. This will do, he thought; it would cover him while he hid, and when the choppers came, he would fling it off so they could spot him. Perfect. Now the hiding spot.

The last jet whined away. He was alone. His clock had run out. And as soon as the skies grew silent, the shouts of soldiers filled the void. They were coming. And they were close—much closer than he had thought.

He dragged himself with his arms as fast as he could. They were trembling with exhaustion; his elbows, where they jabbed into the pebbled streambed, felt bruised to the bone; and he was finally starting to feel the broken bones in his ankles. Each movement caused a wave of pain up his legs. He craned his neck for a hiding place.

He saw it, a dozen feet away. Beside a decent pool, a small bush hung over the creek and cast a shadow onto the pool's placid surface.

The shouts were close. Angry, halting words in Chinese.

He slithered into the pool and rotated onto his back. He drew the leather jacket over his Mae West, hoping it would blend in with the mud of the bank. The bush and the pooled water mostly covered him, but the toes of his boots jutted out of the surface. There was nothing he could do about that. For just a moment, he flashed back to his childhood. His parents had raised his brother and him on a rural homestead in California. There was land all around them, including a creek just like this one. He and his brother would play hide-and-seek in it; when one found the other, they would pretend to shoot each other with their toy cap guns. Ward even remembered hiding just like this, in a small pool, hoping his brother wouldn't find him.

But these men weren't his brother. And the gun in his hand wasn't a cap gun. He positioned the .45 across his chest, pointed it in the direction of the searching soldiers, and lined the sight up with the stream.

CHAPTER 4

Jae Pil darted from tree to bush in a crouch, putting more distance between himself and his unit. The air was hot and muggy. He paused against a trunk and let himself get his bearings.

He should have been afraid, but he wasn't. His former unit no longer felt like a threat. The men he'd served with were, like him, forced into the army, trained to fight for a cause and a man they barely believed in. They were as children, without thoughts of their own. If any of them had survived the Americans' air raid, they wouldn't care about catching Jae Pil. And even if they did, what were they except flesh and bone and blood and sinew? After the miraculous escape he had experienced two days prior, a literal parting of reality so he could walk away unnoticed, how could anyone scare him now? Plus, he was sure almost all of them thought him dead, burned to a crisp in his truck.

Still, Jae Pil felt he needed to be cautious. His faith, taught by his father and grandfather, was a practical one. God might part the sea, but He wasn't going to keep the walls of water at bay forever for someone who refused to march through quickly.

He peeked around the gnarled tree and surveyed the landscape. The sun would set soon, and then everything would be cloaked in darkness. After two days of hiking, his village was just over the next rise. People would recognize him, of course—they had lived there together since he was a baby. But would they care? He still wore his military uniform, which was a problem, but if he had to guess, the other families in his village would just assume he had returned with permission. He closed his eyes. Lord, help me go unnoticed.

Once nightfall descended, he was moving through the trees again. Despite all that had happened to him, notwithstanding the Communists that might actually be hunting him, a feeling like happiness was coursing through him—a heart-pumping, tingling, emanating energy, more powerful and full-bodied than anything he had felt in years. He figured it was the by-product of finally returning to the place where his family was, the home of his ancestors.

He came to a break in the trees. His little village lay before him. A road to the left descended sharply. A series of small homes dotted the mountain, their insides glowing. From far below, in between several of the houses, the stream trickled. He could see no Communist trucks or tanks. No sentries walked among the houses, although that would have been unlikely, since this wasn't a village in the traditional sense, with a square or central area. Jae Pil's ancestors, along with those of all the other families in the area, had settled here before any could remember. Those ancestors were now buried on the mountain opposite where Jae Pil stood. Each had taken a small portion of the mountain, built a shelter, then found a way to grow the crops they needed to survive along the hillside. Snaking trails connected the houses to each other. One road in, one road out.

Jae Pil took a moment to acknowledge his ancestors, then descended the road.

He listened and watched for any sign of the Communists: the low rumble of a truck or jeep, the idle chatter of soldiers standing watch, the prick of a cigarette glow in the dark. He detected nothing and approached his house.

There was a light on inside. It didn't appear to be electric but from a flickering lamp. That wasn't surprising. They did have electricity, but the war had knocked much of it out. He snuck to the door. It was wood, with cracks that let him see inside if he peered carefully. All he could make out was the stove and fireplace where his mother would boil water and stew at mealtimes. He pressed his fingers to the door and nudged. It was latched, locked from the inside.

"Father!" he hissed.

Nothing. He sidestepped to the window, which was covered by a thin sheet of brown oilpaper. "Father!"

Inside, someone shuffled, reached the door, fiddled with the lock. The door swung open. A gasp—it was not his father, but his mother; she had sucked in and cupped her hand over her mouth. "Jae Pil!"

"Mother!"

"Hurry!" she said. "Come!"

He stepped into the entry, tore off his boots, and gave his mother a hug. She held him for longer than he expected. Even after he tried to let go, she refused, clinging to him, her arms squeezing tightly around his neck. At first he resisted—it was not their way, this open show of affection—but then he yielded to it and embraced her back. The silence between them spoke as much as any words either might have shared. And Jae Pil knew many of those words would never be spoken. The hold would do it all.

Finally, his mother let go. "Why are you here . . . how?"

"There was . . . a way for me to come," he said. He scanned the room. Little had changed, but some of the minor adjustments spoke volumes. Their home was just two rooms. They slept in the back. In here, they did all of the cooking, eating, studying of scripture, praying, fighting, and talking. Jae Pil noted that the cross, a treasured family heirloom given to Grandfather fifty years earlier by one of the first Christian missionaries in Korea, was no longer on the wall, and the family Bible, which usually rested on a small block of wood near the fireplace, was missing as well.

Mother was alone. "Where's Father?" Jae Pil asked. He glanced to the back room, hoping that, perhaps, everyone was asleep.

She turned her eyes to the floor. "Gone. They're all gone."

"Gone? Where?"

She motioned for him to sit. He did, folding his legs underneath him on the floor. She tucked her knees under herself and sat across from him. "I prayed," she said, smiling down on him. "Oh, I prayed."

"Mother?"

"They went south, I think. If they made it. You have to go with them."

"South? Where? Why are you still here?"

"I was waiting for you," she said. "I knew you would come. I knew if I waited, and if I prayed, you would come."

"I'm not understanding," Jae Pil said. "Where did they go? Why did they leave?"

His mother adjusted herself to sit more on her rear. "The Communists wouldn't stop. They kept coming and coming. First they only wanted young men, so they could make you fight for them. When they took you to jail, we thought that would be the end. But they made you fight, yes?" She pointed at his military uniform.

Jae Pil nodded. "And I will need to change my clothes soon. Do you have something?"

"Yes," she said. "You can wear Grandfather's old clothes. He left some behind." Tears formed in her eyes, and she bowed her head. "Oh . . . I didn't know where you were."

"They took me from the jail, Mother. They trained me and told me I had to fight in the army or they would kill me. It was my only choice." It hadn't occurred to Jae Pil before that moment that his parents had never known where he was. The last they had seen of him, he had been led away from his home to prison because he was seen as a threat to Socialism. He had been part of a Christian group of students who had opposed the Communists early on, and when the Communists had seen the students as a threat and couldn't force them to disperse, they had fired on them. Jae Pil had escaped and come home, but he'd been tagged as a risk to the regime ever since, right up until he'd been thrown in jail. As far as his parents knew, he was still in prison. Or dead.

"How did you get here?" his mother asked. He gave her a brief explanation.

"They'll come for you," she said with a heavy breath.

"They think I'm dead," Jae Pil said. "I'm certain of it. No one has chased me for two days. I saw no one following me. But, Mother, where is Father? Did Sister go with him?"

His mother nodded. "The Communists kept coming," she said again. "First you. Then all the boys who could fight. It didn't matter how old they were. Then some of the men, if they were strong enough. After they had the fill for the army, we thought they were done. We thought we could go back to our lives and look for you, but then they started hunting for anyone they thought was sympathetic to the Americans. Of course, everyone knows who the Christians are. That's when we decided we had to escape to the South. Before it was too late."

"But you're still here," Jae Pill said.

Once again, she began to weep. "I knew you'd come back," she said.

"You waited?"

She nodded. "Father had to leave, but I told him you would come. He took our cross and the Bible. Sister and Grandfather too. But I told them I would wait. I would wait for you, and we would follow them. Now, the Communists leave me alone. They think my whole family is fighting in the war or dead, and I guess I'm not important enough to worry about."

"When did they leave?" Jae Pil asked. "How long ago?"

"Months."

"Have you heard from them? Did they make it?"

His mother shook her head. Once again, her emotions were clearly close to the surface. How could she know, Jae Pil realized. How could any of them know? They may have made it south and found someone to protect them, but it was just as likely they were killed along the way, either by American plane attacks or by Communists who knew they were deserting. And even if they made it across the front to the southern troops, they might have been fired upon by the south as well.

The voice in Jae Pil's head whispered, *Just believe.*

Jae Pil brushed away his doubts. There was no point in letting them drive him now anyway. "Do you know which way they went?"

His mother nodded.

"We have to follow them. We can escape together."

CHAPTER 5

One thing about studying nuclear physics: you had to do a lot of math problems. And Ward felt like he was living one now. *Ward Millar is hiding under his flight jacket in a shallow pool of water. An unknown number of Communist soldiers are approaching from an unknown distance. His .45 has seven rounds in it. A United Nations helicopter with air support will arrive in approximately twenty to forty minutes. How does Ward survive?* The good news was that Ward liked doing math problems; the world was one massive, complex question, and he enjoyed solving it one equation at a time.

His mind churned through the possible permutations. None of them ended well for him. If he pulled the trigger at the first man he saw, he would end up in a shoot-out and would certainly be dead before help showed up on the scene. He calculated that the chances of the enemy somehow missing him were close to zero. They would find him. When they did, they might just execute him on sight, so perhaps firing first was his best option. On the other hand, they hadn't sniped him when he was in the air or crawling across the field, so they might consider a downed pilot a valuable prisoner. In that case, perhaps he could delay them long enough for the cavalry to show up.

He peered down the sight of his pistol. If they fired, he would shoot back and fight 'til the end.

A number of random thoughts flew across his consciousness as he waited for whatever hand fate would deal him: Barbara and their honeymoon in Monterey; little Adrian first learning to crawl, how every time she was about to take her first move, she would giggle and fall on her face; the way he and his brother used to hunt for squirrels with their .22s when they were kids, and when they killed one, how they would take it back to the family garage and use the microscope their dad had bought them to dissect it and learn all about its innards.

What a weird thought. But it was a cherished memory.

The first Chinese soldier burst into his sights. He was an old man in a tan Chinese army uniform; in his arms, with his finger on the trigger, was a Russian PPS submachine gun. He looked twitchy and nervous, but thorough and methodical. He plodded down the center of the streambed, pausing at every rock and cranny.

Ward figured he could have blown him away where he stood. The man had no idea Ward was there. It would have been so easy. But he held his hand; he wanted this to play out.

Seconds later, the man saw him. Or, as far as Ward could tell, he saw Ward's boot toes jutting up out of the water. He screamed in Chinese—a one-syllable, halting word over and over.

Another soldier burst through the brush, this time directly across from where Ward lay. He looked like a teenager, and he was carrying the same gun as the old guy. The Russians must have provided weaponry for every able-bodied man and child on the whole worn-out peninsula. You can pull a trigger? Go kill some Americans.

The boy's eyes darted to Ward's pistol.

Ward tensed. Just a good boy—maybe only thirteen or fourteen—doing what his elders had told him. But Ward could feel the nervousness pulsing from the boy, like waves of radiation. For a brief moment, he felt a tinge of pity.

The old man muttered from the side of his mouth to the younger boy, and it seemed to have a calming effect. Ward had no idea what they were saying. He knew they were Chinese, not Korean. He had learned some Korean over the past months, so he could detect the language when he heard it. These men were definitely from China. And there was a different vibe. It was a distinction Ward hadn't appreciated before he'd been called up to serve, but the Japanese, Chinese, Koreans—each had their own unique cultures, customs, and even facial features.

As Ward watched the older soldier approach, still talking from the side of his mouth, he felt an intense anger toward the Chinese. This war should have been over. The North had attacked the South a year earlier. General MacArthur had led the UN troops in response, and they had routed the North all the way back to the deepest parts of their land. That should have been the end of it. Then the Chinese joined the fray, and everything escalated again.

The old man had been approaching Ward the way someone might an injured animal. But now he gave what sounded like an order.

Ward had no idea what it meant.

The man said it again. The boy just looked on, his nerves less palpable than before.

Ward figured the safest interpretation of whatever the old man wanted was that he surrender. He pushed his .45 into the mud, then flashed both his hands. They hadn't killed him; now the question was whether Ward could stall them until the jets came. He scooted out from under the bush, his hands still raised.

The old soldier yelled. Ward didn't move.

The old man shouted again. As far as Ward could tell, the soldier wanted him to stand. Ward pointed at his ankles, which were submerged under the water, and tried to sign that they were broken.

The soldier released an exasperated sigh, slung his gun over his shoulder, and stomped to Ward, who went limp, figuring his deadweight would slow everything down.

After a few minutes of fumbling and grunting, the soldier waved the boy over. Together, they heaved Ward to a standing position, but as soon as he was up, the old man let go.

To keep from falling, Ward stepped forward with his right leg. As soon as he did, his legs cracked like he had stepped on a wrapped candy cane. He looked down just fast enough to watch a broken bone puncture through his skin and out the side of his leg. He collapsed back into the water, landing on his side. He screamed. Clinging to his leg, he swore and growled at the old man, "My legs are broken!"

The soldiers appeared stunned.

Good, Ward thought. There was just one thing he wanted now. A clean delay until the jets could come. "I'll go myself!" he snarled, pointing at the bank. He clawed at the mud and dragged himself forward.

The two men seemed unsure of what to do, so they trailed him. The old man mumbled.

A plan had formed in Ward's mind: he would crawl away from the creek so they were all exposed to the skies. When the jets came, the soldiers would flee for cover, and Ward would be able to fire the flare in his Mae West. Smooth as butter. He clawed and dragged his way out of the creek, wasting as much time as possible. Several times, he let himself slip in the mud. His legs and feet were truly throbbing, but he occasionally let out an exaggerated moan, just to sell how hard he was trying to get out of the creek. He finally reached the field and paused.

"Get up!"

Ward froze. That was English. He craned to see a North Korean army officer marching toward him from his parachute, which a number of Chinese soldiers were cutting up with their knives. The man wore the full uniform of the North Korean army, a duck-billed cap with a red star, and shoulder epaulets that suggested he was a second lieutenant.

"Get up!"

Ward collapsed on to his side and pointed at the bone jutting from his leg. "My legs are broken," he said.

The Chinese soldiers behind him yelled something in their own language, and the North Korean paused, seeming to assess the situation. He then shouted orders at some of the men around the parachute. They sprung to action, sprinting in Ward's direction.

He was clearly in charge. The Chinese soldiers all appeared to be peasants at best, poorly clothed and less rigid and precise in their posture and stance. But not this new character, this English-speaking Korean. His eyes looked sharp. Perceptive. A college student before the war, perhaps, who had bought into the socialist rhetoric, then signed up and quickly moved up in rank.

Disciplined and doctrinaire. The only aspect of his entire presence that looked off was his hair: it was longer than Ward would have expected, poking out from under his cap and down to his ears.

Three of the Chinese soldiers jogged to Ward. One, a stocky man, squatted, and with seemingly impossible strength, pulled Ward by the shoulders onto his back. He rose with a grunt and huffed along the creek side. The man stunk worse than the feces in the field, and Ward's face was pressed to his ratty hair. With every bounce, Ward felt and heard his bones grinding against themselves. The pain shot up his legs and into his lower back like waves of electricity. The North Korean barked orders at the rest of the men, and soon they were all together. In minutes, they would have him away from the field, and Ward would have no chance at being rescued. He closed his eyes. *Goodbye, Barb.*

Then his carrier paused. He mumbled something through heavy breathing, then lowered Ward to the ground. It was clear the man needed a rest. Ward flopped onto his back. Two of the Chinese poked his Mae West. They seemed fascinated by it. Ward saw an opening, a chance for delay. He untied the Mae West's straps and motioned for them to look closer. When they did, they noticed his C-3 vest, with its many pockets, underneath, and they seemed even more fascinated by it.

One by one, Ward unzipped his pockets to show them his belongings. He pulled out a fishing kit, flares, a smoke grenade meant for sending a signal, a pen, even his sunglasses. Each time he pulled something from a pocket, he noticed that the Chinese soldiers assumed that pocket was then empty.

The North Korean officer seemed to have only a passing interest in the fun. Instead, he stood a few feet away, his eyes on the skies.

Ward saw it in his face; he knew. He would tolerate this break, these minor distractions, but if a threat came from the skies, he would spring into action. While the soldiers inspected each of Ward's treasures, Ward managed to glance down at his watch. It had been twenty minutes since the last jet had left him. Twenty minutes. The choppers should have been here by now. Unless their escorts weren't jets. The other flights needed to scramble from Pusan; if they were jets, they would have been here already. If they were prop P-51 Mustangs, they would need another ten minutes.

All Ward's hopefulness collapsed inside him like a deflating balloon. He continued to go through the motions of unzipping pockets and handing over items. A Japanese watch. A carbine bayonet for a hunting knife. Maps. Each soldier took his turn inspecting the items; occasionally, one would make some sort of joke and the others would chuckle.

The minutes ticked by. Two. Five.

In the arm pocket of his flying suit, the soldiers found Ward's wallet. He pulled it out and handed it to them. In the same pocket was a letter he had penned for Barbara. The soldiers didn't seem to notice the letter, however. Like before, they seemed to think the pocket was empty after inspecting just one item taken from it. The letter sat untouched. Ward hoped that wouldn't change. One day, he would mail it. Personally.

He normally didn't bring his wallet with him on missions because it carried all of his identification in it. But this time, he had meant to send the letter to Barbara, along with a money order, and he had needed his wallet to do that. He hadn't been able to send it before the flight, so he'd tucked it into his pocket for later. Now, the Chinese soldiers knew exactly who he was.

Name, rank, address, training profile—all the information he was supposed to keep secret was no longer a secret.

Nine minutes had crept by.

For a moment, Ward thought the delay caused by his pocket trinkets might actually save him.

Then he heard two conflicting sounds simultaneously: one was the whir of the Mustangs; his boys were coming. The second was a gunshot. He twisted back to see a Chinese soldier standing near the creek—he had found Ward's .45 and had fired it into the air with a smile. The North Korean shouted out to his men, and before Ward could bask in the sound of his friends coming, he was picked up and thrown onto the back of another soldier. The entire unit charged to a grove of trees, and within seconds, they were under thick cover.

The man carrying Ward tossed him from his back like a sack.

Ward thudded into the dirt, and bursts of pain shot up his legs. He gritted his teeth and twisted to look out at the fields. The planes were close now, zeroing in. He couldn't see them, but he could hear the engines echoing off the valley walls.

"Americans are very bad," the North Korean said.

Ward ignored him, focused instead on the skies. What he wanted was for the Mustangs to unleash a barrage of bullets all over this valley. *Just strafe everything, and I'll take my chances*, he thought.

"Look at me, you dog," the North Korean said. He grabbed Ward's shoulder and spun him.

Ward had no choice.

"Americans are very bad. They should all be killed." He didn't seem to have the most extensive vocabulary, but his words were pronounced with precision, almost no accent at all. After the world war, he must have been exposed to Americans in the South—but then something had attracted him to the North.

"You think so?" Ward said. "I don't." *Come on, fellas. Unleash everything you've got.*

The Mustangs were there now. They had found Ward's chute and were circling the valley. The North Korean stood, his face calm. He stepped to the man who had found Ward's .45 and took it from him. He waved it at Ward. "They will not find you. You will become my prisoner. Then we shall see."

The Mustangs, four of them, roared over the field just above the trees.

Ward heard the welcome chop of a helicopter in the distance. All he needed was something to get his captors to scatter. That was his only hope.

The Mustangs circled again.

Ward turned back to the field. He saw the chopper. It rose up over the far hill. A second followed, much higher. The Mustangs circled.

The urge to make a run for it surged inside Ward like a wellspring. How far could he get? Then he remembered his ankles. He watched as the first chopper hovered in low over the field. It landed right next to his parachute, kicking up dirt and weeds. From his hiding place in the trees, Ward could see the pilot through the windshield and another soldier hanging out the open side door, scanning the field. They must have noticed where Ward dragged himself across the field because they immediately elevated and drifted over to the creek.

Ward wanted to scream, to wave. Please! Please!

But just as quickly as they had come, the chopper pushed away from the creek and started to rise in the air. Not to circle around and keep looking; not to prepare a landing crew to search for him. They were leaving. And Ward knew what they were thinking: Captain Ward M. Millar, Acting Squadron Operations Officer, had either been captured or killed behind enemy lines after his plane malfunctioned during a routine mission. It was time to notify his family.

Soon, the chopper was high above the field, where it joined its friend. They hovered for a moment, then turned back the way they had come. Ward felt a tap on his shoulder.

He dared a look back at the smug North Korean. "Your friends are leaving."

CHAPTER 6

Jae Pil had stripped off his army uniform, buried it far away on the mountainside, and then adorned his grandfather's ragged left-behind clothes. He had now been in his ancestral village for a week without incident—it was as if time had ended, and the boy he once was had receded from all memory, vanished from view like the sun dipping below a distant mountain.

The other villagers, who hadn't been forced into the army, knew who he was, of course, but they didn't seem to care. After his arrival, they maneuvered about their daily hopes for survival just as they had for years—working modest fields, cooking what food they had, tending to dogs and pigs, fixing their homes—and they did not seem to be bothered by this young man who had suddenly appeared in their midst. If anything, they were grateful for some extra muscle around to help.

Twice, trucks from the Supreme Leader's army had bumped along the road that wound through the small huts. The first time, Jae Pil had sprinted to his family's house at the first rumble of the engine, diving through the door and out of sight. But the second time, when it became clear no one was looking for him, he didn't even bother moving. He was assisting his mother in stuffing a kim-chi pot. The truck banged past, soldiers in the back looking on with empty faces, and not one said a word. That was when he realized that, as far as the North Korean army was concerned, he was dead.

So he and his mother started planning. A few more days of getting ready, and they would flee the place of their ancestors. Their goal was to reunite with their family in the South. Jae Pil had seen the routes during his time in the army. He would follow the unmarked roads that would take them deeper and deeper into the mountains, where there would be no towns, no farmers, no villages, no people at all, and eventually through the gaps in the front. He found himself, during those first few days, thinking of his grandfather. Strangely, his worries didn't linger on the army hunting for him, or what was happening out there in the broader war. His time was consumed by chores and getting ready to leave, and debating with his mother, who had come to believe the better decision was to just stay here and wait for the war to end. She was convinced that the Americans would eventually win, that if they just stayed quiet and avoided battles, eventually the Communists would give up, and the Chinese would retreat. Why risk going to the South when the South would come to them? Jae Pil would honor his mother; in the end, the decision was hers to make, and he would obey it . . . for that was their way. But after many conversations, she had come around to seeing his view: even if the Americans won the current battles, the Communists would never relent. They and the Chinese army harbored an admirable devotion, one born of confidence that they were on the right side of history, that their philosophy, and theirs alone, could rid the world of inequality and truly create a people fully equal in the Land of the Morning Calm.

Perhaps that was why his thoughts returned so often to his grandfather. Devotion. It was true that Jae Pil respected his father, as any boy should. But it was his grandfather whom he adored. If he could become anyone as he matured, it would be the older man: soft-spoken but powerful, restrained but forceful, confident but humble. When Jae Pil was little, he and his grandfather would take walks while his parents tended to chores at the house. His grandfather would place his hands behind his back, and with a small arch in his stance, invite Jae Pil to walk alongside him at sunset.

They would follow a trail, behind the house and up to where their ancestors were buried. "Do you know why we don't pray to them anymore?" his grandfather asked him one time. Jae Pil had no idea. Most of the people he knew in the village prayed to their ancestors at least twice a year. They made offerings to them and honored them. But his family did not.

"Because God has said we should pray only to Him," his grandfather said. "So we honor our ancestors; we respect them. But we pray to God only."

At the time, the only world Jae Pil knew was one in which the Japanese colonialists had tried to dominate every aspect of Korean life. They had given Jae Pil a Japanese name and told him to use it at all times. They had forbidden him from speaking Korean. They had even demolished an ancient gate and wall not far from his village, announcing that Korean-unique architecture would not be allowed to stand in the new Japanese empire.

"What about the shrine?" Jae Pil asked.

"We do not bow to it either," his grandfather said, "even if the Japanese have built it, even if they demand it." He then stood tall, a rarity for him. He spoke calmly, pronouncing each word with a ferocity that Jae Pil still remembered all these years later. "You have heard they are killing Christians who will not bow to the shrine?"

Jae Pil nodded.

"And if they come here and build a shrine—what will you do?" Jae Pil looked on but said nothing, afraid to say the wrong words.

"Then let them kill us," his grandfather said. "We have only one God."

• • •

The third time a troop transport truck entered the mountain village, Jae Pil didn't think to hide. There were two jeeps accompanying it. Unlike the others, this unit did not simply push through. With a squeal, the lead jeep jerked to a halt at the road's nadir. A sturdy looking man stepped from it. Clearly an officer—and one who had seen combat. From his shoulder boards, he looked to be a lieutenant. He surveyed the scene with hips on hands like a farmer looking over his crop. Many of the older villagers didn't even acknowledge him. If it bothered him, he didn't show it.

Jae Pil stayed frozen. He and his mother had taken all precautions to ensure any signs of their planned trip South would be obvious to no one. One day they would be here; the next they would be gone. Plus, Jae Pil was certain the army thought him dead. They were in total disarray—the chances of their actually searching for him were zero.

His confidence dissipated slightly when the officer paused, eyes locked on Jae Pil. Then he marched along a trail through some potatoes until he stood just feet away. Up close his face appeared crusty and lined, covered with dust, even some blood.

"How many years are you?"

"Twenty-seven," Jae Pil said, refusing to make eye contact.

"What is your name?"

"Kim . . . Seok Jin," Jae Pil said.

"Why aren't you in the army?"

"I was sick," Jae Pil said, which was technically true. At the very beginning of the war, immediately before the Communists had invaded the South, they had started recruiting soldiers. Jae Pil had been in prison at the time as a Christian and a potential American sympathizer. They had wanted to draft him, but he had some sort of illness in his lungs that forced him to hack and cough constantly. They decided he was unfit. It was only later, when he healed, that they had finally forced him into the army.

The officer considered this with narrowed eyes. Then, "You seem fine now."

"I'm . . . better," Jae Pil said, then instantly regretted it. How could he be so stupid? Hack, cough, wretch, pretend to spit up blood—his mind continued down a list of things he could have done to turn this officer away.

"If you are better, then you can serve the people's cause."

He pivoted and screamed back to the truck, "Bring me a uniform!"

Moments later, two soldiers, both privates, leaped from the back of the truck. They trotted forward, one with a bundle tucked under his arm. With a bow, he handed it to the lieutenant with both hands.

He immediately thrust it into Jae Pil's stomach. "Get dressed. We move in five minutes."

Jae Pil hesitated for only a second. He had seen what anything less than absolute loyalty would bring upon him. He bowed, then spun to his family's home. As he walked, he refused to make eye contact with his mother.

Inside the house, he surveyed what was available to him. His quick conclusion: nothing. The door opened and his mother entered. She slid off her slippers and stepped to him.

The lines around her eyes were so pronounced, it seemed she had aged a decade in just ten minutes. "What are you going to do?" she whispered.

Jae Pil had no answers as he unbuttoned his shirt. And after two minutes, he saw etched onto his mother's face the same conclusion he had reached: she knew. He had no choice but to go with this unit.

"Mother—"

"No." Her voice was quiet—not panicky, simply conveying

facts. "Don't say the words. You will go, and you will find your way back to me. You know you will." Jae Pil couldn't bear to look at her.

I'm sorry was all he could feel, but it was not their way to show their emotions. *I'm sorry I couldn't save you,* he thought, sending this message through the air between them. He wanted to pour the words from his heart, to let her know how much he loved her, but, like so many things, they would be felt but unsaid.

After he donned the North Korean uniform once again and pulled the duck-billed hat over his forehead, their eyes met. Hers bore a simple message: *We were given this time; wasn't that a blessing enough?*

"I'll do all I can to get back to you," Jae Pil said. "If you hear airplanes, hide away from the buildings. In the trees. The Americans do not attack civilians, but if there are military here, they might hit you also. Always listen."

His mother nodded. "I'll be safe. And the South will win, and you will find me again. I'll be here waiting." And together, they exited the house.

Jae Pil, with the lieutenant five paces behind him, maneuvered through the potato patch and, once again, asked heaven for help to escape from this constantly closing trap. But for the first time, he began to wonder if anyone was even listening.

CHAPTER 7

The Mustangs were not finished. The helicopters may have retreated, but it was clear to Ward that his pilot friends were not happy believing the Communists had killed one of their own. They circled away from the valley, then returned, clearly ready to fire. When they passed over, they unleashed their machine guns on a hill rising from the other end of the field.

From the trees, roughly a dozen Chinese soldiers scurried in every direction like a colony of disturbed ants. Some of the Chinese soldiers hiding in Ward's grove of trees did the same, running away from the field and up the mountainside.

Ward saw an opening, perhaps his last one. If he could just make it back to the field in the confusion, the Mustangs could call the choppers back.

This was clearly a revenge attack. The Mustangs circled again and again, strafing every possible hiding place. The English-speaking North Korean had darted to the trunk of a nearby tree, perhaps preparing for when the Americans' fury might fall on him. Some of the Chinese milled about, clearly unsure of whether they should follow their friends, or stay under cover.

Ward calculated that if his captors were going to kill him anyway, he might as well die on his own terms, a clean exit, crawling his way back to his family. He forced himself onto his hands and knees and crawled like a wounded dog down the trail to the field.

"Stop!" the North Korean screamed.

Ward glanced back over his shoulder. The man was pointing Ward's pistol at him. It certainly seemed possible he might shoot Ward right there on the spot. And after this reprisal strafing from the Mustangs—which had likely killed who knew how many Communist soldiers—Ward again figured he was a dead man anyway.

He ignored the North Korean and crawled even faster.

Just as he was about to shuffle from the shade of the trees, he felt a violent yank on the back of his collar. He was lifted off the ground and onto his backside, the front of his vest cutting into his throat. The North Korean then began dragging him back into the trees. Two of the Chinese soldiers jumped forward and screamed at the North Korean, who released Ward. He collapsed onto his back and tried to cough the choking sensation in his throat away.

Above him, the North Korean and the Chinese men seemed to be arguing over what to do with Ward. After a few seconds, it seemed as if they couldn't agree on who should take him. Finally, the North Korean stepped aside, and the two soldiers looped their arms under Ward's shoulders and continued to drag him away from the field.

The next sound caused everyone to pause, including Ward. At first, he thought it was anti-aircraft fire, coming from the Communists. Then he realized it was something far more deadly. "Those are rockets!" he screamed at the North Korean. "We have to get out of here!"

If the North Korean was troubled, he didn't show it. Instead, he yelled an order at the two soldiers, and they jogged further up the mountain with Ward in tow.

Ward was certain the entire place was about to get lit up with napalm, and that was how he would die: burned alive by his fellow pilots. The two men carrying him dragged him even faster, out into a clearing. Ward twisted his neck to see where they were taking him. About sixty feet away was a mud house with a small stone wall around it. "They'll hit that!" he screamed.

But the Chinese couldn't understand him, and the North Korean had pivoted away into a foxhole that, until then, Ward hadn't noticed.

Two seconds later, Ward was falling backward into darkness. He crashed into the carved-out dirt floor of another foxhole, his legs and arms jutting out toward the sky. He lay like a turtle on its back, unable to move. Above him, engines and explosions rocked everything as the other pilots released their fury on the landscape. All Ward could do was wait and hope that fury didn't cook him alive trapped in this pit.

• • •

By the time the planes had left and all had settled, Ward was certain he would be summarily executed. How much damage had the planes done? How many soldiers had they killed? If they had unleashed their revenge tour because they thought him killed, what would these Communists do to him as retribution?

Several faces appeared above him and blotted out the sky. Then strong hands clasped onto his wrists and ankles. The pain exploded in Ward's leg, and he let out an involuntary yelp. The soldiers yanked so hard the jolt and the pain caused dark shadows to pass through his vision, and he knew he was on the verge of blacking out.

This was it. Their friends were dead. Their fellow soldiers were slaughtered. In their view, the evil Americans had come and drunk their fill, and they had left one behind as an offering. It was time for them to accept that offering. Ward writhed on the ground. The North Korean had emerged from his hiding place and was stomping toward Ward with the ferocity of an angry playground bully about to beat his nemesis. He yanked Ward's .45 from his waistband.

Ward prepared for the bullet that would end him.

The two Chinese stepped in between Ward and his executioner. The three of them scuffled while others looked on.

Then, to Ward's surprise, two other soldiers crested a hill behind the group with something in their hands Ward never, ever expected to see: a stretcher.

The North Korean continued to shout, twice trying to force his way past the Chinese men.

But, eventually, he relented.

The two new arrivals moved briskly to stand beside Ward, lowered the stretcher, and lifted him onto it. They bounced him past the North Korean, whose eyes narrowed when they met Ward's. The intent was clear: I will come for you, sooner or later; you will not have protection.

Ward's thoughts lingered on the man's deathly stare for only a moment. Then he realized his carriers were moving at an impressive pace, sprinting him deeper and deeper into North Korean territory. In a matter of minutes, he would be so far from his parachute and crash site that no one would ever find him.

● ● ●

Where was he? What drugs had the Communists given him? How was it possible to feel this good? Everything that had happened since his capture was a blur now: a bouncy ride over numerous hills to some mud hut in the woods; an English-speaking Chinese medic who jabbed a needle with some sort of milky liquid into Ward's arm; a euphoric numbing and lightness that made all the pain go away when the medic jerked Ward's bones into place and wrapped his wounds; Chinese soldiers giving him water; the various soldiers going through his things; another ride on the stretcher and the humorous drug-induced thought that he was some ancient emperor being carried by servants across the antiquated Korean landscape; the murderous glare of the angry North Korean lieutenant who seemed to always be there, an omnipresent gloom always hovering nearby, his eyes always hinting: when the Chinese are done with you, I will execute you properly; and finally a stop at a mud-hut village on a hillside somewhere hours away from where he had crashed, where civilians dressed in white cotton outfits had looked at him like an animal in a zoo, whispering, "Mi-guk . . . mi-guk," the way children might whisper, "A tiger! A tiger! Look, Mommy, a tiger!"

With the drugs wearing off, the realization of where he was, what had happened, and the precariousness of his situation settled on Ward like the coming nightfall. He had the vaguest memory that his carriers had brought him into a room at the back of one of the huts alongside the mountain. Now that he was coherent, he realized the room was sparse. Just Ward on the ground, a waist-high clay pot in the corner, a ceiling of thatch darkened from smoke, and mud walls. No windows. He had no way to see outside.

Interrogation, he thought. *Then they'll kill me. Or give me to the North Korean. Or ship me to Siberia, like the Russians had done with the Germans and Japanese after the war.* His mind shifted to escape— its impossibility, all the routes he might take on all fours with no working legs. Finally, he rested on Barbara.

How strange it would be, he thought, never to see her again. Never to hold her or Adrian again. That outcome had always been a possibility, of course, but in his mind it had been nothing more than a theoretical prospect—one of an infinite number the universe might conjure up. Its probability seemed so low that he had never really considered it seriously before he'd realized the need to eject.

He reached to his arm and patted his pocket, then jabbed his finger into it. The letter to her was still there. Somehow, it just never occurred to these peasants in this army to empty all his pockets.

That wasn't surprising really—the Chinese called themselves the People's Volunteer Army, but everyone knew it was filled with poor men and boys who had been forced into it against their will. Who were they kidding?

Ward drug himself to the door and peered outside. From what he could see and hear, no one was nearby. Perhaps they were waiting for him to wake up before the questioning began.

He lay back on the stretcher and tried to get comfortable. Every part of him still hurt; every position he tried only made a different spot ache. He needed to take his mind off the situation. He couldn't resist; he pulled the letter from the pocket on his arm and unfolded it. In the dying light, he read his words:

> *My Darling Barbara,*
>
> *I've included a money order for you. I will send more soon. I keep thinking of our last conversation about little Adrian, about how we'll raise her.*
>
> *You are so perfect for me. Do you remember how amazed we were when we first met that we liked all the same books, movies, and sports? The guys here can't believe you let me crawl under the car and work on the engine as much as I do (I didn't tell them I give you total control of the house decorating).*
>
> *Still, I don't like this strange silence between us. I love you. I promised I would allow our children to be raised in the Catholic tradition, and I will keep that promise. You know I will. I will keep going to church with you. I enjoy the pageantry of the service, and I don't want to accentuate our differences like some men do who just drive their wives to church, then sit outside.*
>
> *But I think we must wait for our children to reach the age of reason and let them decide for themselves their reli-gion. That's what my parents did for me and Monroe, and*

we figured things out. I like to think we turned out okay—I mean, you married me, didn't you?

I know how much it means for you to have me join you as a convert and to support you in raising our children in your faith. I can't. I won't. I wouldn't be true to myself, or you, or them if I pretend to be something I'm not, and I'm not someone who believes God is involved in our lives. That God is some being we can pray to, as if he's just waiting for all of the hundreds of millions of us to pray to him. And if we do, he'll just go ahead and change the physics of the universe to help us.

There may be a God who put this universe in motion, who organized all these creatures and the rotation of the earth and the planets in the heavens with such mathematical precision. I truly believe that is the case.

Some God, some master, some higher intellect may be responsible for this universe and all its marvels, but that is all I know. That being has some master plan that none of us can comprehend. I can't believe this vast system, that spans cosmos and galaxies and millions of lives is going to change one iota because of the prayers of insignificant people on this one inconsequential planet. All those times prayers seem to be answered are just coincidence. There is no meaning in any of it.

You knew that when we married, and I cannot change it now. You also knew how much I loved you, and I cannot change that now either. I am yours 'til death parts us. I will support you. I will love you and cherish you. I will be a faithful husband alongside you, and we will keep our family united and together. I wish I could do more, my love. I wish I had your faith, but that has not come to me. Nothing I have seen supports it.

Know that I love you. Please tell Adrian how much I

love her. Give her a big kiss from her Dada. I'm about to set
out on my thirtieth—one flight closer to the flight that will
bring me home to you.

Love, Ward

Ward folded the letter. Barbara would have been saddened to read it, he knew, but he meant what he'd written: he couldn't become a convert just to do it, even for her. The grind of boots on gravel snapped him back to his situation.

He tucked the letter into his arm pocket and left it unzipped, so his captors wouldn't get curious and want to search it again. He also realized that he was still wearing his platinum wedding ring. He tugged it over his knuckle and off his finger, then slid it into the folds of the letter.

The door creaked open.

A Chinese officer entered the room. A small paunch stretched the buttons of his sand-colored uniform. Behind him stood the North Korean lieutenant.

"You are awake," the Chinese officer said. "Good."

Ward was taken aback by the officer's English for just a moment, but he didn't let that show on his face.

"It is time for you to answer our questions." Ward glanced over the man's shoulder.

The North Korean stood with arms at his side. He just stared, lips pursed, not even at Ward but into the back of the head of the Chinese officer.

"Okay," Ward said. He even smiled. A plan was forming in his mind.

"What is your name?"

"Ward Millar. Captain. Serial number . . ."

The man waved his hand dismissively. "We already know that information. It is of no value."

There it was: the key to his staying alive, or at least staying away from the execution-hungry North Korean. He needed to provide value. So he would give them what they perceived as precious—information. Information they could easily find. Information that was unclassified and available in any number of newspapers and magazines. As long as he kept talking, they would think they'd found their greatest treasure—an American who would reveal any secret he could to stay alive.

"What is your responsibility in the army?"

"I'm a special observer."

"What is that?"

"My job is to fly over the lines and identify friendly units that have been cut off, then report their locations so our planes don't bomb them by accident."

The officer placed his hands behind his back. "If that is so, why did your plane have machine guns?"

The last thing Ward wanted was for these men to think he was responsible for all the carnage the U.S. had inflicted on their army. "Strictly defensive."

The officer didn't react, seemed only to consider this lie. The one perceptible change in the room came from the North Korean, who narrowed his eyes just slightly before returning them to their normal stoicism.

The three of them danced this dance for over an hour. The officer was curt, firing question after question. Ward offered long, laborious answers filled with information that had long since been made public. With a stab of wariness, he weaved a tapestry of lies and partial truths, unsure of whether either of these men believed him.

When it was over, the Chinese man squatted. "You are a captain. That means you have information we want, and we will obtain it."

He stood, spun, and burst from the room. The lieutenant

lingered for just half a second longer, then followed. A few seconds later, another new, rank-and-file soldier entered the room and stood with his back to the wall. Three other guards carrying rifles with fixed bayonets stood outside the door.

For the briefest of moments, Ward was thrilled: his strategy was working.

Then he felt a rumble and pain in his stomach and the undeniable pressure of his guts wanting to empty themselves. He thought of the water the soldiers had given him when he'd been under the drugs, and he knew what this was: the first signs of dysentery.

CHAPTER 8

Barbara Millar—known to many in the greater Portland Catholic community as the strongest woman they had ever met, the one who knew what she wanted out of life and out of a man—heard the knock at the door before anyone else.

She sprung to her feet and waved everyone else in the room to stay seated. It was a pipe dream: you couldn't keep twelve people (her six younger siblings, her mother and father, Adrian, and two neighbors) in one spot all together for more than a second at a time without some sort of divine intervention. Food did the trick, a secret Barbara had figured out and mastered years before. But the knock at the door broke the spell of the roast and rolls that had brought everyone to the table, and many of her siblings fell in line behind Barbara as she made her way to the door.

This was how she passed her time now that Ward had been called back up: helping her father with his heating and air conditioning business, working with her mother to keep their mammoth family in order, tending to Adrian, who received no shortage of attention since she was the first grandchild. It kept her mind busy.

And it gave her plenty of fodder for letters to Ward.

She wrote him every day, and he wrote her back every day, which was fitting, because when they were in the same place, they were inseparable. It was their running joke; literally from their first blind date during World War II, for the following six weeks, they had spent only one evening apart. "Love at first sight" was too easy and too much a cliché for a description of their relationship. It was a connection, a deep bond that seemed to have formed almost instantly, woven together with unbreakable threads of conversations over dinners and walks and time spent at parks. Others saw it. What's with you two? their friends would ask. Barbara had no clue—she just loved being with him.

Even after that first six weeks, when Ward was called up to serve in France against the Nazis, the bond lasted. Which was remarkable, now that Barbara thought about it, because she hadn't intended to sit around and mope for Ward in his absence—not after just six weeks. When he shipped out, she'd flat out told him: I intend to date other people. Don't think I'll just be sitting around.

He hadn't liked it, but what was he going to do? It's not like he could come home and stop her. Plus, she'd felt Ward carried the kind of confidence that, deep down, he probably knew he wouldn't lose her to someone else. She had never been one to obsess over looks—they just didn't interest her. But she knew how handsome he was, mostly because everyone else said something about it on nearly a daily basis. "Where did you find him?" one of her friends had whispered when Barbara first brought him to Mass after that first date. Barbara only smiled in response.

What really made him attractive was his intellect, his kindness, his charisma, which he never really acknowledged; it just emanated from him and filled up a room the same way cuteness shines off a baby. When she talked with him, he listened, really listened, and always commented back on what she had to say, as if it were the most important subject in the world. So they could talk for hours about anything: religion, movies, baseball, families, music, cars, philosophy, what annoyed them, their dreams and fears. Unlike so many other men she knew, Ward rarely drank, so they didn't go to clubs or bars. For them, it was enough just to be together.

From the start, he'd assumed they would get married. When he got back from France, after two years of writing letters, he proposed almost immediately. Barbara put the brakes on that. Calm down, fly boy. I don't even know you. She wasn't about to marry someone she'd known for only six weeks who'd then gone off to war for two years. In her mind, that was like buying a house you'd never set foot in. People changed from war, and she didn't know if Ward was the same man she'd been so infatuated with when he'd left.

After a year of her dragging him along, he threw down an ultimatum: we either get married, or I'm moving on. That did it. And they never looked back.

Her parents —two strong-willed Nebraskans with German roots (her mother had literally moved to Oregon in a covered wagon as a little girl)—had purchased the house in which they raised Barbara and her siblings. When they found out the next-door neighbors might be running a brothel out of their house, they bought it too. The homes were identical: three levels, with room on each floor for a separate apartment. In one, they raised their family and operated their business. The other they converted into apartments they could rent out, and they let Ward and Barbara start their life together in one of them.

Barbara remembered that period of their life as twenty months of married bliss, followed by little Adrian. Ward went to school at Reed College during the day and worked as a janitor at night to make ends meet, and he joined the Portland Air Force Reserve as a way to add a bit more to the family budget. Their old Hudson was so dilapidated, Ward spent most of his free time out under the engine trying to make it work until Barbara demanded they get a new car. It didn't need to be fancy, didn't even need to have a radio. It just needed to get from point A to point B without breaking down. So they bought a new bronze-colored Mercury. Every night at 1 a.m., she would set Adrian in the front passenger seat in her little portable bassinet and drive to pick up Ward from his job. He offered to take a bus, but she wanted to see him. It was a small but pleasant life.

Then, of course, the world ended. Or at least it seemed to for Barbara. Alone in her apartment, with no furniture beyond a used couch, a bed, and a radio, she received a phone call from a mutual friend of theirs, a colonel, who called and said a conflict had broken out in Korea. He wanted Barbara to hear it from a friend, instead of from cold, official, formal channels. The Communists in the North had invaded the South, trying to take over the entire country. The United Nations was intent on stopping them. Ward's unit was being called up to join the fight.

He would be gone in a matter of weeks.

For just a moment, it seemed she couldn't breathe.

• • •

When the knock came at the door during family dinner, Barbara hadn't even suspected something might be off. After all, her connection with Ward was as strong as ever; that was the only way she could think to describe it. Yes, the letters flowed with regularity, a daily reminder of their love. But there was something more than that—a string that penetrated both time and space and that instilled in her a feeling that he was alive and well.

By the time she reached the front door of her parents' house, her younger siblings and parents had begun to coalesce around her, all curious to see who this visitor was. It wasn't until Barbara opened the door that she fully understood.

Standing on the step was an old high school friend of hers. He had gotten a job working for Western Union delivering telegrams. He stood there, wearing his ridiculous uniform like he was some sort of four-star general. In his hands, he held a piece of paper. In his eyes, he told her what the piece of paper said.

"Hi, Barbara," he said. That was all she needed. She had lived through the big war. How many of her friends had endured this same visit? The piece of paper that always began with the same words: "We regret to inform you . . ."

She put her hand to her mouth, then let out a sob and flung herself onto her parents' sofa. If she'd felt she couldn't breathe when Ward had received orders to ship out, now it seemed all the oxygen in the world, and all the light with it, had been sucked away.

Her parents, her siblings, the house, Adrian, the dinner, the very world itself—all of it seemed to vanish. Her mind plunged. She saw faces; she relived their first blind date and the electric thrill she'd felt the first time he touched her hand. She felt as if she were choking; her gasps could find no air.

From a distant place, she felt arms envelop her. They were warm like hot cocoa on a winter night, but she didn't want them. She wanted only one embrace, and that was now lost to her forever. She batted the arms away, but they refused to budge. They were as strong as anything she had ever known.

"We're here," her father was saying. "We're here. We'll get through this together."

It took some time, minutes, hours, the entirety of the night with all the stars pouring their ancient light upon her; how long it took was unimportant now that her existence had ended. But she eventually released herself into her father's embrace.

"We won't leave you," he whispered.

It was a strange sensation. All her childhood, her father had been a strong man, a presence who could be defined by one word: there. He had been there for her, but he was not one to show his affection. He did not offer hugs, or words of empathy. It was not his way, or the way of his ancestors. Still, in that moment, all things fell away: cultures and customs and personalities and traditions. All that remained was the strength of his voice and of his embrace. *We're here.*

CHAPTER 9

Willing his fingers to stop trembling, Jae Pil forced himself to salute his new commanding officer, a pudgy man ten years his senior with a scar on his cheek. Jae Pil's heart was beating so hard against his ribs, he was certain everyone in the camp knew he was an imposter. It didn't help that the army had found him hiding out in his village after every other able-bodied young man had already been forced into service. It made things worse that, somewhere, on some list, he was a known Christian who came from a family of Christians perceived to be a threat to the new world order.

"What skills do you have?"

Jae Pil paused. "Sir?"

"Have you been trained to fire a weapon?"

"No, sir," he said, though of course he had, during his first stint in the Supreme Leader's army. "But I can drive a truck."

"Where did you learn to drive a truck?" the man asked.

For a fraught moment, Jae Pil realized his mistake. Where else would he have learned to drive a truck but in the army? He stared into the distance, as a proper underling should, grateful there was no expectation that he look the officer in the eyes. For if he did, he was certain they would know he didn't belong, that he hated everything about this, about them. They were simpletons, like overgrown, brain-washed children playing dress-up. And as soon as they realized what Jae Pil was, they would execute him, just as they had others who had not proven loyal.

"I received some training . . . before I was sick."

The officer considered this for a second. Whether he believed Jae Pil or not, he didn't say. "Have you driven at all in combat?"

"No, sir."

"But you can drive in rough terrain?"

"I think so, yes."

"Good. We will be shipping armaments to the front. You will drive the truck. We will train you for combat before we leave."

Jae Pil saluted. He waited for the man to walk away before he allowed his body to release. How could he keep this up? His first stint in the army had been easier. They had dragged him in along with almost all the young men in the North. Everyone was clueless and just following orders, whether they agreed or not. This time was different. He was a deserter. He had been planning to escape to the South. There was no doubt some of these men were watching him, looking for any sign of his disloyalty.

The real danger was someone recognizing him—either a person from his region who knew his family's religious beliefs or, worse, an army member who knew he had already been in the military.

Jae Pil trudged across the dusty camp. In his mind, a plan was formulating. If he could convince them to let him be a truck driver again, that would give him a vehicle. In every village they passed, he would search for his family. If he couldn't find them, he would pray they already made it south. Then he would try to get as close to the front as he could. Once there, he would cross over. He was a strong swimmer. If he could get the truck close enough to the right river, or even to the coast where there were American ships in the waters, he would be able to swim to safety. It was all about timing. But first things first.

• • •

Jae Pil held the rifle like a boy who had never seen one before. When his junior lieutenant instructed him to fire rounds at a target, he intentionally bungled things. At first, he tried to pull the trigger with the safety on. Then he missed the target entirely. He needed to strike a middle ground: if he was too incompetent, they would assign him to manual labor—foxhole and ditch digging; if he was too quick of a study, they would ship him to a direct combat position. He wanted to appear good enough to be in combat but with his best use being a truck driver.

"Again," the junior lieutenant said, barely paying attention.

This time, Jae Pil squeezed the trigger and hit the very edge of the tree at which he was aiming. In all reality, he could have hit the trunk every time.

"You must line up the sights," the man said. "Or you will never hit anything."

Jae Pil made a calculated risk. He pulled the trigger again, and this time, on his third bullet, he hit the tree dead center.

"Good," the lieutenant said. "You're a quick learner." Jae Pil closed his eyes and cursed himself. Too fast. "Again."

I can be a slow learner, he thought. This time, he aimed far wide of the target, and high, firing a bullet off into the hills, where it disappeared into the scrub.

"Consistency takes practice," the junior lieutenant said. "Fire ten more rounds." Then he turned and ambled away. With no one watching, Jae Pil felt the urge to blast the tree into a billion pieces, to puncture the trunk with so many bullets the entire thing would topple to the ground in a great heap of cracked branches and moaning wood. Instead, he kept up his inconsistent target practice, hoping it would be enough.

• • •

The next morning, Jae Pil glanced up with a start when he heard an engine sputtering into camp. He had been sitting next to a fire eating a mixture of rice and pork, waiting for his first assignment and pondering on why the military enjoyed pork but no one else did. Whether his performance from the day before had worked remained a mystery.

A 4x4 utility vehicle rolled into camp. Jae Pil tightened.

The two men in the vehicle were security forces. They had many roles in the Supreme Leader's army, but one of them was intelligence. If anyone would know Jae Pil's secret or history, it would be these men. A private was at the steering wheel, wearing a pair of goggles that would let him see even if the tires splattered mud into his face. The other, based on his shoulder boards, was a sergeant. Their vehicle ground its way into the camp and stopped a hundred feet from where Jae Pil sat.

He glanced around at the other men to see what their reactions might be. Nothing. If anyone was worried about these security forces, they didn't show it. Jae Pil decided his best course of action would be to pretend the men didn't exist. But he watched them in his periphery.

The sergeant exited the vehicle, carrying some sort of clipboard. At first glance, his face was indistinct, one Jae Pil had seen a million times, ordinary and forgettable. But with those security shoulder boards attached sharply to his uniform, he radiated a sense of menace as incontrovertible as the sun. To take him in was to feel oneself sinking.

The man scanned the camp as if searching for something. "Wait," he said over his shoulder to the private at the wheel.

After another second, he strode into the officers' tent and disappeared.

Jae Pil lost his appetite. But to leave even a grain of rice uneaten or discarded was sacrilege.

He forced it into his gullet and choked it down, then trudged over to where a large mound of potatoes had been piled. The one duty he'd been given so far was to stuff these potatoes into burlap sacks and load them into the bed of a nearby truck. They would eventually be shipped to the front.

He did so, but the task itself was removed from his reality—all that mattered was what was happening in that tent. His hands and arms moved of their own accord, while his mind and eyes focused on the opening where the security sergeant had entered. What were they discussing? What was on his clipboard? Did he have a list of deserters? Did he have a list of dissidents?

After twenty minutes, the tent flap opened.

Jae Pil suppressed the instinct to stop what he was doing and watch. Instead, he threw himself into his assignment with more gusto.

"Private Kim Seok Jin," his commanding officer, the one with the scar, called.

At first, Jae Pil didn't react. Then he remembered he'd given them a fake name. He looked to see the officer staring at him. He immediately stood at attention.

"Come here!" Jae Pil marched the way a trained soldier should until he was several feet from the officer. He saluted.

Behind his commanding officer, the security sergeant emerged from the tent. He seemed more interested in his clipboard than in Jae Pil.

"We will need your skills on the front," the officer said.

Jae Pil's heart sank. He was going to be heading into combat as an infantryman. An intense sensation of biological alarm washed over him, tsunami-like in its power and scope—the hope of finding his family began to vanish from him like a beach eroding after a storm.

"You will finish loading this food and supplies," the officer continued. "Then you will drive this truck and a regiment of men to this location." The officer waved the security sergeant forward.

On his clipboard, the man carried a portion of a map that showed a particular location far to the south of their current location.

"This location," the sergeant said, "is where we are amassing our troops for a major offensive. They will need this food and supplies. You will drive it to them. Once there, you will receive new orders."

Just as quickly as his hopes had vanished, they returned, like the miracle of the rising sun.

All of Jae Pil's senses fashioned around this new mission, something that had seemed impossible only seconds before. He would drive a truck. His route would take him through numerous small villages, any number of which might be hiding his family.

"You will need training," his commanding officer said. "You must avoid enemy attacks and aircraft." And on and on and on, Jae Pil barely heard any of it, just enough to throw out an occasional "yes, sir." It was as if these two men were speaking to him from a radio on the other end of the peninsula. After all, he'd already had all this training before. He just needed to fake his way through the conversation as if he were new.

He let his mind stretch out across the distant landscape, to his father, and sister, and grandfather: *I'm coming for you. And when the war is over and the Americans have won, I will come back for Mother as well.*

CHAPTER 10

O*kay,* Barbara thought. *Okay.*

This was always a possibility. If anything, it was long overdue. Her husband had now been shipped to two wars without a single negative thing happening to him. How long did she really think they would be able to beat the odds? She lay on a bed in her parents' house. After hours of sobbing, Barbara had allowed her father and mother to convince her to stay with them for the night, forcing some of her siblings to cram into a room together. She had fallen asleep alone on her sister's bed.

She checked the clock: 11:34 a.m. The day was nearly half gone. Wasted. Time to get herself moving again.

She was still wearing her clothes from the night before. She snuck down the stairs and crept quickly from her parents' house to her own apartment next door, trusting that someone in her family was watching Adrian. She dressed herself in a fresh dress, brushed her hair, washed her face, and put on a dab of fresh make-up. In a matter of minutes, she looked exactly as she now felt: a woman in charge.

And why shouldn't she be? The telegram, when she finally brought herself to read it, had merely stated that Ward was missing in action, that he had been on a mission and needed to parachute behind enemy lines. It didn't say he was dead. There was no confirmation of his execution or capture. For all anyone knew, he was making his way back home right then. And if anyone could do it, it was her Ward—his mind was as sharp and quick as anyone's.

None of that really mattered, though. Not to her. Those were just the talking points she would share with all the busybodies when the inevitable deluge of questions came. What mattered to her was that feeling that still percolated inside her. She knew Ward was alive because the universe was telling her Ward was alive. She still felt her connection to him. It was so palpable and real it might as well have been a tangible cord connecting her body to his. He was out there, and until she felt that connection vanish, she wasn't going to let anyone tell her otherwise.

From the chartreuse radio cabinet in the front room, she snatched a piece of paper and a pen. From her bedside table, she gathered her rosary.

She had taken the time to collect herself—a little over twelve hours to process the horrible news. Now it was time to help bring Ward home. She shoved open the door to her apartment and marched down the stairs, weapons in hand.

CHAPTER 11

Ward could endure what they were doing to him. Those acts came with pain, and its relative, the anticipation of pain. But he could bear it. For a long time, they asked him nothing, just allowed him to linger in his cell, suffering from the blood and stink of dysentery. They made no demands. They played with him, toyed with his mind. *We intend to take you back to your people.* Then they carried him all night on a stretcher only to bring him back to his prison, his shattered bones grinding and aching. *We have no more use for you, we will kill you in the morning.* Then he watched all day as men dug and planted an execution pole in the ground outside his hut cell. *You will not be shot; we will take you to Antung, in China, for questioning.* Then they laid him in a truck, which broke down after a day or two of driving, so they put him in yet another mud hut. The yo-yoing continued. *We will give you medicine for your wounds. You are of no use to us so you will receive no medicine.*

He bore it all stoically, refusing to give them any satisfaction. He silenced his cries of pain when his bones scraped one another, smiled when he could, refused to show any fear. When they finally did ask him questions, he wove a story of lies and information that he figured might keep him alive. The only time he told the truth was when they asked of his youth in America: born in Los Angeles, raised in a rural homestead near Oakland with one brother, attended UC Berkeley for a time, joined the air force in World War II, married a girl from Portland in 1947, reentered college in 1948 but was called to active duty because of the invasion, never had enough money because his family was poor. He played up his family's lack of wealth so they would think him part of the proletariat, but he left out his study of nuclear physics, for fear they might blame him for the atomic bomb or assume he had knowledge worth prying from his mind.

The worry was the worst part. Strange, because Ward was not a worrying sort of person, never one for anxiety. He'd always taken on problems as they arose, rather than anticipating the universe of things that could go wrong and stressing over each one of them. But in this instance, every time his interrogators asked him questions, he fretted over whether he was pretending to be too valueless. Whatever he was doing seemed to be working. In his most positive moments, he told himself it might not even be possible for him to appear as just another grunt soldier without any value. Barbara had always told him—although he didn't really believe it—that he had an air of brilliance about him, that people knew he was bright and discerning the moment they met him. There was, in her view, nothing he could do about it; that, combined with his good looks, made other men so insecure they would take an initial disliking to him until they got to know him. It's just going to be the curse of your life, she had whispered to him one night in bed as a joke. It always made him uncomfortable when she told him those things. Now he hoped it would save his life. Perhaps, no matter what he said, these men would perceive him as someone of high value.

His strength had ebbed noticeably as the days passed. It was only a slight slide each day, but enough that his prospects of ever escaping seemed dimmer and dimmer. They occasionally offered him food—a pasty slop of rice and strips of unknown meat so tough

Ward could barely swallow it—and they let him keep his canteen with some water in it. It certainly seemed that their intention was to keep him alive so they could get whatever they needed from him. They never took his clothes: his G-suit, his Mae West, his flight suit, his vest. But they refused to treat his legs any more than they already had. He struggled to eat the rice and meat; instead he sucked on candy from one of the pockets in his vest, which they still had never fully searched. He had begun to wonder if all they had in mind for him was this endless repetition of tortuous mind games. A few days later, the cadence of it was interrupted by the appearance in prison of the North Korean lieutenant who had threatened Ward's life the day of his capture. Once again, he was dressed in his officer's uniform. Now that Ward looked on him with clearer eyes, he could tell that the lieutenant wasn't a day over thirty.

Ward squirmed as soon as the lieutenant walked into the room. The man's eyes still held a contemptuous gaze. "You don't like the accommodations here?"

"They are reasonably good," Ward said. "But how long am I to stay here?"

"I will ask the questions," the lieutenant said. This man. Ward had thought himself rid of him. As soon as the Chinese had decided to move him to Antung, he figured this problem was in his past. The lieutenant squatted. "You will be here as long as we see fit. Then . . . I will decide what to do with you."

Ward let that sentence hang in the air, still determined not to show an inkling of his emotions.

"My name is Lieutenant Kang," he said. "You are not like other Americans."

"How so?" Ward asked.

"I served with Americans. After we were freed from the Japanese colonialists. That is how I learned English."

A question snuck to the edge of Ward's lips, obvious and poignant, but he choked it back.

Kang anticipated it. "The Americans were not our only liberators."

"So you sided with the Russians?" Ward asked.

"Your system always results in a favored class and a poor class. And the favored class exploits the poor for its gain. The rich become richer, and the poor become poorer. Our system will ensure everyone is equal. We will all rise together."

Ward had all sorts of arguments as to why that wasn't true. As far as he could tell, Communism and Socialism made everyone poorer; yes, all were equal (except those in government), but they were equal in their poverty. In free markets, there was inequality, but even the poorer were better off than the people in a Communist system. He stifled his arguments. His immediate thoughts were on survival, not winning philosophical battles over which economic system was better. He pointed to his ankles. Flies buzzed about them. In fact, the flies had been a constant source of torture, swarming about him now for days, the threat of their laying maggots in his wounds making sleep impossible. Both of his ankles were swollen, the flesh purple and red around the wound where his bone had pierced the skin. He hadn't pulled back the bandages yet, but he was certain he would find a putrid collection of pus and blood underneath if he did.

"Is it possible for me to get some medical care?" Ward asked, hoping to shift away from debating the values of communism versus capitalism.

"No," Kang said. "There is no medical care here. And our medicine is reserved for the People's Volunteers." He spun away. When he reached the door, he turned back. "If you do not like your accommodations, perhaps I can find you something better."

• • •

Ward didn't have to wait long. Shortly after dark, Kang appeared again. This time, two Chinese soldiers were with him. Without a word, they heaved Ward and his stretcher off the ground and marched out of the hut, as if they were in a terrible hurry. Given their pace, Ward figured they had decided to transfer him to a different location, or perhaps they had received intelligence that an air raid was imminent.

They strained over a small rise, then down into a ravine. A hundred yards in, they dropped Ward to the ground.

His ankles throbbed, and he chewed his lip to keep from showing any reaction to the pain. Before he could gather where he was, the soldiers shoved him into an opening that had been dug into the side of a hill. It was a little larger than a coffin. *So this is where they will kill me?* Ward thought.

"Perhaps you will like these accommodations better," Kang said.

Ward lay on his back, looking up at the muddy soil that was the roof of his new cell, now barely visible in the fading light. He looked out the opening to his left to see Kang squatting. He met the man's eyes. "They want to ask you questions. But when they have finished, I will end what I started."

Then he trudged out of sight, and the only sound Ward heard, menacing and final, was of his own breath.

CHAPTER 12

Most times, Barbara Millar was like a pressure cooker—outwardly, she displayed only the smallest inkling of what was boiling inside her. But not this time. She didn't care who knew how mad she was.

Immediately after receiving news of Ward's disappearance, she had written him a letter.

The next day, she wrote another. The third day, the same. Every day, she wrote to him, determined to keep up what had been her practice before his jet crashed. That way, when he made it back into friendly hands, all her letters would be waiting for him, and he wouldn't miss a thing about what was happening with her, or Adrian, or anything else in his life. More important, he would know that she never gave up faith.

But on this day when the mail had arrived, always in a pile, with her personal letters mixed in with the envelopes for her father's business, she'd found something in the heap that made her want to scream. It was one of her letters to Ward—one she had drafted before his jet had gone down. In the cool bottom floor of her parents' house, she looked at it carefully, trying to understand fully what it meant. She recognized her own handwriting, the envelope now cluttered and covered by a series of stamps. One was of a red, mostly closed fist, only the index finger pointing; underneath it were the words: "Return to Writer." The stupid hand almost looked like a cartoon— like something from one of those new movies Walt Disney was pumping out.

Beneath that was another stamp. No cartoonish picture. Just text: "VERIFIED MISSING IN ACTION."

Barbara spun away from the desk as if it had personally offended her and marched back up the stairs. She burst through the door to the living room with such ferocity that she only barely registered her younger siblings, who were playing with Adrian in the living room, jump back with alarm.

"I need a pen," Barbara said.

"What for?" Her mother was in the kitchen, standing over a boiling pot of something on the stove.

Barbara barely heard the words. She yanked open a drawer and found a pen amidst a pile of pencils and other junk. "They sent my mail back to me," she said under her breath. "They must be crazy." She snatched a piece of lined paper from a small stack in the same drawer, then slid out a chair at the dining room table and started to scratch her message into it.

Dear Colonel Tyer, she wrote.

> *I recently received one of my letters to my husband with the "Missing in Action" stamp on it.*

"Barb?" her mother asked.

"My name is Barbara," Barbara said, without looking up.

"Excuse me?" her mother said.

Only then did Barbara realize the icy tone her mother's voice had taken. It shook her from the letter just long enough to realize how disrespectful her behavior was. She looked over her shoulder.

Her mother was staring at her with a look that was a mixture of both coolness and concern. In her hand, she held a long wooden spoon that likely would have already paddled Barbara's bottom were she ten years younger.

"I'm sorry, Mother," Barbara said, releasing a breath she didn't realize she'd been holding in. "They're sending my mail back to me, as if Ward will never read my letters."

The anger in her mother's face dissipated into empathic regard. "That's what they do when men go missing, sweetheart."

"Not to me, they don't." Barbara returned to her letter.

> *Please do not return my letters to me. Ward will return, and when he does, I want him to find all my letters waiting for him. I want him to know he was not forgotten. You have no proof that he is dead, and I am certain he will either escape or be released back into your charge.*
>
> *Sincerely,*
> *Barbara Millar*

The letter contained one simple, unyielding, cosmic truth: Ward was alive. Barbara knew it even if no else knew it, and she knew it because she could feel him. A soft sensation, gliding atop every surface of her being, kissing her skin like a ray of sun on her face, hands, and neck, even her hair and the tips of her fingers. A gentle nudge that came from within her and without her all at once. The connection between her and Ward that had yet to be severed.

She realized that her mother had sidled up behind her to read over her shoulder.

"You know," she said. "He's a colonel, and Ward's commanding officer. You might want to take a respectful tone."

"I don't care if he's the president," Barbara said. She stuffed both the new letter and the returned one with the stamps into a fresh envelope, then scooted from the table and stomped to the door.

"Where are you going?" her mother asked.

"To the post office," Barbara hollered over her shoulder.

CHAPTER 13

Jae Pil found himself, in those first days driving the truck, thinking about life in the South. His time was exhausted by navigating the rugged dirt and rock roads of the North and surreptitiously looking for his family every time he stopped in any sort of village or encampment. That left his mind free to roam wherever it wished, and it chose to move over the future, like an animal freed into a field for the first time.

In contrast, for much of his youth, Jae Pil's mind was in a sort of prison. His family was Christian, true, but it was a sort of pent-up Christianity that they were forced to keep hidden from the Japanese. The colonialists did not tolerate any dissent in their empire, so they allowed for the inclusion of Christianity as long as it was bland and did not call for devotion to anything other than the emperor. Following his grandfather's teachings, Jae Pil would have died before bowing to or worshiping the emperor, but that didn't mean he needed to strut around his village and school broadcasting his religion either. Instead, he and his family kept it quiet and largely lived it in secret.

The first time he felt a sense of his mind escaping its cage was when Japan left his homeland in defeat. The Japanese flag, that burning disc with blades of red emanating from it, was ubiquitous in his youth. He recalled it flapping in the wind on the flagpole near his village, but one day, after he was already a grown man in his early twenties, it came down. Jae Pil stood by with his grandfather, watching it slide the pole to the ground.

In a sort of impromptu ceremony, some of the elders in the village built a fire and threw the flag into it.

Jae Pil had watched its emblems burn and then ride the smoke into the evening air. "It's over," his grandfather had said. That was all anyone needed to say.

That night in their home, for the first time, their grandfather pulled out his copy of the Holy Bible and read it to the family without anyone keeping a lookout at the door. For the next few months, the wider world rumbled. Korea was divided at the 38th parallel, with the Americans setting up some governmental structure below that line, and the Russians doing the same above it. Everyone should have seen what a problem that divide would become, but Jae Pil, at least, did not. He just figured Korea would be one country again soon, once all the political wrangling after the war was complete. The Russians and Americans would negotiate things out, but eventually, Korean leaders would rule over the land again, and all these foreigners would go back to their own countries. After all, wasn't that the whole point of this great war that had thrust Japan out of the land?

To Jae Pil, that was all distant talk. What would happen would happen; in the meantime, he found himself thinking for the first time about what it truly meant to live his religion. What would he do with his newfound freedom? How should he use it? Should he pray on the hill near the ancestors, or only in his home? Should he pray aloud, or only in quiet? Should he kneel in the fir trees, or stand with arms raised?

"So," his grandfather had said one night during dinner. "We should build a church here."

"Here?" Jae Pil's father had asked. "In this little place?" Everyone always commented on the remarkable resemblance between Jae Pil and his father. *How handsome!* the old, toothless grandmas in the village would say. Both boasted full heads of hair and thick, full cheeks. Both were surprisingly tall as well. *Ooooooh . . . long legs!* the grandmas would say, causing Jae Pil to bow his head sheepishly. And their smiles—they put people at ease, his mother would say.

"Why not here?" his grandfather said. "We can do whatever we like now. Even if it is small, it will be an invitation to anyone who comes."

For a time, that became the family mission: to build a church, no matter how modest—a place to worship openly.

• • •

But the illusion of freedom vanished as quickly as that Japanese flag. Talk of Communist "ideals" slowly spread through the villages. In the early days, the conversations were intellectual, theoretical even, something Jae Pil found he enjoyed. During mere survival under Japan's rule, it had never occurred to him he might one day enjoy allowing his mind to explore heavier subjects like economic theory or the role of government power. But working in the fields of his village or laying the bricks for the new church and allowing his mind to ponder such issues felt like eating a hearty meal after months of starvation. There was something about finally having the freedom to think about how he should live his life, and the tenets he would follow, that made him feel better about things. He was in control of his ship for the first time, instead of being tossed about by every wave and gale of life.

What the Communists offered seemed not just plausible, but beneficial: equality for everyone; no overlords like the Japanese hoarding all of the country's resources only for themselves; the government working for the people and assuring everyone received an equal share of the land's bounty; no exploitation of workers; free healthcare and food and education for all, not just the elite. Jae Pil was not well educated, but he could read, and all of this sounded reasonable to him. Who would not want it?

Then, the Communists had marched into his village to put it into practice.

They came in the evening. He, his grandfather, his father, and even his sister had worked tirelessly for months building their small church. It was difficult labor and finding supplies was a challenge. The fact that they were the only Christians in the area also made finding other like-minded workers almost impossible. But Jae Pil had found that tremendous burdens felt exceptionally light when he was passionate about the end goal. They had managed to lay a foundation of concrete. Upon it, they had nearly completed three walls. Jae Pil and his family could see those three walls in the distance that night as they gathered in the center of the village to hear what news the newly arrived regiment of soldiers had to share.

Prior to that pivotal evening, Jae Pil had heard vague talk of the Communists consolidating power. But he didn't really know what that meant. Messages had reached the village that a man named Kim Il Sung had been chosen as the new leader of the North. He would make the grand vision of a unified Korea built by the people and for the people a reality.

"Attention, citizens!" announced the regiment's leader, a young man, not much older than Jae Pil. "A new era is upon us! Rejoice! We have come to bring the grand vision of our Great Leader Kim Il Sung into fruition." Jae Pil listened intently, his hands still aching from working both in his family's plots and on the church building. "Come forward and learn of the new vision for our land!" The soldiers then had the villagers form a line, so each family could report on their livelihoods and property.

When Jae Pil and his family reached the front of the line, a soldier asked them their occupations and if they owned any land.

"We own those three plots," Jae Pil's father had said, pointing to his land.

"Excellent," the Communist soldier said, his face beaming a cheerful smile. "They will now be used for the People."

"What does that mean?" Jae Pil's father said.

"Half of all land will be used to support the people. Two of your three plots will be for that purpose. The new government will give you directions on what you must do come harvest time. You will also receive instructions on which crops to plant. What is your name?"

Jae Pil's father handed over the information, a confused look on his face.

Jae Pil watched the man scratch the family information into a notebook. He asked Jae Pil's father several questions about which plants the family had grown on the land. "And what is that structure?" he asked, indicating the partially constructed church.

"That is a church. We are building it."

"A church?" the soldier said, his brow furled.

In the twilight, the building up the hill looked almost mystical to Jae Pil, something from a fantasy.

"Christian?" the soldier asked. "Jesus? Mary?"

"Yes," Jae Pil's father said. The last hint of a smile vanished from the man's face. He scribbled something into his notebook. Some of the other soldiers behind him perked up, as if they had heard something interesting for the first time.

"What is it?" Jae Pil's father said.

"You will tear it down immediately," the man said.

"Tear it down?" Grandfather asked. He had been listening quietly behind his son, but now he pushed to the front of the family. His hands behind his back, his shoulders hunched, he stood a little taller. "We are only just building it; we cannot tear it down."

"That land is to be used for the people, and the Workers' Party of North Korea will determine its proper usage. You may not use it to build any sort of church or other building without permission from the Party. Any church activities must be authorized by the Party to ensure they do not undermine the primacy of the people."

"But we are the people," Grandfather said. "Are we not?"

"Each individual must give up his personal interests for the betterment of us all," the man said.

Grandfather seemed ready to argue. Jae Pil could see it in the way he freed his hands from their clasp behind his back.

But the men behind the primary leader had stirred to the point that they were now standing behind him in an organized line. Several carried rifles. Grandfather seemed to notice this, his eyes darting between the leader and his men.

"We will return in one week with instructions for how the land is to be used," the leader said. "That structure must be removed by then. Save the bricks and whatever you can of the foundation. We may have use of those for the people as well."

• • •

Grinding along a heavily pocked dirt road north of Changpung, Jae Pil couldn't help but think of what it would be like to taste that freedom again. Even if it had only been for the briefest of moments, it had left a hunger inside him he couldn't satisfy. There was something about working on a vision of your own creation, or one given by God, that drove him to an enthusiasm for life and his work that simply couldn't be matched. When he was working for the People's Party, that enthusiasm had left him, as if small parts of his spirit had been slowly siphoned away by an unseen force. He couldn't explain why; it was just how it felt.

In the passenger side of his truck, Private Pak slept with his head against the window. Jae Pil realized he knew nothing about the man, except his age. He was younger than Jae Pil, though they were the same rank. They had both received orders to drive this shipment of armaments close to the front lines. As far as Jae Pil knew, that was all they had in common. If Jae Pil drove the truck across the lines to try to surrender, would this private go with him? Would he shoot Jae Pil? Did he agree with the Communists? Had he been forced to fight like so many others? Did he believe in God?

The questions forced Jae Pil to pause. Did he even believe in God? That was a stupid question—of course he did. But for a being that was supposed to care about His children, God had seemed remarkably silent through Jae Pil's suffering. Trials were meant to work for Jae Pil's good. That was the promise, was it not? "And we know that all things work together for good to them that love God, to them who are the called according to his purpose." Wasn't that what Paul had written? So far, Jae Pil hadn't seen it. Not even once. He had issued more prayers and pleas to heaven than anyone he knew. Still, he had been taken from his mother. He'd seen no sign of the rest of his family. And the road ahead most likely led toward nothing but death and mayhem.

CHAPTER 14

Ward lay in his carved-out cell, alone, except for the centipedes, worms, spiders, and ants that he imagined were in the soil all around him. He pulled his ankle to him—a herculean task given how little space he had—and unwrapped the bandages around it. The infection was getting worse. In the brightening light of dawn, he could see the swelling growing. The area around where his bone had penetrated the skin felt warm.

He had spent all night thinking about the lack of medical care. His captors didn't need to torture him or execute him; they could just let him die from the infection.

Then he remembered something in one of his pockets. Twisting to get at his vest, he fingered underneath the zipper. Once again, he was thankful the Communists hadn't thought to search every pocket. At last he touched what he'd hoped were still there: two bottles, neither bigger than a thimble, filled with halazone tablets. He took all but one of the tiny tablets from one of the bottles, and then let a few drops from his canteen fill up the bottle before recapping it. After letting it sit for a moment, he shook until he was confident the pill had fully dissolved.

The halazone was meant for purifying drinking water, not for disinfecting wounds, but Ward figured it couldn't hurt . . . might even work. He dribbled the liquid over the wound.

• • •

After a restless hour, one of the guards thrust some soupy rice into the pit. Ward was still hesitant to eat anything his captors brought him, so he set it aside and instead sucked on some pieces of candy that were still in his vest. A short time later, Kang appeared. For the first time, Ward saw him smile. "Good morning! I have brought you a paper to read." He thrust a dank, dirt-stained newspaper through the opening.

Ward glanced at it for just a second. It was in English. The words *Shanghai Times* stretched across the top. Ward accepted the paper. As long as Kang was smiling, Ward figured he might as well try to be friendly back. "Thank you."

"You do not like your rice?" Kang asked.

"Just saving it," Ward said.

Kang considered this, then nodded, seeming satisfied. "My ankles are quite bad," Ward said.

"Oh, yes," Kang said. "I have been talking with the commanding officer about your wounds. We had a long discussion over breakfast this morning. He even said they might be able to provide you some medical services. There is a hospital nearby. Of course, your answers during interrogation must be . . . satisfactory."

Ward lay in the dirt, considering this proposal. He didn't believe it; most likely it was an interrogator's trick—convince Ward to talk by dangling medical care in front of him like a carrot before a mule, then never let him reach the carrot. But what did he have to lose? If he refused, would they leave him in the pit? Would they execute him? Would they drag him all over the countryside until his festering infection killed him?

These thoughts were interrupted when Kang shifted his

squatting stance. He was still smiling, but a hint of impatience had crossed his brow.

"Deal," Ward said.

"Good." And Kang walked away.

Ward was reading the *Shanghai Times* when he heard the Americans.

Obviously written for propaganda, the paper had informed him of all sorts of developments in China: the Catholic Church was being purged; redistribution of land was occurring at a rapid clip through "land reforms"; anyone who mistakenly thought Americans were "friends" of the Chinese was being reeducated. It all seemed nonsensical to Ward. If the paper was meant to be propaganda, all it did for him was prove how problematic Communism was, which begged the question: who was the propaganda for?

He was pondering this when he heard, "Okay, Mac. Take it easy" coming from somewhere outside his pit.

For a blink, it didn't register that the words were English, the shear impossibility of it preventing his mind from processing it. Then he heard Kang say, "This is where you will be kept . . ." and it hit him. "Hey!" he hollered out of his pit. "Hey! You out there! Are you an American?"

"Yes. Two of us. Are you in there?" The voice carried a thick southern twang.

But before Ward could respond, Kang broke in: "Hey! Be quiet. No talking." His head suddenly appeared beside Ward's pit. "OK. OK. No talking."

Ward decided not to push his luck.

"We'll see you later," he heard the American voice outside say.

• • •

Hunger finally won out. Ward choked down the rice he'd been given. As he finished, Kang appeared at the entrance to his pit. "We have captured two infantry sergeants. We want to help them, but they haven't answered my questions very well. I want you to talk with them. If they answer my questions well, we will give them good treatment. Otherwise . . ." Kang let the word dangle in the air like a grenade with the pin pulled.

"I'll talk to them," Ward said. He wanted to get with them anyway, so this seemed like a plausible excuse.

Minutes later, the sound of scraping boots drew Ward's attention. "Well, I'll be . . ." a voice said in a thick southern accent.

Ward rolled to face the opening of his pit and saw a pair of figures backlit so they seemed like hovering shadows.

The first squatted. "Hi there, captain."

Now that he was closer, Ward could make him out. He was tall, with sandy hair and long, bony fingers that looked like branches on a tree. "I'm buck sergeant Thomas A. Ward. Feller over there says you can talk to us. Wanna come on out?"

"I can't," Ward said, pointing to his ankles. "They broke when I ejected."

Thomas considered this. The other sergeant stood silently behind him, his face dour. "That's horrible," Thomas said. "Well, maybe we can get in there with you." Then he leaned in and whispered, "Talk quietly, you know, so they can't hear us."

He slithered into the pit until he was lying right next to Ward, practically on top of him. "This here is Lester . . . Lester McPherson from Maine," Thomas said, motioning to the other American. "What city did you say you was from, Lester?"

"Rumford, Maine," the man said.

"Lester don't talk much," Thomas said. "How'd you get here?"

Ward gave him the story. "How about you?"

"We was part of a seven-man patrol in the U.S. First Calvary. Crossed the lines and was spyin' on a village where a bunch of commie troops was. We was crossing back over the river, and our boat capsized. Lester and me swum back to shore, but we was on the wrong side. Kept tryin' to cross over, but the river's too high right now. Finally, a buncha Chinese surprised us. Took us before we could even fire a shot."

"How have they been treating you?"

"Not too bad, I guess," Thomas said. "They just been askin' us questions for the past three days and ain't given us a thing to eat."

"You look good for not eating," Ward said.

"Yeah, well, we're some tough bucks, but we're both feelin' pretty weak. We ain't been givin' 'em any information. Just name, rank, and serial number. You know the drill."

At this, Lester squatted next to the opening. "How about you? I see you got some rice there."

Ward told him his strategy about spewing all sorts of useless information, lies, and details already made public.

"Not me," Lester said. "Army tells us to give name, rank, and serial number, and that's all I'm giving them."

"Air force gives us a bit more flexibility," Ward said.

"Well, I ain't changin' nothin'," Thomas said. "They can kill me, but I'm followin' orders."

"Enough!" The voice came from nearby. It was Kang, who had never really left. He marched up to the pit. "You two go back."

"We'll talk more later, buddy," Thomas said, patting Ward on his chest. Then he crawled out of the pit, and just as quickly as they had come, they were gone, hurried off to wherever they were being held.

"So," Kang said. "You convinced them to talk to us, yes?"

Ward shook his head. "They refused. They are under orders and cannot disobey them."

Kang offered a close-lipped smile. "There will be consequences," he said with a shrug.

• • •

"You will dig, or you will die," Kang said.

Ward couldn't see him, but he heard the command from somewhere nearby. He squirmed and twisted to get a glimpse out of his pit, but his ankles wouldn't give him the leverage he needed to see what was happening. Soon enough, three Chinese soldiers appeared out of nowhere and dragged him from his hole. With piercing grips, they clawed under his armpits and pulled him into the light. The sun blinded him. Blinking to see, he felt them tug him across a short space. The next thing he knew, he was sliding into another pit in the ground. When he hit the bottom, he was staring at Thomas and Lester.

"What is this?" Ward said.

"Bastards made us dig a pit big enough for all of us," Lester said, his face and hands covered in grime. He was panting heavily. "I wish we'd just killed all of them."

Ward grimaced but did his best to hide his discomfort. He fought in this war because he was under orders, and, because, in the long run, he felt he was saving innocent lives. But he took no joy in killing anyone, even the Communists.

The pit was open air, with enough room to sit up. Ward tried to adjust his position to lessen the throb in his ankles. Nothing worked.

Kang appeared at the edge of the pit. "If you continue to refuse to answer questions," he said to Lester and Thomas, "you will be given more labor. You will also receive no water or food." He pointed at Ward. "You will care for this man. If he has bowel movement, you will drag him to latrine for it." He spun away.

Ward examined Thomas and Lester more carefully. The dehydration and lack of nutrition were finally showing on their faces, which had begun to appear gaunt. "I'm sorry, fellas," he said.

"It's okay, cap," Thomas said. The muck on his face matched the color of his hair. "We all gotta meet the good Lord at some point."

CHAPTER 15

The threat of American bombers continued through the day. Jae Pil drove hunched over the wheel of his truck, peering up through the windshield's glass. Private Pak did the same, alternating between poking his head out the window and glancing through the front for any sign of the enemy.

The enemy.

It was strange for Jae Pil to think of the Americans that way. It wasn't just Americans. He had heard there were Australians, British, Canadians, Filipinos, and armies from other countries completely unknown to him. His only goal was to join them. Of course, they didn't know that, and therein lay his problem. He was wearing a North Korean soldier's uniform and driving a truck for the people he hoped to fight against. It was all so disturbing. Just five years earlier, all Koreans had been united in their hatred of the Japanese, but now they were fighting against each other like dogs in a cage. Jae Pil rotated his shoulders. His neck ached. His back was sore. Craning constantly to detect jets and bombers in the sky, all while navigating the road and keeping the truck from careening into a tree or a boulder, was an arduous task. He was tired.

After days of driving, he had seen no hint of his family. All he could hope was that they had made it to the South, and that he could soon join them. He was creeping closer and closer to the front lines. The broad valley he was traversing now inclined at last to a tree-covered mountain, towering and dark in the summer sunlight, beneath a cerulean dome of sky. Once he hit the trees, he could relax, take cover beneath their branches.

His convoy was small—it was only he and Private Pak in the truck. Two other pairs of drivers in two other trucks were behind them. They moved across the bomb-pocked terrain like trespassers on an emperor's land. Their own army had covered this particular valley floor with mines, so it was crucial no one veered off the road. The summer air, both in the truck and outside, was oppressive and thick—Jae Pil could feel sweat trickling down his back and into his pants at a regular clip.

His plan was taking shape. As far as he could tell, they were not far from the various United Nations encampments. The People's Army troops to whom he was delivering these supplies had taken the high ground on the mountain in front of him. Below that was a narrow valley with steep walls, and on the next hill over, salvation. The thought of reaching it seemed beyond Jae Pil's power to dream. He was surprised to realize that he did not miss his mother as much as he thought he would. As with the rest of his family, his home, and their modest parcels of land, thoughts of her seemed to be slipping away, gobbled up by the exhausting work of simply surviving.

When the sun was at its zenith, he entered the shade of the firs lining the road. He leaned back in his seat. Then, almost immediately, he spied the irregularities he had expected in the mountainside—to an untrained observer, they would be nothing but shadows among the fallen logs and undergrowth of the forest. To Jae Pil, they were clear signs of foxholes, the barrels of rifles jutting from them like sticks from a small bush.

He hit the brakes. The truck squealed to a stop. Behind him, the other trucks followed his lead. He exited the cab. As soon as he did, a soldier emerged from the bush. A captain.

After balancing his rifle against a tree, the man marched through the undergrowth to Jae Pil, who immediately saluted. "Private Kim Seok Jin, sir."

The captain saluted back halfheartedly. "What did you bring?"

"Armaments, sir."

The captain nodded, seeming less interested and enthusiastic than Jae Pil would have expected. He walked around to the rear of the truck and untied the canvas flap hiding the contents. Then he peered inside.

Jae Pil saw no reason to follow. The man was simply confirming what Jae Pil had said, and then would give them the necessary orders.

Private Pak jumped from the cab, looking anxious. He stared across the hood of the truck to Jae Pil, but his eyes immediately started searching for the captain. He clearly wanted a chance to impress his superior.

Jae Pil pointed with a nod to where the superior officer had gone, and Pak dashed away. "Private Pak Byung Ho, sir," Jae Pil heard from the rear of the truck.

Whatever response the captain gave, it wasn't verbal, for a period of silence ensued.

In that void, Jae Pil stood patiently, merely waiting for the captain to finish whatever assessment he was making. After a moment, he noticed, for the first time in a long time, the buzz of insects in the trees and plants. He even noticed a few dancing in a shaft of sunlight that made a group of leaves glow as if electrified. It was odd, especially this close to the front lines. "It is quiet," he said, almost to himself. Come to think of it, how was it he had driven so far without seeing even one jet or plane? He and Pak had scanned the skies for hours.

"It is quiet for now," the captain said, returning from the rear of the truck, Pak on his heels. "It won't last." His uniform was covered in a layer of dust, making its already drab color appear even more so. Under his eyes, halfmoon shadows revealed a man who likely hadn't slept in days. Jae Pil had seen it—and felt it—before. "Peace talks," the captain said.

"Peace talks?"

"In Kaesong. That is the rumor. Supposed to be starting any time now."

"So there is a ceasefire?" This would put a major complication in Jae Pil's plans. His thinking had finally turned positive as he and Pak had driven along together all those hours. His assumption was that the front lines would have all the chaos of old. And in that bedlam, he would be able to escape, just disappear into the night, wait for the right moment, then escape across the lines and turn himself in. It was a crazy plan, he knew, but in the pandemonium, especially in the dark, opportunities to vanish could easily present themselves. He had been praying for that very thing: one more miracle, a parting of reality that would allow him to walk away, just as he had before. God had done it once; He could do it again. Jae Pil considered his luck, being assigned to this trucking route, for this very assignment that would allow him to come this close to the front lines. It couldn't have been a coincidence. God had brought him here, and God would deliver him. How, exactly, he wasn't sure, especially with a ceasefire in place.

"Perhaps," the captain said. "Nothing official until terms are reached." He pointed for Jae Pil to climb back behind the wheel. "Deliver these to our men on the top of the mountain. They are expecting it. You can only drive the trucks so far before the road is bombed out, then you will need to carry the crates from there. Follow orders when you get there."

Jae Pil saluted and climbed back into the truck, worried he might seem a little too eager.

"Yes, sir," Pak said with a hearty salute. Jae Pil waited for Pak to climb back in. All he needed to do now was wait for an opening. It would come; he knew it.

As for Pak, did he have any sense of what Jae Pil was planning? Would he even care?

Soon, Jae Pil was following the road as it wound up the mountain. It had morphed into more of a trail at this point, narrowed into deep trenches and jutting rocks, the decay of time and lack of maintenance. The truck careened and dipped, at times leaning so much that Jae Pil worried it might topple over. Eventually, it could grind no farther. The trees had encroached too closely. In one place, an American bomb had clearly blown a maw so large it looked like it might swallow Jae Pil's truck in one gulp. This was the spot the captain had referenced.

"We carry it by hand from here," Jae Pil said.

"Yes," Pak said, jumping from the passenger side.

The other trucks pulled up behind them, and their drivers jumped out, with no option but to follow Jae Pil's lead. Out of the trees, other soldiers from the strategic position at the top of the mountain appeared. Jae Pil scanned them all for the person he was to salute. He spied him: a senior lieutenant who had somehow managed to keep his uniform cleaner than Jae Pil's, despite being stationed here on the front lines for who knows how long.

The senior lieutenant gave them both a sharp salute. "Lieutenant Lee Ji-Hoon," he said, his words sharp and deliberate. This was a man of precision. Jae Pil could sense it, could see it in the crispness of his uniform, could feel it in the discipline of his salute. He was shaven; his face clean.

Jae Pil perked and offered as crisp a salute as he could. Private

Pak had leaped from the cab and offered the same with a grunt of extra effort. Down the line, the other drivers followed suit.

"Haul the crates to our trench positions," the senior lieutenant said. "You will see where to put them." Jae Pil nodded.

"Yes, sir!" Pak said, a little too enthusiastically for what was bound to be hours of painful, hard labor. The two of them pulled the first crate from the back of the truck, one on each end, and started the slog up the mountain, where they deposited it as directed.

Jae Pil was out of breath. But as soon as they set the crate down, Pak sprung back to his feet and started jogging down the path.

Did he really plan on running the whole time? Jae Pil thought. But before he could say anything, another voice chimed in. "You don't need to run," Lieutenant Lee said, flat and emotionless. "Just steady."

"Yes, sir," Pak said, stuttering to a halt and waiting for Jae Pil to close the gap between them.

"You should work harder," Pak whispered when Jae Pil reached him. "Then you will be recognized."

"Do I want to be recognized?" Jae Pil asked.

"It is the only way to progress in the Great Leader's sight."

Jae Pil considered Pak. When they had first met and were in the truck, their conversation had been sparse, mostly nonexistent. Jae Pil hadn't wanted to talk because he was afraid of revealing too much about himself and his family. Pak had seemed a bit disgruntled that he was not assigned as the lead driver, but he also seemed content to sit in silence, so Jae Pil didn't see any need to push the issue. Now, however . . .

"So you are hopeful to progress in the ranks?" Jae Pil asked as they traversed back down to the trucks.

"Of course," Pak said. "We all should be." His tone was one of disdain, a hint of disrespect below the surface. Jae Pil couldn't identify its cause. Pak was young, quite a bit younger than Jae Pil, barely over twenty-one.

"Indeed," Jae Pil said. "You are from Pyongyang?"

"Yes," Pak said. "How did you know?"

"Just a guess."

They walked in silence for a few more meters before Pak said, "How is it, at your age, you are only just a private, driving trucks?"

There it was: the cause of his disrespect. In this young soldier's mind, Jae Pil, at twenty-seven, should have been so much more. A soldier on the front lines. Even as an enlisted man, someone rising in the ranks. A seasoned servant of the Great Supreme Leader Kim Il Sung.

Jae Pil needed to be careful with his answer. Who knew if young Pak would report if he perceived even the slightest hint of disloyalty. "I was sick," Jae Pil said. "I wanted to fight, but commanding officers decided I was too ill to join the People's Army, so I had to wait. I only recently joined. I am certain I will move up in time."

"That must have been frustrating," Pak said.

"What about you?" Jae Pil said, trying to shift the conversation off himself. "Surely you could have joined before now."

"I was in a factory," he said, the words spilling from his mouth like he was spitting out warm milk. "I was serving the People's Cause there until I was old enough to fight." Suddenly, his air of arrogance had deflated into self-defense. His eyes were big, and he spoke with both hands in front him, like a little boy trying to convince his parents of something.

"A factory?" Jae Pil said, pleased with himself for shifting the tone of accusation. "What kind of factory would have been more important than serving the People?"

"It was a vehicle factory," Pak said. "I was helping make vehicles for the People's Army."

"Huh," Jae Pil said. "Well, hopefully you will serve in the army with as much gusto as you made vehicles."

Pak offered no response to this, and Jae Pil allowed himself a modest smile. But it didn't mirror what he was feeling inside. Pak was clearly enthusiastic about the Communist cause. He plainly believed in this fight and what they were doing. In short, as Jae Pil planned his escape, Private Pak was going to be a problem.

CHAPTER 16

Ward had been drifting in and out of a shapeless dream when a shadow crossed his face. He blinked his eyes open to see Kang standing there.

Lester and Thomas lay next to him in their hole.

"The commanding officer says you will go to receive medication," Kang said. Then turning to the other two, he said: "The interrogations here are complete. You two will be sent to a POW camp at Pyongyang."

Ward couldn't believe it. Kang was actually going to keep his promise. He didn't look happy about it. It had been five days since he'd made the deal with Ward. During that time, the homemade antibiotic Ward had crafted from his halazone tablets had done wonders for his infected wounds, and Kang and the Chinese commanding officer had asked him enough questions to fill a book. Kang's thoroughness was astounding. He didn't stop simply at Ward's mission or rank. Width and length of runways, locations of bases, sizes of buildings, the conditions of facilities, numbers of windows, statistics concerning the various installations, the organization of the air force, squadrons, units, command structure—nothing was off limits. It all occurred in a hut not far from the pit. Ward spewed up as many made-up facts as he could; if he knew something had already been made public, he offered that as precisely as he could. During all of it, a stenographer—an impish private whose uniform looked two sizes too large—sat in the corner, scribbling down every word.

For Ward's cooperation, Kang continued to reward him with rice and water. Ward shared all of this with Lester and Thomas, an act Kang either didn't mind or simply didn't consider. As a result, the two did not dance with death nearly as quickly as they had planned, even though Kang had repeatedly given them heavy labor assignments that seemed to accomplish nothing—digging holes that never seemed to get used, hauling sticks from one pile to another.

Time in the hole hadn't been nearly as painful as Ward would have expected. He, Thomas, and Lester lay nearly on top of one another, their legs intertwined. During the days, when Ward faced interrogation in the hut, the other two did their tasks. At night, the three shared Ward's food and drink and fantasized together about returning home. More often, they fell asleep before even getting to talk very much.

Now Kang pegged Ward with a cold glare. The illusion of friendliness was over. Kang seemed to guess at the question in Ward's mind. *Why are you keeping your promise? Why not just kill me?*

"It seems," Kang hissed, "that you have cooperated so fully it will make a very fine mark on the commanding officer's record."

So that was why he wasn't being turned over to Kang. Good news, but at some point, the report of this interrogation was going to reach more sophisticated parties. Someone would realize his "information" was nothing more than a mound of manure. When that happened, they'd be coming for Ward. The clock was ticking.

Kang waved to someone Ward could not see. A moment later, a private appeared with a bucket. "Use this to clean yourselves," Kang said. Then he was gone.

Lester and Thomas crawled from the pit, then dragged Ward from it as well. There in the sun, the three of them stripped down and used rags in the bucket to wash their bodies. Ward hadn't cleaned himself since hiding in the creek, and while it wasn't a hot shower, just getting the muck and grime off his skin felt soothing. When he finished and re-dressed, he glanced at the nearby guards. The closest looked more bored than anything. He certainly didn't seem to be in a hurry to force Ward and his friends back into their hole.

Ward lay back in the grass and let the sun wash over him. Its heat felt like a warm tub. Waves of cozy pleasure radiated from his head and down his arms and legs. For that moment, the world seemed right. He knew his journey was far from over, that this moment of contentment was a passing gift, and he basked in it. His body felt clean and robust. The pain in his ankles faded to some distant part of his consciousness. He pondered the workings of the universe in all its expansion and rotations and perfect mathematical circularity. All the days in his youth, dissecting the world with his brother, he had become so certain that whatever force had constructed the vast eternity of it all would never take the time to tweak its many complex workings only for him. It would be like a major factory changing its schedule to help two fleas trapped inside a machine. It would be ridiculous.

But recent events—surviving an exploding aircraft, having his execution cancelled, the Communists leaving his pockets unsearched so he could treat himself with the halazone tablets, the truck breaking down on the way to interrogation in China so he could meet Thomas and Lester, the commanding officer ordering his medical treatment to spare him from Kang—all seemed nothing short of miracles to Ward. Too improbable to have happened by chance.

For the first time in his life, he felt a nudge within him, an impulse fighting to emerge. It was the desire to pray. A need, really, to thank his creator for saving his life. It occurred to him, in that moment of gratitude, that he knew precisely no formal prayers. He just spoke to God in his mind, an informal conversation, like two friends shooting the bull with a drink in hand on the porch on a hot summer day. Almost immediately, he felt guilty, as if the being he was now talking to for the first time in his life deserved more. But what could he give? He had seen Barbara pray a thousand times. The Sign of the Cross. The Hail Mary. The many prayers during Mass. He had never internalized any of them. He tried to recite the Lord's Prayer: *Our Father,* he thought, *Who art in heaven . . .* but his mind trailed away into hopeless oblivion. He knew only a few phrases at best.

Nearby, Thomas stretched, stirring Ward from his thoughts. An idea alighted on Ward like a butterfly. "Tom?"

"Yeah?"

"Are you a praying man?"

"My family always goes to church, yeah. Tell you what: I been prayin' a lot more since I got caught out here, boy."

"Do you have a Bible on you? One of those little ones they give to soldiers?"

"Nah," Thomas said. He leaned up on his left arm and looked at Ward. "But I got somethin' like it." He fingered a small black book from his breast pocket and handed it to Ward.

"What's that?"

"It's a prayer book. Picked it up at the Y."

"Baptist?"

"I don't know," Thomas said. "Might be."

Ward flipped through it. The more he read, the more he realized it was a non-denominational book, filled with prayers and instructions on how to pray from various religious traditions. Ward flipped until he found the Lord's Prayer and the Hail Mary—those were the two prayers Barbara would be saying. "Can I keep this for a second?"

"Sure thang," Thomas said. Ward lay back in the sun and settled into reviewing the two prayers. By the time the guards meandered over to force the three men back into the pit, he had memorized the prayers and given the book back to Thomas.

That night, after darkness had fallen and Thomas and Lester had drifted to sleep, Ward lay on his patch of soil and looked up at the stars in their almost imperceptible twinkling traverse of the night sky, their ancient light upon him. The forest hummed, in rhythms that Ward was making his own. He was surprised to realize he had memorized the prayers so thoroughly.

He fingered his wedding ring in his pocket and pulled it free, leaving the letter to Barbara in place. Its metal felt warm in his palm, and he held it to his heart.

In his mind, he recited the prayers, while simultaneously giving thanks—for the miracles that had kept him alive, for the chance of coming into the orbit of Lester and Thomas, for Barbara and Adrian, for living another day when the time of so many was not extended. In those prayers, his mind went into a place beyond perception, drifting away from his body and broken bones to another plane of existence.

Or at least it seemed so.

There, in that place beyond knowledge, he talked with Barbara. In a quiet voice, or perhaps no voice at all. *I've prayed, Barbara,* he said. *I've prayed.* He wanted so badly for her to know that. Somehow, he knew the message would get to her. He didn't know how, whether she would feel it or see it or hear it like a whisper carried by a soft breeze, but he knew it would reach her.

When he returned and felt the earth beneath his aching body and a nighttime breeze blowing in directionless bursts just strong enough to reach him in the hole, his eyes were brimming with tears.

CHAPTER 17

From the passenger seat of the cab, Barbara watched the front door of her in-laws' house. The weather was warmer in Los Angeles than in Portland, at least on this day. She had flown from Portland to LAX, Adrian crawling all over her, occasionally reaching out her hand for some more crackers. "Mo'. . . Mo'. . . Mo'."

Barbara's reality had gone numb, and her body seemed to be giving out on her. Since she had received the news of Ward's crash, she'd struggled to breathe. It was as if someone had placed a pillowcase over her head and made it impossible to untie. She felt constantly constrained.

Tight, perhaps, was the word for the way her lungs felt. Or *squeezed*. She wasn't sure; she just hated it.

She had fallen into a routine in Oregon: Mass every morning; a letter to Ward every night; prayers in between, with her parents, her siblings, her girlfriends, anyone who would pray with her. But her mind, her thoughts: they were not her own. They would cheat and detour if she let them, sometimes wandering down paths she had tried desperately to block from her mind.

That was why she was here, why she had made this journey. It occupied her mind. "Come on, Adrian," she said. She swung out of the taxi, paid the driver, and gathered her things.

106

Adrian climbed out. Her shoes had fallen off, so Barbara bent down and swooped her up. "Oh my gosh," she said. "You're getting heavy."

"Eeee!" Adrian said, pointing.

"Yep, that's a tree," Barbara said. "Let's go see Grandma and Grandpa." Lugging Adrian across the dirt drive, Barbara reached the door and knocked.

Ward's stepdad answered. "Hi, Ben!" Barbara said. The pleasantries were over quickly, and soon Barbara found herself in their living room, resting on the sofa after the long trip. Ward's mom, Lysbeth, had brought her some coffee.

"Thanks so much for coming down," Ben said.

"Oh, of course," Barbara said. There wasn't any question that she would. In fact, in the history of her relationship with Ward, she had been the bridge builder in his family. She had helped Ward keep a strong relationship with his mom and his stepfather, and when she'd learned that Ward had never even met his biological father, she'd put a quick end to that. She'd tracked down Ward's father—an orange rancher and golf pro in central California—and reunited father and son. So, bringing a grandchild to visit her grandparents was a no-brainer.

"How are you holding up?" Ben asked. He was a kind, skinny man, with thin hair and a warm smile.

"We're doing okay," Barbara said. "It's just gonna be hard until they find him."

Lysbeth coughed. She was a slim woman, with sharp eyes, her hair naturally curly in a medium-length bob pushed from the back to frame her face. She was also brilliant; everyone in the family knew that Ward got his brains from her. She didn't have his charm or warmth, but she was as intelligent as they came.

"You okay?" Barbara asked.

"Oh, yes," Lysbeth said. "We . . . are you still writing him every day?"

"Yes."

"And you're . . . they haven't sent the letters back?"

"They tried," Barbara said, "but I wrote the colonel and told him I didn't want the letters back because I knew Ward was still alive."

"You did?" Ben said. "What did he say?"

"I haven't heard back," Barbara said. "But I also haven't gotten any other letters either, so maybe he listened to me."

"Well, good for you," Ben said. "Not many wives would have been that bold."

Lysbeth shifted, eyes down, then adjusted her skirt, fidgeting with the edge as if it were coming undone.

Barbara just watched her, then braced for the comment she knew was coming. It was as inevitable as her next letter to Ward.

"Barbara," Lysbeth said without making eye contact. "Honey, don't you think you should be preparing yourself that he might not make it?"

"No," Barbara said, perhaps a little more forcefully than she intended. "Because he's still alive."

"Well, honey, we all hope that, but chances are—"

"Don't talk to me about chances," Barbara said. "He's got as good a chance as anyone."

"Yes," Ben chimed in, "but even then, the chances aren't great. Most of those men don't make it."

"Plenty do," Barbara said. She felt herself heating up, as if someone had just lit a fire in the room in the middle of summer. Though she tried to control it, she knew her volume was rising as well. "Take my cousin: her husband was shot down over Germany. Everyone said he was dead, but when the war was over, he came home. Happens all the time."

Lysbeth nodded and pursed her lips. In the silence that followed,

Ben scooped some sugar into his coffee and pretended to be fascinated by something on the rug at his feet.

• • •

The rest of the night passed in awkward chitchat about mundane things no one cared about until, finally, Adrian was asleep and Ward's parents had gone to bed. Only then could Barbara unleash the anger she was feeling inside. The only problem: there was no one to listen to her. She stepped out the front door of the house and walked across the dirt driveway to a faded cedar fence. She leaned against a post.

She looked up at the stars and wondered if Ward was looking at them as well. Could he see them? Or was he trapped in a cage somewhere?

For just a moment, a fleeting blip in the long expanse of eternity that might as well have been an eternity itself, she entertained her mother-in-law's warnings. Could Ward be dead? It was impossible. My cousin, she thought. Her husband came back. Ward will too. You'll see.

Even if it's not until the end of the war, he'll come back. That's what POWs do. The thoughts pinged in her head like marbles—venomous retorts she wanted to fire back at her mother-in-law. As time passed and the stars snuck along in their voyage across the sky, she realized none of those arguments mattered. Her cousin's husband, Ward's brilliance, his instincts for survival, the news of peace talks in Korea—none of that was why she knew Ward was alive.

It was her connection to him. That invisible power, perfectly munificent, still tugged at her heart, at her soul; it was the link to Ward. It seemed to stretch from her innermost core, up into those stars and through the heavens, then back to wherever he was. It was as strong as ever, a spiritual joining. A gift from God perhaps?

Maybe, or just an unexplainable transcendent bond that no scientist or philosopher could ever explain.

Barbara didn't need them to. She didn't need anyone else to understand, although it would have been nice if her mother-in-law did. They would all come to see it in time; the passing of the days and weeks and seasons, even years if necessary, would prove her right.

There at the fence, her anger dissipated. How could she blame them for putting their trust in statistics and likelihoods and probabilities? Wasn't that the way of the world? Didn't that help people make sense of their reality? That she had been given a gift to perceive a deeper existence required her to have patience. So she would, she determined. Right there, in her in-laws' driveway, she found her way forward: patience and love, until Ward walked off a plane on a tarmac somewhere, and she held him in her embrace. When that finally happened, an I-told-you-so wouldn't even be necessary.

That was her path.

With her new resolve, she pushed away from the fence and walked back into the house.

CHAPTER 18

O600 hours: Thomas, Lester, and Ward lay in their pit, awaiting the dawn. Ward had told the other two to sleep, to gather their energy for the journey ahead. They would be marched to a POW camp, if Kang's word could be believed, and the voyage would not be easy.

But none of them could sleep.

"What about you, cap?" Thomas said.

"We'll see," Ward said. "Hopefully they stay true to their word. They claim they're gonna take me to a hospital and get some medical care. I'm not worth much to them now, and eventually they're gonna find out everything I told them wasn't helpful."

"I hope we see you again," Lester said. It was one of the rare times the boy had spoken. At first Ward had thought he was angry or bitter, but it turned out he just didn't talk unless he had something to say, in stark contrast to Thomas, who could chat for hours, seamlessly transitioning between topics like a child telling a story.

"I do too," Ward said. "You two don't know what you've meant to me. I thought I was all alone out here."

"When this is all done," Thomas said, "we'll find each other, sit back and drink a cold one together, and remember our good ol' times in Kang's pit when we had to drag you to the crapper."

111

Ward chuckled. Lester cracked a smile. "It's a deal," Ward said.

A half hour later, just as the sky shifted to a shade of gray, two guards appeared over the rim of the hole and ordered Thomas and Lester to climb out. As soon as he was on his feet, Thomas glanced back. "Hang in there, cap. If we get back, we'll reach out to your family."

"No," one of the guards said, shoving Thomas forward. And just like that, Ward was alone again.

Later in the day, his ride appeared. Two soldiers Ward had never seen, one officer and one enlisted man, wearing the same drab, olive-colored uniforms as all the rest, reached into the pit and pulled Ward up by his armpits. They lifted him onto a stretcher that had been fastened to a metal frame, which connected to two bike wheels. The officer walked in front, with the soldier pushing the stretcher.

They made their way along a dusty oxcart trail, through thickets of trees and streams littered with bloody bandages and other human filth. They bumped along in silence until, eventually, a village appeared through the brush like a promise.

As it came into shape, Ward had hope that this was his final destination. In his heart, he knew it was unlikely. When he saw another Russian-made transport truck, his suspicions were confirmed.

Quickly, the soldier and his commanding officer loaded Ward into the back of the truck and, soon enough, it roared to life.

Ward found himself in the canvas-covered bed surrounded by three new guards. Night fell.

The ride was rough. Ward's legs bashed into the sides and against the floor, projecting waves of pain up his thighs and into his hips. From what he could see in the dark, they were in a landscape of pure namelessness; they could be going anywhere.

By midnight, the truck slowed and its airbrakes hissed. The tailgate dropped with a clatter. Four guards materialized out of the black and dragged Ward from the bed. He tried to take in his surroundings, grasping for any hint of where he might be, but the night blanketed everything. All he could make out in the glow of the truck's headlights was the vehicle itself and the looming wall of a mud hut.

The soldiers carried him through the door of the hut. What hit him first was the stench. It was overpowering, enough to make him gag. Vomit, feces, urine, sweat, pus, mud, straw—all mixed together in a pungent stew Ward could barely stomach. It was like someone had taken one of Adrian's stinky diapers and multiplied its aroma by infinity. They didn't need to torture him, he thought. He would give up anything to get away from this.

He resisted the urge to put his hand over his mouth and instead sucked in shallow breaths.

It didn't help.

Inside, one burning kerosene lantern provided just scant light. It was enough to make out his new surroundings, which were anything but a "hospital." The hut looked to be an old stable. Half a dozen men lay on straw beds scattered about a twelve-foot-square room. The roof was made of straw, which culminated at a high peak. On one end, hanging from it, was some sort of wooden storage area. Beneath that was a shallow pit filled with the detritus of a world at war with itself. The walls were mud, pierced here and there by bullet holes.

Ward dangled in the soldiers' hands, his arms and legs held aloft as if he were floating on air. It was clear the men didn't know what to do with him.

One man was tending to a soldier on the floor. He glanced up and, without expression, nodded for the soldiers to place Ward by the pit.

They sidestepped to the spot, then dropped him to the ground with a thud. He did his best not to groan. Without comment, they walked from the room and into the night.

Ward took in more of his surroundings. There was the door through which he had entered. Opposite it, another door led out into a poorly lit courtyard. Six Chinese soldiers lay silent on the floor of the hut, and two others navigated among them, apparently checking on their wounds. In the pit and scattered across the floor, except in the high traffic areas, lay bloody bandages, discarded food, and what looked like vomit mixed with excrement.

One of the workers made his way to Ward. "We fix your legs," he said.

"OK," Ward said, but he was doubtful.

Within minutes, the two men—both Chinese soldiers—knelt by Ward's feet and began their work. One cut free the splints that had been holding his legs together. The other used a thick stick to stir what looked like plaster of Paris. They didn't bother washing or even inspecting his ankles or legs in the dull light.

Ward considered saying something but decided against it. No use offending the men who said they were going to help him.

Soon, the men were dipping strips of cotton cloth in the plaster and wrapping Ward's ankles.

He had no idea if they were doing it right. "What happens now?" he asked as they finished up.

"This is hospital," the first man said. "You stay here until you heal. Then you go to POW camp or Pyongyang."

"When will that be?"

"Two month," the soldier said. Two months, Ward thought as the two medic-soldiers exited the room. Sixty days. Plenty of time for Kang and the commanding officer to realize everything Ward had told them was worthless or, worse yet, an outright lie. They were probably already in Pyongyang now going over it all with Chinese intelligence officers. Now that he thought on it, where was Lieutenant Kang? Had he not followed Ward here? Was he, in fact, poring over Ward's interrogation transcripts so he could use anything he found against his American captive? Perhaps the commanding Chinese officer had thwarted Kang's murderous execution plans. It was a possibility, but something told Ward it was a slender reed on which to rest his hopes.

Pondering these questions, he drifted off to sleep.

• • •

I've got to get out of here. He knew it when he woke the next morning to a boot in his gut. He coughed and gasped for breath.

"Wake," a voice from above said.

Ward opened his eyes to see a Chinese soldier standing over him. But as soon as Ward stirred, the man just limped away and out the door that led to the courtyard. Bloody bandages bound the man's right knee—he was one of the wounded in this makeshift hospital.

That, by itself, isn't what pushed Ward to his resolution. It was the entirety of the situation: the filth in the room and the likelihood that if his captors didn't kill him, infection would; the hostility of the other soldiers; the likelihood that Kang would return with a wind of fury and vengeance at his back; the loneliness Ward now felt and the devastating longing for Barbara that left him feeling as if every part of his inner person had been stripped by some unseen force and could never, ever be filled again; and, just as bad as the rest of it, the swarm of flies that had decided to make this place their home. They were everywhere.

They had kept Ward awake most of the night. Now, from the shafts of light coming from the doors and bullet holes in the walls, he could finally see the magnificence of their number. The flies swarmed about the room in shifting clouds, alighting anywhere and everywhere. A few feet away, one of the Chinese soldiers slept, snoring with his mouth open. The flies walked all over his face, in and out of his mouth and nose, picking at the corners of his eyes. Another soldier sat cross-legged on his bed, shoveling rice into his mouth. Several times he swallowed flies with it; he didn't even seem to notice.

The fleas and lice were just as aggressive. They seemed to be in an all-out war with the flies, unwilling to be outnumbered.

At first, in the night, Ward hadn't noticed them because he couldn't see them. Then the itching started. Now he found both all over his body—in his hair, his casts, the seams of his G-suit; on his head; around his privates. He swatted at them, picked them off whenever he could, but more and more charged, as if he were lying on a wellspring of them.

The itching in his cast was the worst of it. He found a twig on the floor and used it to scratch the bites; but he knew that, in the end, all he would do was scrape his skin raw, inviting further insects and infection.

The bathroom situation only added to his desperation. There wasn't one. After he woke and surveyed his surroundings, he realized how bowel movements were taken care of. The medics walked into the room with shovels of dirt and stopped at each injured man, who would then squat over the shovel and poop into it. The medic would then take it outside and dump it somewhere. Ward could have lived with that, but when one patient missed the shovel, the medic kicked the feces aside and didn't even bother scooping it up. Ward's dysentery made using the shovel impossible. As soon as the medic realized this, he marched out of the hut and returned with a flute-topped flowerpot. He set it next to Ward and pointed. Ward held out as long as he could, but eventually, he had no choice. He found a way to support himself against a wall and sit on the pot at the same time. He used strips of the cotton from his cast for toilet paper, but it did little good.

He needed to get out of this place. Escape or die. The only middle point between those two options was somehow surviving and ending up in Siberia, where the Communists were sending many of their enemies to work. That would only postpone death by a short time.

Ward glanced around the room, taking in his resources, calculating how he might escape. He would need help. In the end, he realized, he had nothing. No one. Just the flies and the filth and the vermin.

Then, a quiet moment passed—a sacred second, he thought, because he felt her.

Barbara. She was always with him, for the minutes, hours, days of his captivity, the one who followed him. She was always nearby, though distant, through all the oceans and mountains and war-torn hellscapes that stretched inside him. The one whose melancholy was his melancholy.

It was a feeling of a world beyond himself, a reality breaking down borders both seen and unseen, seeming to penetrate the very laws of physics and mathematics he had studied so diligently. A spiritual plane just beyond his five senses. In that moment, he was certain it was there, finer and deeper than this reality—he could discern it if he looked with purer eyes.

Tranquility. Followed by prayer.

This time it came to him as naturally as a walking baby who has finally made it past taking the first tenuous steps. When he was alone, with nothing in the world that could help him, there was only one place he could turn for help. For peace.

—*Help me. Help me.* Quiet.

—*Help me escape. Help me.*

He felt it then: a new thought to replace the ones that had left his mind. *God helps those who help themselves.*

He pondered on this for much of the day amidst the insects and enemy combatants. As the evening settled in and swarms of mosquitoes decided to join the insect hordes, he came to one precise conclusion. It was time to go to work.

CHAPTER 19

The "ceasefire" lasted as long as burning rice paper.

At the top of the hill, pandemonium reigned. Earlier in the day, in the predawn darkness, someone fired a shot. Some screamed that the Americans fired first; others said the North Koreans had. It didn't matter to Jae Pil. He just wanted to live. What followed was hours upon hours of shells, both exploding and being fired.

Jae Pil and Private Pak had been assigned the duty of hauling new boxes of artillery ammunition to the top of the ridge, where soldiers fired it as fast as they could get it.

In the middle of the day, the two lugged the latest crate through the trees. Jae Pil's fingers ached and gave him the sense they might remain in a permanent claw the rest of his life. At first, he'd faced no problem pushing up the trail. Now, he struggled to keep his grip with his boots.

His feet slid from underneath him as if the dirt had a mind of its own. "Keep moving!" Pak screamed. "They need this!"

Jae Pil dug in his toes and forced himself to his feet. *Please, God.* They were the only words his mind could muster. The rest of his mental energy was consumed with the task at hand.

Most of the blasts had hit on the face of the ridge, showering Jae

Pil and his unit with dirt but otherwise doing no damage. Whether his fellow soldiers were hitting the American targets was a mystery to him. He had hoped that if a skirmish broke out, he might be able to escape in the chaos, hide until things calmed down, and then sneak across the border.

It was a fantasy. Right out of the gate, he and Pak had received the assignment that forced them to stay together. And with his seeming devotion to the Communist cause, Pak was never going to let Jae Pil slink away.

They reached the top of the ridge and dumped the crate. Jae Pil sucked in a long breath.

"Hurry!" Pak screamed, pivoting to jog back down the mountain. His energy seemed boundless. He'd never once slipped or even leaned against a tree—not a single sign of fatigue.

"Hold," the captain yelled. Jae Pil looked back at him.

"We have enough," the captain said.

Then Jae Pil noticed that things had grown quiet again. Smoke wafted along the ridge. It weaved in between the trees like a specter.

"Stay ready!" the captain barked.

"Rifles, captain?" Pak asked.

The captain grunted yes. Pak spun like a child playing on ice and sprinted down the hill. Jae Pil shook his head, then followed, thumping down the trail and feeling like gravity might knock him over.

Soon, both had taken position in a foxhole that gave them a view of the distant ridge where the American army was positioned. It could have been Americans, but it might have been South Koreans—Jae Pil didn't know. From his vantage point, he couldn't see anything. The opposing mountain was nothing more than a giant shadow bulge in the distance. As far as he could tell, no one was even on it. "Do you think it's over?" he finally asked.

"Not sure," Pak said.

In time, the adrenaline of the battle gave way to the heat of the sun. It cooked Jae Pil's back like an open fire. He finally flipped over and rested his rifle on his chest.

"We must stay ready," Pak said.

"I'll be ready. We can be back into position immediately if anything happens."

Jae Pil didn't know what Pak would think of this, but he was too tired to care. It was possible, he supposed, that the private might report him, so he was relieved when Pak turned onto his back as well.

"Did we lose any men?" Pak asked.

Jae Pil shrugged. "Not sure."

"I wonder how many of theirs we took out."

"Hard to say," Jae Pil said.

The entire ridgeline had grown quiet. Jae Pil could hear people whispering in nearby foxholes; occasionally, he noted the footsteps of someone walking below them or the crackle of a radio in the distance. The captain, he presumed, was talking with command.

Nothing to do but wait.

"How is your ammo?" Pak asked.

It was a silly question. Neither of them had fired a single shot. Jae Pil chose not to argue the point. "Fine. Still fully loaded."

"Did you grow up in Pyongyang?" Pak asked.

"No," Jae Pil said. "A small village."

"Ah," Pak said.

"What is the city like these days?" Jae Pil asked.

"Things were getting better before the war," Pak said. "The Japanese were gone. We kept what was ours."

Jae Pil considered this, remembering the Communists ordering his family to tear down their fledgling church and give half of their fields to the People. "It is nice not to have to give ourselves to the Japanese."

Pak nodded. Neither spoke for a long time. Then Pak added, "They took everything from us when I was little."

"The Japanese?"

Pak nodded. "Who else?"

"Yes, yes," Jae Pil said. "They did. What did your family do?"

Pak snorted. "Survived . . . some of us."

"Not all of you?"

"My mother died."

"I'm sorry," Jae Pil said.

Pak continued, "My father worked in a factory. As soon as I was old enough, I worked there too. We made clothes, but we enjoyed none of the profits."

"Did they pay you?"

"Not me," Pak said. "They paid my dad some, but not enough. We could afford nothing. We all lived in one room and shared rice. The Japanese took all the rest. The Great Leader has changed all that."

"You are paid better now?"

"He gives us hospitals. For free. We don't have to pay."

"There are no hospitals in my village," Jae Pil said, adjusting in the dirt and using his hand to block the blinding sun. "The closest is half a day's walk away."

"When this is over, you should come to the city. There are many there. We couldn't afford any sort of doctor before now. That's why my mother died."

"She was injured?"

"Sick," Pak said. "And when we tried to get help, we couldn't find any. There were almost no doctors, and the ones there were wouldn't see us because we didn't have any money."

"What was her sickness?" Jae Pil asked.

Pak shrugged. "We never knew. Fever, couldn't breathe, sweaty.

Her hands shook . . . I remember that. I was little. I remember my dad saying we had no medicine."

"I'm sorry," Jae Pil said again.

"Now we all have medicine. We never need to worry again. Instead of the Japanese taking everything from the workers, we will all keep what we earn. It is better, is it not?"

"But do we keep it?" Jae Pil asked. "I thought everything goes to the Party. Half of our farming we must now give up immediately."

"It goes to the Party to be redistributed," Pak said, impatiently. "Instead of any of us getting richer and richer while others go poor, the Party will ensure everything is spread among the people, so we will all be equal."

Jae Pil nodded. He didn't want to argue with Pak, who had clearly thought about this far more than he had. Something about all of it felt wrong. It sounded nice: equality, no one poorer than anyone else, the Party acting as a kind of grand and benevolent over-lord to help everyone receive the benefits of their production. But he couldn't help but think of his own family. After the Communist officers had seized half their land and, once again, forbidden church worship, the brief period of time where Jae Pil had felt truly alive had dissipated like smoke in the wind. It hadn't taken long before working the field morphed into drudgery. Life had become a mean-ingless toil of nothing but work so the Party could take it from him.

As he bottled up his comments to Pak, a familiar frustration came over him: the need to stay cloistered, to hide his true thoughts and feelings. It was this way every time he spoke to a diehard Communist. Only in his home, with his parents, behind closed doors, had he ever been able to speak freely about his beliefs, his hopes and dreams, the direction he would follow in his life if no one were controlling it. He never expected such forced silence to be so aggravating, but buttoning up his true identity and hiding it deep down was like sealing the lid over a pressure cooker. It was building inside him, bulging, until he felt he might explode.

And it brought anxiety with it.

Day after day, week after week, he worried about saying the wrong thing. He had seen people imprisoned for even hinting they were not utterly and completely loyal to the Party. He had witnessed others get shot or executed. But how long could he keep the core part of who he was silent? Faith in God the Communists interpreted as fealty to something other than their cause. Dedication to family they saw as a threat to putting the People above all else. Wanting to work your own land and keep the fruits of your labor meant you were just a capitalist pig with selfish desires and should be dealt with accordingly.

So he locked it inside, afraid of exposing himself.

He closed his eyes against the sun. His mind floated, gliding here and there. What would it be like to just be himself? Nothing less, nothing more. He had enjoyed that only once: during that blink of an eye when the Japanese had been overthrown but before the Communists had taken control. He was determined to enjoy it again.

CHAPTER 20

The crunch of boots on dirt, the scuff of a hesitant person.

Ward opened his eyes to see a shadowy figure standing in the doorway.

He was lying on his straw bed. He was tired, so tired. For days, his mind had churned over all the items he would need for a successful escape: sixty cubic inches of uncooked rice, enough for three weeks; water; matches; his halazone tablets to purify the water; boards he could kneel on to use as sleds to crawl across the countryside; most important of all: his legs, which he didn't have use of.

It all seemed so impossible. Ward had never been one for despair, but these past days it had been creeping over him like a growing moss, to the point that he turned, again and again, to prayer. He'd even made himself a cross out of two twigs, which he'd fastened together with string and candle wax. It was less than two inches tall, but it had given him a way to focus his prayers—that and his wedding ring. At night, he held both, as if they were talismans imbued with a spiritual power all their own.

Still, the hopelessness had been difficult to keep at bay. His ankles seemed no closer to healing. One time, late at night, he had snuck from his pile of straw to the porch of the hut, swung his legs off the steps, and tried to stand, only to realize that even the slightest weight on his feet fired debilitating pain through his bones and up his legs. Another time he had asked one of the medics to cut a square viewing window in his cast to see if things were healing properly, only to find that some sickening flap of skin had begun to grow off the side of his ankle. Before Ward could stop him, the medic had cut it off with a pair of rusty scissors. The move had caused blood to spew all over the cast and into the wound. Days and days passed, and Ward was still no closer to collecting what he needed to escape.

And now a new spectral figure stood in the doorway.

Ward didn't move. He just watched. He had found that any time new soldiers arrived, they found the American in their midst fascinating—they would pull on his hair, rub his eyes, play with his clothes and the few belongings he still had. Pretending to be asleep seemed to be the best way to keep them at bay until they grew bored with the novelty.

This figure, however, was not leaving. Whoever it was seemed cautious, like a skittish cat.

Ward finally leaned up on his elbow.

The silhouette in the doorway developed some character. He was a boy, perhaps eight or nine. He wore what so many of the Koreans in the village seemed to wear: white trousers and shirt, black rubber shoes with the toes turned up, and a black baseball cap. When he saw Ward prop himself up, he took a step back toward the sunlit path outside.

"It's okay," Ward said, smiling and stretching out his hand. His voice felt trapped in his throat, it had been so long since he'd used it.

The boy refused to move. But neither did he run. He eased down the doorjamb and squatted, positioned for a quick escape.

Ward waited.

Minutes passed in silence. The rest of the room was largely empty; those soldiers who could walk were out enjoying fresh air . . . only one remained, snoring. Even if there had been more in the room, it likely wouldn't have mattered. After the initial fascination with Ward, most seemed to lose interest in him pretty quickly. Ward remembered something an old man had said to him one Sunday when he'd gone to Mass with Barbara: "Son, when I was twenty, I worried what people thought about me; when I turned forty, I didn't care what people thought about me; now that I'm well past sixty I've finally realized something: no one has ever been thinking about me; they've all got their own problems." It certainly seemed to be true here in this "hospital." None of these men cared about the American in their midst.

Finally, Ward remembered the Korean word for "friend." He patted his chest. "Chingu," he said.

The boy managed a feeble smile and seemed to relax. There was something calming about his presence, the sheer impossibility of it. A child. Here. In a war zone. The more Ward thought on it, the more it made sense—of course there were still children around. It was their country at war; where would they go? But it was so rare to see them, especially as a pilot.

Ward acted out his own story, explaining his jet crash and broken legs, the casts. He patted his chest again. "Ward Millar. Ward Millar."

The boy smiled. "Hyun Bong Ho," he said, pointing to himself.

"Hyun Bong Ho," Ward said. He was certain he had butchered the pronunciation, but the boy brightened noticeably at Ward's efforts.

"Nice to meet you, Ho," Ward said.

They sat in silence again, and Ho set something down beside himself and watched it.

Ward could barely make it out, but it appeared to be a small oxcart crafted from straw—wheels and all. It was attached to a large beetle, which dragged the cart behind it.

Ingenious, Ward thought.

Then Ho started humming. It was a tune Ward recognized but couldn't place. It wasn't Korean. Something from home. "For auld lang syne, my dear," Ho sang. "For auld lang syne . . ."

Ward guffawed. He sucked in a deep breath. "Do you speak English?"

Ho shook his head. His face slackened. That was a stupid question, American.

"How did you learn that song?" Ward asked, pointing to Ho's mouth.

Ho shrugged. "Little English," he said. "Methodist school."

Ward nodded. In excitement, he pulled his makeshift cross from his vest pocket and showed it to Ho. "Christian?"

"No," Ho said.

It was a disappointing moment for Ward; for a brief second, he thought maybe he'd found someone who would be sympathetic to him.

"Father army," Ho said. He pointed to the distant hills. Then he pointed to the ground outside. "Mother village." He pointed around the hospital hut. "Uncle house. Communists take."

Ward pointed at Ho again. "Communist?"

Ho made a face like he'd just smelled the inside of the fake hospital for the first time. "No. Hate."

Ward was jarred by voices and the clatter of someone just outside the door. A gruff voice drew Ho's attention. He said something back. Then one of the medics crawled over the boy. He slapped the side of the boy's head on the way in, and then shouted a series of terse orders.

Ho yelled something in return, then disappeared onto the trail.

• • •

Ho turned out to be precisely what Ward needed. Ho hated the Communists, who, as far as Ward could tell, had taken everything from the little village, from their homes to their fields to their family members—and they had been harsh in doing so. In the quiet moments, when the room was empty, Ho also helped Ward build a useful connection. He introduced Ward to a Chinese soldier who hated his army as much as Ho did. He spoke broken English but told Ward there were "many, many" Chinese soldiers and civilians who did not like the new regime. Only a few military men, students, opportunistic politicians, and some powerful businessmen had truly embraced it. The commoners found it did nothing for them.

Ho also introduced Ward to a local trader who gave Ward two hundred won, the Korean currency, for his undershirt and a ballpoint pen Ward had been allowed to keep after his crash. He didn't know what he would do with the money, but he figured it would always be good to have. If he ever did find himself in the countryside, the won might just save his life.

In time, Ward decided he could trust Ho with his plans for escape. It was a calculated risk, but Ward needed help.

It paid off.

Ho smuggled in a container for carrying rice; he convinced his uncle to cut two boards Ward could use as sleds; he procured the rusty blade from a broken scythe Ward could use while on his escape; he found twine; he even smuggled in edible food—some sort of a sweet rice cake—that Ward ate to gather his strength.

One afternoon, while most of the injured Chinese soldiers basked in the sun out in the courtyard, Ho appeared at the door. He scanned the room, ensuring none of the medics were around, and then sauntered over to Ward.

Ward waved him to squat next to his bed, then pointed to the dirt floor. As soon as Ho was in position, Ward drew a map of the peninsula.

Ho immediately erased it, his eyes wide. He shook his head. "No," he said.

Ward flashed both palms, as if to say, *What's wrong?*

Ho pointed to the door, then made the motion of someone shooting, then pointed to his chest.

Ward nodded. "They'll shoot you if they see this," he whispered. He paused for a moment.

He had always known that Ho was taking a risk in helping him, but he hadn't quite realized just how severe it was. The boy was putting his life in danger every time he brought Ward even the tiniest item.

Ward placed his finger to his lips, then waved for Ho to come closer. Looking over the boy's shoulder to show him he understood this needed to be a secret, he once again drew the Korean Peninsula in the dirt. Then he made a dot close to the west coast and indicated he thought this was where they were.

Ho shook his head. He made another dot closer to the center of the country.

That can't be right, Ward thought. Ward tapped his dot again.

Ho furrowed his brow and drilled his index finger into his own spot.

There was no point arguing with him, Ward thought. He wiped away the map, gripped Ho's shoulder, and thanked him with a smile and a nod.

After the boy had gone, Ward lay on his back. His plan depended on one thing: being close to the coast. His hope was to crawl from the hospital and head north, the last direction they would search for him. Then he would cut straight west. If he could make it to the coast, then he could either flag down a UN vessel or, if worse came to worst, inflate his Mae West and float out into the ocean until someone rescued him. The UN boats controlled the seas, so he didn't think it would take too long.

None of that would work, however, if Ho was right about where they were.

• • •

Kang returned with the pomp of a king, strutting into the room as if he expected Ward to rise and salute. When Ward just lay there, Kang looked genuinely disappointed.

For his part, Ward didn't move because he figured the end had come. He didn't know where Kang had been these past weeks. Had it really been weeks already? But the most likely location was a place he could check the veracity of Ward's information. And now here he was again, lazily walking into the room, his eyes trawling down the length of Ward's body to his casts.

Kang scrunched his nose. "You stink," he said.

Ward shrugged. He didn't know how to respond to that.

"You can walk?"

Ward shook his head.

"You will soon," Kang said. "Then Chinese give you to me." He smiled without showing his teeth, his pressed lips thinning almost imperceptibly.

• • •

Ho brought company this time. A woman and an older, balding man. Once they reached Ward, all three squatted next to him.

Ward did his best to sit up, but the woman waved him back to the ground. "Anjaya-yo," she said. They compromised with Ward on his elbow.

"Uncle," Ho said, opening his palm to the man. "Mother," he said with a bow toward the woman.

Ward smiled at both. "Thank you," he said, bowing his head.

"Need favor," the uncle said in stilted English. He was quite a bit older than Ho's mother, with only the thinnest wisps of hair on an otherwise shiny scalp. Moles dotted his face, but his smile was kind.

"Okay," Ward said.

"Boy go with you," the uncle said.

Two feelings seized Ward simultaneously: panic and obstinance. The first because it was now clear to him, as it should have been days ago, that Ho was telling other people about his escape plans. The second because under no circumstances could he take a child with him on his escape.

He quickly realized there was nothing he could do about Ho's loose mouth. And, besides, it had proven invaluable in getting him what he needed.

"No," he said. "Too dangerous."

"Please," Ho's mother said. The look on her face was one of desperation. "Please," she whispered again, seeming only barely able to hold back tears.

"His family in army in south," the uncle said. "They take him."

When Ward didn't immediately respond, the uncle said again, "Family take care of him."

"Please," Ho's mother said again.

Ward probed all three of them. Their faces mirrored each other with a look of hopefulness.

Ward's first reaction dissipated, replaced with both compassion and a new sense of possibility. What must they be facing here, in this place, that would make them so desperate to get this child to the South? How much better must they perceive things to be? Ward couldn't deny them that. Deep down, he did believe, as they seemed to, that what the Americans would provide in the South would be so much better than what was here. And while he was confident his own military could eventually defeat the North, he wasn't so sure that would happen. Even before his latest mission, there were rumors of peace talks. President Truman had already removed General MacArthur because the man had wanted to bring the full weight of America's might against the Communists, something the president saw as both dangerous and unnecessary. It may well be, Ward thought, that boys like Ho will be trapped here and left to a fate decided by men like Lieutenant Kang. How could Ward do that to him?

At the same time, having Ho along for help could prove advantageous. He was young, but he had proven himself remarkably resourceful. Plus, Ward had to embrace the reality that it would be very difficult, if not impossible, for him to carry everything he would need while crawling over hills and across rugged terrain.

"Okay," he said.

• • •

Kang had grown impatient. The day after Ward and Ho had finalized their plans, he marched into the hospital and ordered two men with a stretcher to carry Ward out of the building.

With no choice but to obey, Ward crawled onto the stretcher. *My time has come,* he thought. All his plans, his preparation, had been for naught. "Where are we going?" Ward asked.

"To see if your wounds are healing," Kang said. The men carried Ward down the hill and into the village, through a stream, and finally into a different hut, where two men dressed in white waited. They placed Ward on a table, where he sat, his legs jutting off the edge.

Without a word, the two men sliced into Ward's casts with some sort of a sharp spike. Once they had carved a groove wide enough for a crowbar, they jammed the spike into both casts and pried them apart. Two things, both disgusting, assaulted Ward: the stench of rot and the lice—living and dead, of every size. Neither seemed to bother the men in white.

Ward grimaced.

Kang scrunched his face in disgust, but his abhorrence seemed directed at Ward as much as the casts, as if the situation were Ward's doing.

Ward couldn't have cared less about the North Korean. And after the first two seconds, he didn't care about the stink or the bugs either. What caught his attention were his legs. Once muscular and fit, they looked like nothing more than twigs with loose skin draped over them. All his muscle was gone.

Ward leaned over to get a closer look. The men who had created the casts had obviously butchered the job. The bones and flesh of his ankles jabbed out in great knobs. And his feet. What had they done to his feet? They seemed to have become something else entirely, like the Communists had reformed them into new, grotesque protrusions. They were angled down and away from him, as if it were perfectly natural for a man to spend his days walking on his toes. He tried to move them, to lift his toes out of that awkward, downward point, but they refused to move. It was as if the signal from his mind to his feet had been derailed somewhere along the way.

"This is no good," he said to the doctors.

Kang asked something in Chinese, maybe Korean—Ward couldn't always tell the difference.

The doctors shook their heads.

Kang released an angry, guttural sound, then stormed out of the room and into the sunlight beyond. The doctors watched him go, both slightly amused. Then one of them met Ward's eyes. "We recast."

"No," Ward said. "I'm okay." He wasn't sure if his bones had set at all, but he figured casts would only slow him down. He needed to try to exercise whatever muscles he had left, perhaps bring some movement to his feet.

"No," the doctor said. "We recast."

Ward continued to protest, but, in the end, he couldn't stop the men. Soon they were rewrapping both his ankles. They didn't stop there. They wrapped higher and higher up his leg, past his knee, up his quads.

"No, if you go that high, I won't be able to bend my legs," Ward said. He tried to push their hands away.

"You stop!" one of the doctors snapped. "This better." When they were finished, the casts were well above his knees. Attendants appeared at the beckon of the doctors and slid him back onto the stretcher. On his way back to his hut, his mind clung to only one thought: now he couldn't even crawl.

CHAPTER 21

Barbara's next destination was inland.

She had asked Ward's brother, Monroe, to drive her to visit Ward's biological father. They drove through Los Angeles and up over The Grapevine, twisting down into the agricultural lands of the San Joaquin Valley, then heading north on Highway 99. By nightfall, she and Adrian had reached Ward's dad's house in Visalia, exchanged brief greetings with him, and quickly fallen asleep.

The next morning, in the kitchen, she reopened a letter her priest had sent to her at Ward's parents' house in LA. She had already read it a dozen times, but something about the words touched her:

> *Yesterday at Church, your mother told me of Ward . . . and requested that I offer the Holy Sacrament of the Mass for his safety.*
>
> *My heart goes out to you at this time, Barbara, and I assure you of my prayer. I shall pray that Ward will be kept safe, and I shall pray that you be given strength to carry the cross which has come your way from the loving hand of a good God. And while I know that it is difficult to see the designs of God in a trial that comes so close to home, yet I know*

your faith in God and in his Goodness will tell you that even out of this cross great blessings can and will come to you and Ward and Adrian Ann.

I am beginning this evening to pray to St. Francis Xavier to return Ward safely to you, if this be God's will, and to give you the strength to be the "valiant woman" the scriptures speak of, who knew how to carry the cross.

Barbara tucked the letter into her dress pocket, then walked to the back porch with some lemonade she had just mixed. She watched while her father-in-law, John, played with Adrian in the grass by the fence. Was he her father-in-law? Was that the right title? She wasn't sure, and it didn't really matter to her. Growing up, Ward had never known John, because his parents had separated when he was little, and his mom had remarried. Ben, the man he had called Dad all during their courtship was actually his stepdad. But which of the two men was her "in-law," Barbara had no idea. Maybe they both were.

To her, the whole conversation was academic. John was Ward's father, and she should get to know him. John was also Adrian's grandfather, and he should get to play with her. Case over.

Over the fence and beyond an expanse of tall, brown grass, an orange grove stretched on for miles. John cultivated it. He was both a golf pro and an orange rancher. It was the family business. "Doesn't pay well," he'd once said. "But I've got enough for our needs."

That first time they had all met, it had been a little awkward. Barbara had hunted the man down through Ward's mom, who wasn't overly thrilled about handing over the information. But she eventually relented. Barbara was persuasive that way. When they had arrived at the house, Adrian was not even a twinkle in anyone's eyes. Both Ward and John stared at each other awkwardly like two teenagers who had never been in a relationship before. They shook hands like they were about to buy and sell a used car.

"Oh, this is silly," Barbara had whispered to herself before moving around the edge of the Mercury and enveloping John in a warm hug. "It's so good to finally meet you, Johnny!"

John seemed genuinely taken aback. Then he released a slight laugh and said, "It's good to meet you, too." She felt all the muscles in his body relax then, like a statue coming to life.

"I want you to know," Barbara had said, pulling back so she could look him in the eyes. "I love your son. He's the finest man I've ever met." Barbara thought she detected tears in John's eyes. Regret? Frustration? Joy that his son had turned out fine even though he hadn't been there to contribute? It didn't matter to her, and he had quickly coughed them away.

From then on, Barbara had ensured that she and Ward had a relationship with everyone in his family.

Now, in the backyard, Adrian had become obsessed with following a butterfly from plant to plant. "Bee!" she squealed. Roly-polies, ants, flies, bees, hornets, butterflies, spiders—they were all "bees" to her. Barbara had written a letter to Ward telling him all about it. She was certain he would want those letters once freed, so she pumped them out at an epic pace.

After watching Adrian toddle away after another bug, John groaned to his feet, wiped his hands on his jeans, then tromped up the porch steps.

"Lemonade?" Barbara asked.

"Don't mind if I do."

"He looks like you, you know," Barbara said. He and Ward did look alike: same sharp eyes, handsome features. Ward got his brains from his mother; it had become apparent to Barbara the first time she met Lysbeth that her mind was working on a level most people couldn't even dream of. She wasn't necessarily intellectual, but shrewd. John, on the other hand, was a romantic, often quoting poetry and the classics.

"I suppose he does," John said. Then after a long pause, "Just when you finally brought him back into my life, I'll never see him again."

"Yes, you will," Barbara said. "I know it."

He looked at her. Unlike Ward's mother, he did not have an air of superiority or condemnation. Lysbeth's eyes always seemed to suggest that Barbara was naïve—a young girl with her head in the sand. John's was a quiet look. Pensive. "I hope you're right." A gravid quiet. "But how long can you keep up your hope?"

"As long as it takes," Barbara said. "I'll know if and when I should give up hope. I'll tell you what I told his colonel: he's still alive, so don't act like he's dead."

"Then maybe you'll have enough hope for both of us."

"You know I do."

CHAPTER 22

The night had come.

Ward lay on his straw bed. At his feet, his blanket covered both his legs and Ho. The boy had arrived a short time before, and Ward had instructed him to get under the blanket and lie perfectly still. They were waiting for the medic to make his final rounds.

The preparation had been intense. Now, everything was ready: the canteen filled with water, the rusted scythe blade, the halazone tablets, the sleds, some matches provided by Ho's uncle, a five-pound sack of rice Ho had brought with him that evening, and, finally, a bowl of freshly boiled rice the two of them could eat for energy before starting their journey. It was all stuffed into the pile of hay next to them.

His newly cast legs, immobile from thigh to toe, had been a problem. But Ward had realized he could use the scythe blade to cut the upper part above the knee free. He had done this in the middle of the day, hoping he could keep it secret, but the medic had still noticed. When he did, he paced in a panic, as if he were about to be executed. Ward explained to him that it was the only way for him to squat on his toilet pot, and the man immediately calmed himself.

Strange, thought Ward, but it worked.

Now they were ready.

The medic entered the hospital for his ten o'clock rounds. The dark was impenetrable, and the man hadn't bothered to bring a flashlight. Ho under the blanket was nothing more than another shadow in the night.

As quickly as the man came, he left.

Ward waited another ten minutes, then pulled the blanket from Ho and nudged him. The boy had fallen asleep. Ward poked him in the ribs.

"OK," Ho whispered. "OK." He sprung to his feet and pulled the blanket aside, then moved gingerly to the center of the room.

The injured soldiers in the room snored in a steady rhythm.

Ward handed Ho the bowl of freshly cooked rice. In the blackness, he could barely see the boy, but he whispered, "Eat."

Ho accepted the bowl.

Ward pulled his sleds from under the pile and fastened them to his knees and ankles using the twine Ho had found for him. Once he had them secured, he pointed to the bag of rice.

Lugging that would be Ho's main job, while Ward would handle everything else in a burlap sack tied around his chest.

Ho stepped closer and handed the cooked rice back to Ward. Then he bent to grab the bag of rice—

A scrape at the door.

Ho sprung up and away from Ward's bed.

A Chinese officer sauntered into the room, flashlight blazing. As soon as the beam landed on Ho, the man's face contorted in rage. He screamed something in Chinese. One step, and he had closed the distance between himself and the boy. He snatched Ho by the arm and spun him around.

Short bursts of language. The man's face pressed right against Ho's. His finger jabbed the boy in the chest.

Ho tried to respond but never released more than a syllable.

Ward knew Ho was in trouble, but he also knew things could get much, much worse. At that moment, Ward's skids were naked for the soldier to see. All he had to do was scan down with his flashlight. If he saw Ward's legs, he would know they were trying to escape. Both would be executed.

The soldier was screaming so loud that the other men in the room stirred, several leaning up on their elbows.

Ward inched his blanket over one leg.

Another soldier burst into the room. Then another.

Ward pulled his blanket partway over the next leg. Any sudden movement would shift the soldiers' attention from Ho to Ward.

The first man fired what sounded like questions at Ho with the rapidity of a submachine gun.

Ward finally covered both legs.

"What's happening in here?" a voice said from the doorway. It was Kang.

"The boy and I were just talking," Ward said. "That's all."

Kang charged into the room and grabbed Ho by his shirt collar. He fired off something in Korean.

Ho's response was short.

Kang answered by yanking the boy from the room and out into the night. The other soldiers followed.

Ward knew his window was narrow. He ripped the blanket from his legs and untied his skids. In the dark, the other injured men couldn't see what he was doing. He started to stuff the skids into the straw, but a thought stopped him abruptly: the soldiers would search in here next. He hunted for other options.

Nothing. The straw was obvious. His blanket—the same.

The pit. The pit under the hanging closet. He had seen it the day he'd come in but not really thought much of it since then. It was filled with all sorts of random garbage.

Ward pivoted onto his hands and knees and scurried to the edge of the pit. He shoved the skids over the edge. Then he threw in the matches and the scythe blade. He scooted on his rear back to his bed to grab the rice, but he was too late.

Kang had returned. Two Chinese soldiers followed him.

Ward lay on his bed so that his body covered the bag of rice, and he scooped up the bowl of the cooked stuff and pretended to be eating it.

Kang blasted Ward with the flashlight. "Did the boy give you that?"

Ward tried to block the light with his hand. It blinded him to the point that Kang was nothing but a disembodied voice hanging in the air behind the shine. "No," Ward said. "This is Chinese rice left over from my dinner."

"Move," Kang said.

Ward pretended to shift aside, but he was careful to always keep the rice bag under his back.

Kang thrust his hands into the straw and tossed it aside furiously. Just then, his flashlight flickered, then blinked off.

Kang cursed. The words were crisp, terse. He slapped the end of the flashlight, banged its handle against his raised thigh. It flickered back on.

Kang dove back into the straw.

Ward tried to act helpful, pulling aside the straw so Kang could get a closer look. "I don't have anything," Ward said.

"Quiet," Kang said, his voice not loud but focused.

Ward shifted and adjusted, always helping move straw and always sliding so the rice stayed underneath him.

The flashlight sputtered, then turned black. "Ah," Kang said, banging it again.

It blinked and flickered, stayed off, then returned to a steady beam. "Move," Kang said, resuming his work.

Ward had no choice. He moved off the bag. As he did, he pulled some of the straw to cover it, but he knew it was pointless. Kang would spy it, and they would die.

Kang worked leftward through the pile, searching as thoroughly as the light would allow him. He must be enjoying this, Ward thought. This is his chance. If he can show the commanding Chinese officer that I've been planning something nefarious, the Chinese will give me up.

The beam moved closer and closer to the bag.

Please, Ward prayed. *Please, God.*

Kang was inches away now.

Please. For me, for Barbara, for Adrian, for Ho. Please.

Just as the light hit the bag, it shut off. Kang fired off a series of short Korean words and pounded on the flashlight. It refused to turn back on. He slapped it, on the side, the top, the bottom. He unscrewed the end, pulled the batteries free and slid them back inside. He shook it.

Nothing.

Ward held his breath. He didn't dare move.

Finally, Kang straightened and released a guttural growl, then marched from the hut.

As soon as the lieutenant was outside, Ward gathered up the bag and, still seated upright, heaved it toward the pit. It landed. Out of sight. Ward was safe.

His excitement lasted only a second. Outside, Ho screamed. Crying followed.

Ward rotated and crawled to the wall, where he peeped through one of the bullet holes. Kang's fist rose and fell like an oil pump.

Ho screamed and blocked his head and face against the blows. Soon, his shrieking stopped and all he did was cry in a low whimper while the blows fell and fell and fell and fell. All the while, Kang barked like a guard dog. The words flew from his mouth in rhythm to the blows until, finally, he seemed to have exhausted himself.

Ho lay in a crumpled pile in the middle of the trail, looking more like a bundle of discarded clothes than a human being.

Kang said something to the Chinese soldiers, then pivoted away toward the village. They all gathered around Ho, lifted him to his feet, and carried him out of Ward's view.

• • •

Ward was forcing himself to breathe. Had he just gotten Ho killed? What would they do to the boy? What else could Ward have done? He listened to the sounds of the night, both grateful and terrified he was hearing nothing else from the village. Did that mean the beatings had stopped? Or did it mean Ho had been bludgeoned to death? His mixture of conflicting emotions didn't end with Ho's fate: he was also feeling an intense worry that the kid wouldn't be able to keep the escape plans a secret. But how could he possibly be worried about Ho giving up the secret plans when he knew the boy was being tortured? *Forgive me, God. Forgive me.*

He fished into his vest pocket and pulled out his letter-wrapped ring. He fingered out his cross as well. All night, he stared at the two objects in the darkness. He could barely see them—shadows among the shadows. But they focused his prayers. They became lifelines. As the Lord's Prayer echoed in the recesses of his mind, he imagined lines streaming from that ring and cross to Adrian and Barbara and Ho, and he wondered what all three were doing in that precise moment. *Where are you, Barbara? I am here. I am lost without you. Lost. Ho is lost. And where is our little Adrian? What would I do if she, in years hence, were captured by men like these and beaten? How can we save her from that? That's what I'm doing, my love. Stopping men like this. And when I am done, I will come to you.*

These thoughts floated about his mind, bubbles that formed and popped, sometimes before he could even grasp them. Occasionally, he would drift off to sleep only to hear the echo of Ho's cries and screams, which immediately jolted him back awake. There had been nights when praying had helped him fall asleep; something about focusing his thoughts on the words allowed him to free his mind from the physical prison of his body and its current constraints. But tonight, he didn't want that to happen.

How could he sleep knowing how Ho was suffering? The earth rotated through the night. Ward felt every inch of that motion. The darkness seemed to last forever.

• • •

By the time the sun rose, Ward had reached an unbreakable conclusion: he would escape alone. Assuming Ho had survived the night, Ward simply couldn't risk placing the boy in more danger. And planning for two people raised the risk of getting caught exponentially. He wouldn't tell Ho or Ho's mother and uncle; he would simply disappear, and hope they understood.

He watched the door like a cat ready to pounce. Occasionally, he found himself staring so intently that he had to force himself to blink. When the medics brought in his morning rice, he couldn't stomach even a bite.

Eventually, Kang stepped into the room. He shook his head as he stepped to Ward. "You should not be friends with villagers."

"Where is he?" Ward asked.

"With his family," Kang said. He rested his hand on the pistol holstered to his belt.

"What did you do to him?"

"Punished him. For disloyalty."

"He didn't do anything," Ward said.

"If he is friends with you, he is not loyal to the People's Army."

Ward scoffed. Normally, he prided himself on his ability to know his emotions and to keep them perfectly in check. But in that moment, everything he felt hovered just beneath the surface. "The People's Army," he said derisively.

"You don't believe we are the People's Army?"

Ward had done a masterful job of not arguing with his captors; silence and agreeableness had been his allies. But he couldn't help himself. "That child and his family *are* the people. I don't think you're doing much for *them*."

"You believe American army would do better?" Kang asked. "Why?"

"We would never beat a small child."

"But you would take from them?"

Ward shook his head and mumbled, "You don't know what you're talking about."

"I do," Kang said. "Yes, I do." He squatted. "You Americans think your country is great. Freedom! Freedom! Yes? But who is free in your country? If we let you take over our country, some will get rich, but most will get poor. It is the way of capitalism. No better than Japan."

"Everyone would be better off," Ward said. "They can decide for themselves."

"No, no, no," Kang said. "My family was in the South. They had no food. No one to help them. We help people. In the North, people control together."

"Someone always rises to power," Ward said. "And if they aren't stopped, they will always take more and more."

"Not here. Not in Korea."

Ward shrugged. "If your ideology is so great, why do you have to force it on everyone? Why don't they just embrace it?"

Kang only stared, and Ward realized he may have used words outside the man's English vocabulary.

Finally, the North Korean stood. "The boy is fine." And he was gone. Thirty minutes later, the medic left the room, and as soon as he vanished, Ho crept through the door.

Ward perked up.

One of the boy's eyes was black and swollen, as was his lip. Otherwise he looked far better than Ward had expected.

"Okay?" Ward asked.

Ho nodded. He patted his chest, pointed at Ward, shook his head, and put his finger to his lips. *I didn't tell them anything.*

Ward smiled and nodded appreciatively. "Good boy," he whispered. Then, considering the totality of what the boy must have endured, "I'm sorry."

The crunch of boots on the trail made Ho's eyes grow wide. He backtracked to the door and peeked around the frame. Then he was gone.

CHAPTER 23

On a hillside, in the black of night, Jae Pil eyed Private Pak warily.

The two had been assigned to drive inland again, away from the front lines. The skirmish of the previous days had died down completely, and now Jae Pil's unit and the Americans across the valley did nothing more than pass the time staring at each other.

For Jae Pil, the new orders were devastating. He had been certain that, given another day or two, he could find a way to escape into the night. So why this order now? He just didn't understand it. Why would God have led him all the way to this place, so close to freedom, only to snatch back that blessing at the last possible moment. *My God, My God, why hast thou forsaken me?*

"How long is the drive?" Pak asked as he tied down the canvas to the back of the truck.

"It will take us at least a day or two," Jae Pil said. *God, please, give me an escape. Help me to stay.*

"Why are we going?"

"The captain didn't say," Jae Pil said. "Maybe to pick up more supplies."

Jae Pil's mind churned. There had to be a way to stay here. At first, he had hoped the truck would be stuck on the hillside near where he parked, or an American bombing run would ruin the road or take out the vehicle. He'd prayed for it. For days. Nothing. The God in Heaven was as silent as stone.

Now he considered his options. With every passing second, his hopes were dwindling. In minutes, they would be driving back down the mountain. *Please, God. Inspire me. Create the diversion that will lead me to Thy paths.* Pak moved from the rear of the truck to the passenger side.

Jae Pil had an idea: he could disable something. Sabotage. He dared a glance to the gas tank cover. He could never siphon it out without Pak knowing. Even if he could, he didn't have time.

"Hurry!" Pak said while climbing into his seat. "We need to get on the road before the light."

The light. *God, who commanded the light to shine out of darkness, help me.* Pak was right. The glow of the sun would make it too easy for enemy jets to spy them. They would be forced to move slower, hide often. All Jae Pil needed to do was delay them until first light. Then he could make a credible argument that they should wait until the following night. It would give him time, a window to do something.

"Kim Seok Jin!" Pak yelled again.

Jae Pil was out of ideas. He opened the driver side door, crawled in, then yanked it closed behind him like a prison cell. He inserted the key into the ignition. If God was going to intervene, it struck Jae Pil that this was His chance. But as soon as he cranked the key, a great roar bellowed from under the hood, and the smell of combusting diesel filled the cab.

Why? Jae Pil thought.

"Let's go," Pak said.

Why?

• • •

Ward was on his hands and knees outside of his hut. He estimated it was sometime between eleven and midnight. Recovering his skids and the rice from the pit had proven impossible. They, along with his rice and other supplies, were lost forever. The pit's walls were so deep and steep that even if he could have crawled in undetected, he was certain he would never make it out. Still, in the few days since, he had hoarded his bowls, and Ho had brought him a new supply of uncooked rice.

The boy was incredible. Nothing deterred him, and he continued to help Ward even as the risks to himself mounted.

Now it was time to leave. So far, his new escape plan seemed to be working. Amidst the filth piled in the hospital, he had found some dirty black pants he used to wrap around his casts to camouflage their bright whiteness. He had found some other rags to use as knee and hand pads. They were holding up well.

Above, the weather was cooperating. Dark rain clouds had floated in like zeppelins, blotting out the nearly full moon and stars. The entire village was black as ink.

Ward hesitated just off the hospital's porch, watching for any sign of movement. No lights. All was silent. He slid forward; every scrape of his legs against the dirt sounded like an explosion to him. But he pushed himself forward. He knew he needed to be quiet, but he also knew that being overcautious could risk his life as much as being careless. He stuck to the shadows of the building until he reached a steep downward embankment.

He pivoted to swing his legs in front, then slid down, catching himself with his feet. At the bottom of the embankment, he switched back to his hands and knees. He was on a trail that followed a gentle slope down to the creek. He maneuvered it as fast as the ground allowed, but it wasn't forgiving. Rocks bore into his hands and knees, seeming to pierce his pads. He caught his fingers on a root he couldn't see in the dark and stumbled, planting his face in the dirt.

Eventually, he found a steady pace. Slow enough to navigate the obstacles in the night but fast enough to feel like he was making progress. A voice lifted out of the darkness somewhere behind him. Ward paused. He thought he heard the Chinese word for "American," but he couldn't be sure. He lay down in the dirt and waited. Time passed. He didn't have a watch, so he had no idea how long he lay there, but once he didn't hear anything else, he decided to keep going. If someone was talking about him, it wasn't because they were searching for him.

When he reached the stream, he paused and looked back. Nothing. No sign of anyone awake in the village. Ward knew time was against him. He needed to cross the stream, make it over the hill beyond, then disappear into the forests to the north. His only hope was that Kang and the Chinese wouldn't think to search for him in that direction.

He eased into the stream. Once in, he paused and sat on his backside. His breath came in furious gulps, and he couldn't get enough air. How long had it been since he'd left? An hour?

How long had it been since he'd done anything resembling exercise? His body felt far weaker than he'd expected this short distance into his journey. He splashed water onto his face and sucked several handfuls into his mouth. He was not so much tired—it was almost like he'd skipped that step—but more like he was pushing himself on some final reserve of energy human bodies kept only for emergencies. With his hands and arms trembling, he wondered how long even that would last. He'd been wasting away for weeks, just lying there on his bed, and now it seemed he was finishing off the process.

Still, he couldn't give up now. If they found him here, this close to the village, they would surely shoot him. The patience the

Chinese had shown him in allowing his legs to heal would yield to Kang's thirst for punishment.

Ward filled up his canteen in the stream and then turned to the steep hillside beyond the water. The first thing he noticed was how much he missed the rocks from the trail. The vertical climb of the slope would have been bearable with stones to grip, but this was all grass—dew-covered blades as slippery as ice.

After several failed attempts, he realized the grass was long enough to grasp in huge clumps. He spread his legs wide, which allowed him to stop the downward slides, then he pulled on the clumps, maneuvering up the hill one grunt at a time.

• • •

How much time had passed? How far had he traveled? Barbara—where was she? Is this what crawling felt like to Adrian before she started walking? Snakes. One of the Chinese soldiers had meandered over to this hill the other day to bask in the sun, and a snake had bitten his hand. He'd spent two days in the hospital lying next to Ward, breathing hard, his tongue bloated and heavy.

The ground passed by in jerks and thrusts, timed to the groans and snorts that emanated from his mouth, almost beyond his will. Finally, his arms gave out. He flopped onto his back in a spot where the slope flattened for a pace. He looked up into the darkness and panted. With more effort than should have been required, he curled his canteen to his lips and poured the water in. A balm, but it seemed to have little effect. He had brought a small piece of food with him—a sort of pancake-like bread Ho had smuggled him. It was supposed to be for emergencies, for days hence when he was trapped in the wild and needed to survive. Now, he realized, he would need its energy just to keep moving. He removed it from his vest and chewed on it, savoring the softness as it melted on his tongue. There, lying on his back, he sensed, then heard, a rustle to his side, a kind of slithering. He let his head tilt to the side. Nothing. Then he arched his back to peer into the darkness above him.

A monstrous snake moved with remarkable speed, its eyes glowing like candles.

Ward's body acted on instinct, pulling energy from places he never knew existed. He sprung to his feet, out of conscious control. For a moment, Ward found himself standing—actually standing—on his casts.

Then the illusion ended, and he toppled backward. Like an old enemy seeking revenge for a grudge, the ground bashed into his back. Combined with gravity, it thrust him head over heels down the slope. His face, his ankles, his torso—each took turns slamming into the ground.

Mindfulness ebbed and then, like a bright light flicking on, returned to him. He was lying on this stomach. He tasted blood in his mouth; the grass was wet against his face; the metallic smell of soil filled his lungs. He glanced up the mountain. He had rolled nearly thirty feet.

The snake.

He forced himself to a crawling position and scanned the hillside. Nothing. He shook his head and his thoughts focused to a crystalline point of clarity: a snake's eyes would light up only if another source of light hit them and there was no other source of light.

Millar, Ward thought, *you're hallucinating.*

He couldn't believe it. The serpent had seemed as real as anything he'd ever seen. He patted himself down. The tumble hadn't injured him any more than he already was, so he pushed forward. The hike fell into a rhythm then. Every ten feet, he paused for a break and sipped from his canteen. After an hour, the storm clouds that had hidden the moon finally began to cry. Or at least that's what the rain felt like: a million heavenly tear drops. They made the going even more arduous, the grass twice as slippery.

For hours, Ward allowed his mind to journey to different places while his body focused on the task at hand. Finally, he reached the top of the ridge. It was a triumph of humanity. He allowed himself to rest and collapsed onto his stomach like the winner of an Olympic marathon. If not for still having some of his wits about him, he would have unleashed a victorious scream to the heavens. The grass felt so smooth on his face.

How long did he lie there? He didn't know. The rain stopped, yielding to a soft breeze out of the west. In time, the clouds broke, and the light of the moon brought the terrain to pale life. Ward forced himself to sit up and take in his accomplishment in all its glory.

Then he realized it. On the hilltop, panting, drained of all the energy he could ever hope to muster, he could still see his mud hut. It was, at most, 250 yards away. He had been crawling for hours. How long? Five? Six? And he had made it only 250 yards. Below him, the evidence of his escape lay on that hillside like a trail of breadcrumbs. The guards wouldn't even have to search for him in the morning. They would follow the trail of flattened grass on a casual stroll and walk right to him. As he looked around, he realized there wasn't even a place to hide. No trees or bushes for miles, except for the occasional lone cedar.

Ward pulled out his cross. *God, what should I do? What can I do?*

At first, the answer to these questions was an empty darkness in his brain. Then the obvious answer settled upon him like light at the beginning of the dawn: he needed to get back to his hut before any of the guards awoke. He had no chance of escape.

• • •

Every bump of the road mocked Jae Pil. Why was God not helping him? Why was he hiding? They had been driving for three hours, grinding along the pocked and muddied roads. Guards along the way had met them at various checkpoints. Jae Pil spent much of his time on the lookout for them, both eyes and ears. The system was simple: truck drivers couldn't hear approaching American jets over the growl of their engines, but they could hear a rifle shot. The guards along these roads were stationed at regular intervals, lone sentries in the night. If they heard approaching aircraft, they would fire their rifles into the air, and Jae Pil would immediately pull over and shut off his lights. Otherwise, he would be too easy of a target. So far, it hadn't been necessary.

"Is your family still in your village?" Pak asked.

"Yes," Jae Pil said. He saw no need to elaborate to Pak about everyone other than his mother trying to flee to the South.

"They are safe?"

"Yes," Jae Pil said. "We are far enough away from the front that no attacks have come to the village."

"The Americans will attack anywhere," Pak said. "They will do whatever they must to conquer our people."

"Yes," Jae Pil said, but he could only feign a half-hearted enthusiasm. Oh, to be able to talk as freely as Pak did, to be able to share your feelings openly, without fear of reprisal. Jae Pil had become a master of silence, but he envied Pak. The man was where he was supposed to be. It must have been liberating, to be surrounded by so many like-minded people. It was a rare gift Pak likely didn't appreciate.

"What do you think the Americans will do if they win the war?"

"They will not win," Pak said. "We are far superior. We have far more people in our army, and with the People's Volunteer Army at our backs, we cannot fail."

"Yes," Jae Pil said. "But what I mean is this: if the Americans were in total control of our country, what would they do?" A faint hope was starting to brew inside him. If he could keep Pak talking, perhaps he could find a way to use the man's enthusiasm against him. The road they were traveling was windy, never straight for very long. At some junctures, it would come relatively close to the front lines again. Perhaps then, he could find a way to distract Pak and disable something in the engine. If they broke down near the border, Jae Pil might find his opening.

"They will force their capitalism on us," Pak said. "It will be the same as the Japanese. Some few rich companies and government officials will exploit the rest of us for their profit. The people will continue to suffer. You can already see it happening. In the North, we have equal pay for equal work. The Party has ensured only an eight-hour workday. Prostitution is outlawed. The people have received wage increases. We have insurance now for older workers. None of that has occurred in the South with the Americans. The poor are as poor as ever."

"So, you were paid well in the factory after the Japanese were forced out?" Jae Pil asked.

"Yes," Pak said. "Far better than ever before."

"You worked on vehicles?" If the man was an expert in automotive repair, Jae Pil's plan would only buy him a minimal amount of time.

"Assembly, yes," Pak said. "For the Party." Everything seemed to come back to the Party for this zealot. It was almost like a religion for him.

"Did you work in mechanics? Repairing vehicles?"

"No," Pak said. "Just assembly. I helped put axles onto the bodies of the cars."

Excellent, Jae Pil thought, but said out loud, "I'm sure you became quite skilled at that."

"I did," Pak said.

"Who worked on the engines?"

"There were other men who understood them better than I do. I learned some, but it wasn't enough for me to do quality work."

"What did you learn?" Jae Pil asked.

"Just the basic workings, but nothing to assemble them."

This could pose a problem, Jae Pil thought. The reality was that, as a truck driver, he also knew the basic workings, enough to sabotage a vehicle, but not enough to do it in a way that wouldn't be obvious to someone else. And, of course, there was the question of distracting Pak long enough to give him a window to pull it off. With just the two of them, it wouldn't be easy.

"What does the map say about where we are?" Jae Pil asked.

Pak lifted the paper on the seat between them and unfolded it. "We should reach the Pukhan River by daybreak," Pak said. "There is a camp there. We can refuel and take cover."

The river. The river! Why hadn't Jae Pil thought of the river. It was a tributary that ran north to south. If he could get in, or steal a boat, he could float along it past the battlefront and into enemy territory. Again, all he needed was to slip away from Pak long enough to make it happen.

"Good plan," Jae Pil said. "How long until we get there?"

"One hour probably," Pak said. Jae Pil eased down the accelerator.

• • •

Ward flopped into his pile of straw just before daybreak. He hurriedly stripped off his pads and the wrappings around his casts and shoved them all under the pile next to him, then climbed under his blanket. Within minutes, he had fallen asleep.

He woke hours later to find a bowl of cold rice next to him, left by the medics.

His clothes were still soaked. His casts were as muddy as the rest of him. How would he explain all that?

Outside, the clouds had opened up with fury, lashing the village in wind-driven panes. It had cooled everything considerably and given Ward an excuse to stay hidden under his blankets. He just hoped he could dry off and then wipe the dried mud off his clothes before anyone else saw him.

By late afternoon, he lay on his side and decided to pull out his wedding ring. It was perhaps the only source of comfort he had. His fingers felt around in the pocket. His letter to Barbara was there. His cross.

No ring.

He bolted up. Immediately he noticed the muck and grime covering his clothes. But it was dry. He brushed it all off, then dove into the pile of straw. No, no, no. He swept large swaths of the stuff away. Had he lost it on the hillside? Had it fallen out while he was crawling? The pocket had a zipper, so it shouldn't have gone anywhere. Had he accidentally dropped it when he was crawling back into bed?

"What are you doing?" a voice behind him said coolly. Ward glanced over his shoulder. Kang.

"I've lost my wedding ring."

"What?" Kang said.

"My wedding ring," Ward said, sitting back and pointing to his finger. "We wear them when we get married. I've lost it."

Kang dove into the straw. His search was frenzied, almost as if it mattered more to him than to Ward. He came across Ward's pads and even the dark, mud-crusted pants Ward had used the night before, but he didn't even seem to care.

Ward offered a mental shrug, then joined back in. After a good ten minutes at least, Kang rose. "Not here. How big?"

"Small," Ward said. "Just my finger."

"Did you sell it?" Kang said. "We know the boy has been bringing you things. We know you sold your shirt. Did you sell it to someone? The uncle?"

"No," Ward said. He paused his search. "I swear."

"Do not lie," Kang said.

A stark realization came to Ward: this was more important than a mere ring. If Ward didn't find it, there might be more punishment in store for Ho and his family. Ward wasn't sure why, but apparently doing any business with an American was an extreme violation of some rule. It might also mean Kang could use it as ammunition to get Ward shipped out of the hospital early.

Kang turned to leave the room.

Ward craned back to the straw. *Please.*

Then he saw something, contrasting with the golden brown. "Wait!" he yelled. He brushed the straw aside. There it was. He scooped it up and held it out toward Kang. "Found it!"

Kang immediately brightened. He even—did Ward actually see it?—smiled, but a scowl quickly replaced it. He strode back into the room. "Here," he said, stretching out his hand.

Ward placed it in his fingers, and Kang looked at the platinum carefully, spinning it before his eyes as if it held some talismanic value.

"May I have it back?" Ward asked.

Kang slipped the ring into his pocket. "No," he said.

"Please," Ward said. "It's my wedding ring."

Kang did not answer. He spun away, then paused at the door. "You do not go to Pyongyang. For now."

After he left, Ward flopped onto his side. Every part of him ached, as if someone had beaten him with a rock all night long. Somewhere deep inside him, ancient, primal emotions were begging to break free; Ward could feel them. They choked his breathing, clenched his stomach, caused his heart to rage against his rib cage. If he let them, they would explode like some sort of demon horde from the deep, bursting from him in the form of curses and clenched fists and tears. Oh, how those tears would come. In a flood, a torrent, a never-ending tsunami of heartbreak. He beat it all down;

no one could see that from him, especially not here. Only one. His One. Although he had lost his one physical connection to her, that string that stretched across space and time still connected his heart to hers.

"I'm sorry, Barbara," he whispered.

• • •

A single shot. Jae Pil heard the rifle fire thirty minutes before they would have reached the river encampment.

"Rifle," Pak said. "Incoming." Jae Pil reluctantly hit the brakes, bracing himself against the steering wheel. The cones of light from his truck's headlights would be the first thing American jets would target. He shut them off.

Pak was staring up and out the windshield. "Where do you think they are?"

"I don't know," Jae Pil said.

Pak opened the passenger door. No! Jae Pil thought. But it was protocol: first, pull over; second, shut off the lights; third, move away from the vehicle until the threat passed.

Jae Pil climbed from the cab. The sky was as dark as an abandoned hut. With the engine off, he now heard the hum of jets as well. They were up there somewhere, above the clouds most likely, but certainly looking for targets. *Take me with you.*

He and Pak walked across the cratered road, over some rocks, and past a tree leaning like a drunk.

Pak plopped down onto a rock and pinched some cigarettes out of his shirt pocket. His face went aglow from the match and the orange pinprick at the tip of the cigarette. He offered the package.

Jae Pil waved it away. How could the man just sit here? Dawn was approaching like a prison guard. "Maybe we should hike the rest of the way to the river?"

"Why?" Pak said.

Why indeed? Jae Pil didn't have a good reason, so he said, "We can find the encampment. Sleep there tonight. They'll have food. We can get the truck in the morning."

"We cannot abandon our truck," Pak said. "You know that." Protocol.

Jae Pil's mouth was unexpectedly dry.

"What's wrong?" Pak asked. At the words, Jae Pil realized he was pacing, tapping his fingers against the side of his pantleg. An old habit he still engaged in when he got nervous.

"Nothing," he said. "I just want to keep moving. I don't want to get hit out here. How long should we wait?"

"You know protocol," Pak said. "Thirty minutes."

"We don't always have to follow protocol."

Pak rested his hand on his knee. Jae Pil could feel the man's look of absolute incredulousness, as if Jae Pil had suggested they should both take their clothes off and climb one of the white pines together. "Protocols," Pak said, "will keep us alive. Protocol will win the war. We will follow it."

Jae Pil paced again. Thirty minutes. Assuming all was silent for the next thirty minutes, they could start driving again. Then it would take another half hour to get to the river. By then, the sun would be rising. They would park under trees for cover, and any chance he'd have of escaping would essentially drip to zero. Drip. Drip. Drip.

Technically, as the driver of the truck, he held slight seniority over Pak, so he supposed he could just order him to get in and keep moving. But Pak was the type to immediately report such a move to their superiors, and who knew what they would do to Jae Pil once they found out. In the People's Army, protocol reigned supreme.

In the sky above, all was silent. Wherever the American jets had been going, it didn't seem that Jae Pil's truck had been a target. A short distance ahead and behind them, he knew Chinese sentries stood among the trees and rocks, smoking cigarettes and watching the skies. So even if he could get rid of Pak somehow—tie him up or knock him unconscious—they would likely scoop him up within minutes. And his ability to dispose of Pak was questionable. One of the great ironies of this war for Jae Pil—one among thousands—was that he was dressed as a soldier. He was not a fighter. He could pull a trigger, sure, and even hit targets with ease. But the idea of killing another human being, or fighting one into submission, made him recoil. It was not his way. Nor was it his God's way.

There, in the dark, he watched his chances of escape die. From the river, they would proceed north; they would receive new assignments, most likely shuttling cargo and gear from various encampments behind their front lines. He felt detached from everything, like ash floating in the wind. The skirmishes along the front lines would continue, the war would rage on, consuming the peninsula. Years. Decades. Who knew how long? Rain, wind, snow, hail, the greedy maw of time—all would gnaw at him. He could see it in his thoughts. He would become just another prisoner in a country filled with them. The reality of it pummeled him. It was so simple. God was not going to help him escape. He felt it profoundly: the silence of the heavens.

He trudged over to Pak, whose burning-tobacco-lit face reflected contentment, and eased down next to him on the rock, Suddenly, the gravity of the world seemed to be a thousand claws, pulling him to the earth, never releasing.

CHAPTER 24

B arbara was back in Portland, celebrating Mass.

She knelt, rose, and partook of the Holy Communion and offered peace to her fellow parishioners as they offered her peace in return. It was her solace, her sanctuary; the Latin words from Father Schultheis flowed over her like healing water, their import touching her soul. Here, she felt Ward most. Here, she was certain her prayers would fall on listening ears.

Naïve, a word she had been hearing since Ward's disappearance. You're being naïve.

I let them say it, Barbara prayed, to God, to Saint Francis, even to Ward himself. *I let them say it, for they do not understand what we are, our oneness. Our unity. You and I know we cannot be separated; our life together feels ordained, as inevitable as the earth's trip around the sun. What are we, Ward, but the example others of humanity can follow? We are the shining example, held aloft in God's hands. Will not He be our buckler and our shield? Has He not girded us for this time of separation, like a creator moved to pity as He looks on His creations? He will move us where He will. The board is set, the pieces in place, the players prepared to take their roles, to perceive a miracle.*

The long-awaited day will come. I know it, even if others do not. He will return you to me. Flesh of your flesh.

He will restore to me the breath of life.

• • •

When Mass was over, Barbara drove to her parents' house, where Adrian was, and found her mother in the kitchen, preparing food as usual. This time, she was kneading some bread dough while a pot of soup simmered on the stove. Somewhere upstairs, two of Barbara's siblings were squabbling. The rest, she assumed, were on the property somewhere, either down in the basement helping with the family business, watching Adrian, or in the fields behind the house.

"How was Mass?" Her mom asked.

"Wonderful," Barbara said. "As always."

"You've got a letter there."

Barbara found it on the table. It was from the headquarters of the 49th Fighter-Bomber Wing in Korea. "What?!" she said. "Why didn't you tell me?"

"I just did tell you," her mom said. "It's not as if I could call you at Mass."

Barbara was ready to tear into the envelope, only to realize it had already been opened. "You already read this," she said.

Her mom had snuck up behind her, fingers pale from the dough. "Guilty." Barbara took out the letter and scanned it:

> *Dear Mrs. Millar,*
>
> *In reply to your letter, it is my suggestion that I continue to hold your letters to Ward. After all, assuming he is a prisoner and may be released soon, there is a possibility that I may see him. If so, your letters to him would certainly be appreciated.*
>
> *Most Sincerely,*
> *A. W. Tyer*
> *Colonel, USAF Commanding*

Barbara nodded and let the paper drop to the table. "Well at least they're finally showing some common sense." Then she cast a sideways glance at her mom. "I may need to stop getting my mail sent here."

"What if it had been big news?" her mom asked. "Wouldn't you have wanted us to read it so we could come get you right away?"

"If that makes you feel better, Mom," Barbara said, smiling. "I'm just thankful my letters will be there for him when he gets back."

"I'm glad," her mom said. She sprinkled a pinch of flour onto the dough, then continued working it like a woman possessed. Her focus and stamina were a source of constant amazement to Barbara. The woman did more in an hour than most people did all day, and she still had energy at night to clean up the kitchen. When Barbara's little brother had suffered extreme burns in an accident, many years before, Barbara remembered her mom somehow being at both the hospital and the house at the same time. Constantly, for weeks on end. She knew, of course, that was impossible, but somehow her mom made everyone feel that way.

Upstairs, the conversation between the arguing siblings had grown even louder. "What are they fighting about?" Barbara asked.

"Oh, who knows what any of you fight about," her mom said. And she was right: a source of pride in the Robben family was how they could argue about anything and everything all day long without it ever being unpleasant. They were talkers, and they would talk and discuss heatedly about any topic under the sun, then break bread together and laugh about it all the way to bed.

Barbara credited her mom for that. The woman emanated a spirit of love and selflessness that seemed to distill over the rest of the house like a savory aroma. I'm a lover, she said as a mantra, not a fighter.

"Can you still watch Adrian for me?" Barbara asked. "I'm headed over to look at that apartment."

"Of course—I'm sure someone around here can keep an eye on her. Which apartment?" She had moved back over to work the dough.

"The one over in the city."

"The two bedroom?"

"That's the one."

Adrian had toddled down the stairs and into the living room; apparently no one was watching her. Barbara walked over and leaned against the wall so she could see into both rooms at once. There was nothing in the living room that Adrian could choke on, but in a house with this many people, if she didn't keep an eye out, the little girl could get lost in a heartbeat.

"Don't you think it's a little big?" her mother said. "For just the two of you?"

"I can afford it," Barbara said. "I'm still getting Ward's money, and I think I need a job. That will help."

"I know," her mom said. "But it's not just about money."

"What else?"

"Well," her mom said. "It might be a long time before he comes back, if they find him."

"If?" Barbara said. "You too?"

"Honey—"

"No," Barbara said. "I'm not going to do anything different. I'm not going to act like he's not coming home."

"I'm not asking you to," her mom said. "I'm just asking you to be reasonable. His plane exploded. Over enemy territory. The last letter said they have absolutely no more information. If he were captured or in a POW camp, we would have heard something by now."

"Maybe he's hiding somewhere," Barbara said. "Maybe he's making his way back to me right now. Did you ever think of that?"

"Maybe," her mom said. "But if . . . when he comes back, then you can get the bigger apartment. Wouldn't that make more sense?

You can save your money until then. We have no idea how long it will take."

Barbara nodded. Then she blinked to keep her tears at bay. "It's perfect for us. A bedroom for Adrian, one for me and Ward. A new icebox. New oven. The cabinets are all white. He would love it."

Her mom crossed the room in one step. "Then maybe you should get it," she said.

Barbara looked down at her hands; without thinking, she had intertwined and twisted them together. "Do you think I'm crazy, Mom?"

"Yes," her mom said.

Barbara glanced up and caught a mischievous grin on her mom's face. "But no more than I would be."

Barbara chortled.

"Do you think he's still alive?" her mom asked.

"I know he is," Barbara said.

"Then you get your apartment. And if the rest of us think you're being unreasonable, just let us go right on thinking that."

CHAPTER 25

Ward had been recovering for days. With nothing to comfort him but the straw on the hard dirt floor, sleep was all but impossible, especially since the flies and mosquitoes never relented. Ward had grown used to them, their constant presence, but they didn't help with rest. When he did doze off, his wedding ring would hover before him: a great circle of fire and tears that surrounded him, mocked him, sent him slamming back into consciousness. How could Kang have taken it?

The only bright spot was Ho, who still managed to come on a regular basis and smuggle Ward more and more food.

After his failed escape, two ideas had become clear to him: first, there was no way he was crawling back to Barbara; second, he needed to gain his strength.

The first was a problem because his legs weren't healing. The second was doable—it just meant eating more. As often as possible, Ho smuggled food into him, the other soldiers in the room either not noticing or not caring. When he could, he begged the medics for more rice.

Sometimes they gave it to him; sometimes they didn't. On one occasion, the medic even brought him a bowl of some sort of Korean dish with clear noodles and pork. Ward couldn't believe it.

He asked for seconds, and even thirds, and the medic continued to oblige. Ward had no clue as to the source of the medic's generosity, but he would take as much as they would give him. That particular dish seemed to have an unending source, because every soldier in the room enjoyed multiple helpings.

Finally, after a week, Ward felt he might be ready to try another escape. He lifted his head to see the glow of daylight gathering outside the hospital door. One more day. That night, he would try again. With what Ho had been bringing him, and with his new-found strength, he liked his chances.

A shadow at the door. It was Kang.

The man looked more irritable than normal, his scowl deeper, his eyes even more focused than usual.

Ward rose to a sitting position, his legs jutting out before him. For a moment, he considered asking for his ring, but Kang's glower warned against it.

"Why are your casts so dirty?" Kang said.

Ward found the question amusing. It had been days since his attempted escape, and Kang was barely noticing this now?

"My dysentery," Ward said. "I had to go outside because the pot was full. I had to crawl. Two nights ago."

The topic of blood-laced diarrhea seemed to turn the lieutenant off. He shook his head and grimaced. "You will be transferred," he said.

The news hit Ward with the force of a slug to the gut. "What?" he said, trying to keep his tone from revealing the panic seizing his chest.

"We will close this hospital," Kang said. "Not enough prisoners. Too many villagers."

The message was clear. Kang knew. He knew the villagers were helping Ward. It was time to move him somewhere else.

Ward tried to think of some sort of protest, but before he could get the words out, Kang marched away. Two hours later, a truck crawled up to the hospital. Two soldiers appeared at the door and scooped Ward up from his bed. As they carried him out, he craned his head back for one last look. His home for the past month. His pile of supplies hidden under the straw. The place where he'd lost his ring.

Outside, Ho and his uncle were both standing by the road, watching.

The men lifted Ward into the back of the truck. A few minutes later they carried out a few of the other injured soldiers as well.

The truck cranked a few times, then rumbled to life. It pulled away. Ward scooted to the edge of the tailgate.

Ho and his uncle were watching. As soon as Ward's face appeared over the edge, they both bowed.

Ward waved in return, knowing he was saying goodbye not just to a good friend, but to his best chance of escape.

• • •

The truck drove only a few miles—four or five by Ward's estimate. It moaned to a stop at a nearby village of about a dozen mud huts built sporadically on either side of a narrow oxcart trail. Along the way, Ward had marked the landscape in his mind—the ridges, a stream, and, most important, the cornfields with what appeared to be ripe ears ready for an escaping American to harvest. Corn was everywhere; the valley floor was like the middle of Nebraska or Iowa.

When they stopped at the first hut, a well-dressed man stepped from the door and looked on quizzically. When his eyes fell upon Ward, he raised an eyebrow, as if to say, Well, this is unexpected. Ward heard the door to the truck cab open and slam shut. Then Kang appeared. He greeted the man and began talking, pointing to Ward at regular intervals. Ward couldn't understand much, but the gist of the conversation appeared to be that Ward had misbehaved in his previous prison and as soon as he could walk, Kang would transfer him to a prison camp in Pyongyang.

Ward couldn't be certain he'd understood everything. What he did know was that when the conversation was over, the man's raised eyebrow had turned to a scowl. He was not happy to have this American in his midst.

The man barked an order in Chinese, and two soldiers appeared from the hut, marched to the truck, and pulled Ward from it.

Then it happened. Something unforeseen, astonishing even. When the soldiers dragged Ward from the truck, they didn't lift him by his legs immediately. They let his feet touch the ground and, for a moment, the full weight of his body rested on his feet. There was no pain.

• • •

Over the next several days, Ward tried not to draw attention to himself. It wasn't easy. At first, he had been placed in an area with an open-thatched roof in front of one of the huts. Kang was ever watchful, always, it seemed, keeping an eye on Ward's activity. As before, many of the Chinese soldiers in the camp were fascinated by the American—his hair, his now long and scraggly beard, the few things he still had in his possession; they poked, prodded, and pulled, talking over him in a group as scientists might who were trying to understand some new species. One North Korean soldier took to hurling rocks at Ward for sport, tossing them up over the roof to see if he could land them anywhere on Ward's body. Eventually, Ward crawled into a different hut. No one stopped him, but the rock-throwing North Korean jogged around the village screaming as soon as he noticed Ward's absence.

Finally, a pair of medical personnel arrived in the village. The same men who had redone Ward's casts earlier.

Ward saw an opening, but it was a risky one. The lack of pain when standing told him his bones had probably healed. If he was going to escape, he needed his casts off, but if they took them off and all was well, he would fall into Kang's hands. Still, the risk was worth taking.

When the pair arrived in Ward's hut, Ward signed that he thought it was time to take the casts off.

"How long have they been on?" one man asked in seemingly perfect English. He wore glasses and carried a U.S. carbine over his shoulder. The last time the men had applied his casts, this one had stayed silent in the background, dipping the cotton strips in plaster of Paris.

"More than two months," Ward said. It was an exaggeration, but he figured it might help. "I didn't know you could speak English."

"We will see," the man said. Then he walked away.

A short time later, he returned with a rusty saw. He helped Ward up onto a table in the room. "Lie down," he said.

Ward obeyed.

The doctor—Ward didn't suppose he was an actual doctor, but he didn't know how else to think about him—cut a long opening down the length of the entire cast. He paused when he noticed the cuts Ward had made at the knees, but that was the totality of his reaction; they didn't seem to bother him. When he tore open the casts, the motion ripped out most of the hair on Ward's legs. Ward grimaced.

The doctor pounded on Ward's heels. "Does that hurt?"

"No," Ward said.

"Try to stand up and walk," the man said.

Ward sat up. His calves were as skinny as twigs. His feet were still pointed down in that awkward, sickly angle. He eased his rear off the table and let his toes touch the ground.

When he put his weight on his feet, they held him. No pain, but his left ankle made a strange clicking sound.

Ward wobbled, then collapsed into the doctor's arms. What he knew was that his legs were stronger than he would have expected. What he pretended for the doctor was that they were so weak they could barely hold the weight of his emaciated body.

"They will get better in due time," the doctor said. "Try to get some exercise." He helped Ward back to his place on the floor, then exited the hut.

A short time later, Ward heard footsteps outside. The well-dressed Chinese man who had raised his eyebrow at Ward's arrival appeared at the door. In his arms were two wooden sticks just a bit longer than ski poles and a plastic canteen. He set them next to Ward and pointed at the sticks.

Ward gladly accepted the canteen. "Thank you," he said. The man again pointed at the sticks.

Ward shifted to all fours, and the man helped him to his feet, then shoved the sticks into Ward's hands one at a time. Ward tried the sticks. He found they could hold his weight, but he could rely little, if any, on his feet. They were curved at such an awkward angle that even if he could put weight on them, he'd have to walk around on his toes. He leaned his armpits back into the sticks and jutted his legs before him like the tines of a forklift. That let him put some weight on his heels and stand, even if he couldn't move. But it also left him leaning back at a 20-degree angle. He could never walk like this.

The doctor nodded and then walked out of the hut, leaving Ward to slide down the sticks to get back to the floor.

Outside, the man muttered something to someone, and the response came from Kang.

Ward listened, trying to glean anything he could from the two men, who seemed to switch between Chinese and Korean at will. How long would it be before they decided Ward was healthy enough to be turned over to Kang? he wondered. Obviously, someone in the

Chinese army was protecting Ward until he was healthy. For that, he was grateful. But he estimated his luck could run out any day; after all, he could only fake complete immobility for so long. At any second, the angry anti-American lieutenant was going to burst into Ward's presence and announce that judgment day had arrived.

• • •

Ward lay on his back and flexed his ankles. Up and down; up and down. This had become his routine. Exercise his ankles during the day; at night, do pushups and sit-ups. One of the other Chinese patients had offered him a pair of tennis shoes, which protected his skin but did little to help with the awkward angle of his toes. Still, at night, he practiced maneuvering around the room with his sticks, trying to strengthen his leg and arm muscles.

Each day, when the medic arrived, Ward begged for as much food as the medic would give him. Usually, it was nothing more than extra rice, but each grain provided him an extra modicum of strength.

He also asked for boots, every day. Every night, he prayed. He felt his strength returning. The corn in the fields would give him sustenance, as would the many streams flowing through the valleys of the North. But without proper boots to give him ankle support, he could do nothing.

Time trickled by and trickled by some more.

Kang was always somewhere nearby, watching, waiting, so Ward did all he could to feign immobility during those waking hours.

Finally, one of the workers appeared with a pair of footwear in his hands. "OK," he said. "Have shoes for you. American boots."

Ward felt a flush of excitement. But it lasted only a second. What the man threw at Ward's feet were not boots, but four-buckle rubber galoshes, designed to slide over a size ten-and-a-half boot to protect them during heavy rain. Even if they were boots, they would be huge; Ward wore a size eight-and-a-half. He rotated them in his hands. Where did they even get these? Who even makes these things? The Dutch? From a century ago? He tossed them aside.

Worthless.

That night, he looked upon his cross. *Why, God? How long must I be trapped here? I am ready; time is running out.* He wished, as his mind worked through the Lord's Prayer and the Hail Mary, that he understood the mind of God. His timing; His thinking. Why create a universe and leave it to itself? Why not allow the beings that inhabit it to seek out the being who created them? And if God did interfere, why not communicate back when His creations asked for help and guidance? *I need help. Now is the time. A month ago was the time. How long must I wait?*

Will you not hear my pleas? I want something pure—to return to Barbara, to be a good husband and father. That isn't too much to ask, is it? It's not an unrighteous desire. Ward rubbed the cross in his hands. The wood felt dead, silent. And time, precious time, kept oozing away, drop by drop, leaves falling one by one. *Why, God? Why aren't you helping me? Now is my only chance.*

CHAPTER 26

D o you believe in God?" Jae Pil asked Pak.

"No," Pak said flatly. "There is no God."

Jae Pil nodded. He expected the answer. But he needed to talk about something of substance, and he was also curious how Pak could be so sure. They had been driving for days. His hopes of getting to the front lines had faded like fog facing the rising sun. Instead, he and Pak had been given assignment after assignment to shuttle supplies between Chinese units in the west and North Korean units in the east. Shells, crates of rice, uniforms, soldiers, rifles.

Now they sat on a fallen pine log outside a small encampment. A hundred steps away, the truck was parked under the cover of several cedar. They had been ordered to wait there until a new shipment of shells arrived.

"How can you know?" Jae Pil asked.

"God was invented by humans," Pak said. "To control others. The idea of God is only used to control us, to take away our agency so we will not use it to control our own existence. They are trying to control our reality."

"They?" Jae Pil asked.

"Anyone who wants power and wealth and wants to keep the lower classes subservient. So they invented God to do that."

"What about with the Japanese?"

"What do you mean?"

"Well, didn't the Christians fight the Japanese? I heard about that."

"No," Pak said. "The Japanese used the church to keep the people under control. So do the Americans. What better way to force people to do your bidding than to convince all of them to assemble in churches, then tell them how they must behave. The masses follow it."

"It does seem like a good way to control people," Jae Pil said. The words felt like poison. Pak was just wrong. The church had almost always been part of the resistance, and it was never widespread enough for the Japanese to use it to control the people. But now was not the time to set Pak right. The last thing Jae Pil wanted to do was draw suspicion to himself.

"Yes," Pak said.

"So, before the Communists came, back when the Japanese ruled, did you or your family believe in anything?"

"Buddhist," Pak said. "So silly. It did nothing for us."

"Nothing," Jae Pil said. The comment was more to himself than to Pak. Nothing. "Did you ever try to talk with the Christians or pray to their God?"

Pak shook his head. "Once," he said. "They tried to get us to come to their church. My dad took us one time. I said their prayers. Again, nothing."

"Nothing," Jae Pil said again. In that moment, the silence of the forest spoke to him, as loud as if it were a voice. An exclamation from a universe bent on destroying every creature in its midst without compassion or mercy or justice or love playing even a minor role.

Pak stood and stretched, raising his arms high into the sky.

"Do you think any refugees are still crossing the border?" Jae Pil asked.

"I don't see how," Pak said. "The Americans will kill anyone they see crossing."

Jae Pil nodded, thinking of his family. Where were they? Had they even made it to the border? He had now traversed the peninsula multiple times, stopping in villages and encampments at every turn. He had yet to see any trace of them. He considered asking Pak if he had any knowledge about what happened to refugees trying to flee south, but he thought better of it. The man held only hatred for anyone not loyal to the regime, so bringing up refugees would only result in some long-winded rant about what should happen to those who had not caught the vision of the greatness of the Workers Party.

"Do you think the peace talks will work?" Pak asked.

"I don't know," Jae Pil said. "What if they do?"

"What do you mean?"

"Well," Jae Pil said. "Two countries? Will our land become two countries? What will happen to all the families? What about families who have members on both sides?"

"I'm sure we will be able to cross the border," Pak said. "But I hope the peace talks don't work. We have the superior army. We cannot let our people in the South suffer under the Americans. I think we should keep fighting until they are forced out of our land. Then, and only then, can our people thrive."

"There isn't another way?"

"The world has tried all of the other ways. Only an ideology that puts the people first, all people, the commoners, can succeed. Everything else must be stamped out."

A long silence passed between them. A breeze had picked up, cooling the sweat that had formed along Jae Pil's brow. Something in his stomach sunk. It wasn't just the prospect of one view crushing all dissenters. But the silence; so much silence, everywhere.

CHAPTER 27

Ward's mind was full of the horrors awaiting him. The Chinese doctors had so butchered his feet that the only solution he could imagine that would enable him to walk normally again, if he ever did make it home, would be for the doctors to re-break his ankles and set them properly.

He felt it, all of it. The snapping of the bones, the weeks of not being able to walk again.

The stink of casts being ripped from his legs.

The only other solution, it occurred to him, would be for them to create some sort of built-in heel to his shoes, one that would allow his raised heels to rest on something so he could walk about on his toes, the way ladies did in their high heels. He would need a huge pair of special shoes to pull that off.

And there they were. The galoshes. Brought to him by a fool, who lacked the sense to distinguish between boots and rubber boot coverings. They were gigantic. Worthlessness objectified. Yet, could it be? Could they be big enough to hold a false heel?

Ward sprung from his bed and snatched up the galoshes. He scanned the room; the other soldiers were all asleep, snoring and breathing with the cadence of the night. What time was it? How close to dawn? Outside, the only sounds came from a directionless wind. He was alone.

The right galosh slipped over his foot like a bucket; he'd have plenty of room to work with. He grabbed a handful of straw from his bed, wrapped it in one of the many rags lying on the floor, and stuffed it into the galosh over the heel.

He slid his foot back inside. It fit perfectly, the top of his foot stopping snugly against the top of the galosh. He skulked about the room, gathering up other rags. He wrapped them around his ankle and the lower part of his calf. Within minutes, the galosh was secure and it seemed to provide him the ankle support he needed. He fastened the left foot the same way, then grabbed his walking sticks.

He crawled to the door and peeked outside. Nothing. He slipped off the porch and then rose. For a moment he wobbled, but the makeshift shoes allowed him to stand up straight. He put his weight on his feet and held onto the sticks like ski poles. Then, for the first time in eight weeks, he took a step.

• • •

For the next few days, Ward prepared. He lay motionless during the day, stretching his ankles. He knew that if anyone figured out he was mobile, they would place a full-time guard on him or, more likely, hand him over to Kang. He gathered what supplies he could from the medics or his fellow patients: a handful of rock salt, a few scraps of soap, the top of a tin can he could use as a knife, and a small can of meat one of the medics had given him. He also still had his Mae West, his vest, and his leather jacket.

At night, he snuck from the hut and walked up and down the path behind it. His going wasn't fast, but it was far better than crawling. He could cover ten yards in minutes. He moved at a slow hobble, but, suddenly, he was free, at least in his heart and mind. One more day, and he would be ready.

• • •

Jae Pil watched with only mild interest as the convoy pulled into the camp. The commander of the convoy stepped from the cab of the lead truck. He looked as bored as Jae Pil felt. As was his way, Pak gave the man a hearty salute. Jae Pil offered a passable one. After all, the man was a sergeant, not Kim Il Sung himself. A cigarette hung from his lips, and his cap looked as if it had been dragged in the mud behind the truck for days on end. He didn't even bother saluting back to Jae Pil or Pak. "Is your truck operational?" he asked.

"Yes, sir," Jae Pil said.

"Any mechanical problems?"

"No, sir," Jae Pil said. Though he wished there had been.

"Good." The sergeant pointed to the rear of his own vehicle. "This truck is filled with medical supplies. Your orders are to transfer these supplies to your truck, then transport them to the field hospitals in Dong-A-Li and Na-Han-Li. Understood?"

"Yes, sir!" Pak said with enthusiasm, practically skipping to the back of the sergeant's truck.

The sergeant looked at Jae Pil and merely raised one eyebrow. "I was not finished," he said in a calm tone. "Once you deliver the supplies, you will pick up the men at those camps and move them to Pyonyang, away from the front. Understood?"

Jae Pil nodded.

• • •

Ward found he was too excited to sleep or even focus on a thought for more than a few seconds. It was morning. That night, he would make his escape. It had been raining for hours, the kind of long, steady downpour that penetrated the earth and turned every inch of soil into thick mud. None of that bothered him.

But the sound that materialized out of the morning stillness did:

the lashing gears and growing engines of approaching trucks. He lay on his side and listened as they moved into the village. By his estimates, there were at least three. They ground through the mud. Russian—he could tell from the hissing airbrakes.

Someone appeared at the door and conveyed a brief message in Chinese. The other patients stirred all around Ward. Those who could jumped to their feet and began collecting their belongings.

"What's happening?" Ward called.

Of the six other men in the room, most ignored him. One looked his way—a friendly soldier whose arm was in a sling. "Evacuate hospital," he said. "We all go to camp in rear."

This was it. They might not hand him over to Kang immediately, but they were taking him to the North, deep into the North, where evacuation would be impossible. Perhaps all the way across the Yalu River and into China. He would never be found again. His heart shuddered with adrenaline. He couldn't move; his breathing turned shallow. Blood rushed into his face, and he felt a flush of heat followed by a jolt of dizziness. His escape would be over before it had even begun.

What could he do? Should he just run now, in the middle of the daylight? That would be suicide. He scanned the room. The Chinese were already shuffling out.

The head medic walked into the room.

Ward flopped onto his back, an idea budding in his head. He snagged his blanket and wrapped it around himself as if he were freezing.

The medic walked to him. "Up," he said. "Evacuating village."

Ward whispered with a raw voice. "My throat," he said, pointing to his neck. The summer heat had already made his forehead clammy. "It hurts." The medic's eyes widened. He felt Ward's forehead, then muttered something Ward couldn't understand. He flew from the room, seeming almost in a panic.

Ward watched the door. Under the blanket, in the summer heat, he baked, but he kept up the ruse that he had a temperature and was cold. His only hope was that they wouldn't want him to travel sick with the other soldiers and pass whatever was wrong with him onto them.

The soldier reappeared. In his hands, he held a cup of water and a spoon of white crystalline powder. "You drink," he said. "You take."

Ward made a show of struggling to rise enough to take the medicine, which he swallowed. Who knew what it was, but the logistics problem was simple: the risk of the powder versus the risk of leaving on the truck.

"You will drive out tonight," the man said.

Time passed slowly. The sleepy village had morphed into a swarm—soldiers bustled everywhere with the same anticipation Ward recalled feeling before a major holiday. What could he do? Even with all the excitement, he couldn't disappear into the nearby cornfields. Someone would most certainly see him.

Twice Kang stepped to the door and looked at Ward but said nothing.

Finally, as dusk fell over the area, Ward heard the trucks fire up. He waited. Outside his hut, he heard Kang and another man sniping back and forth at each other in an intense conversation. It quickly morphed into an argument. When it finished, one of them stood in the doorway.

It was Kang.

He closed the distance between the door and Ward in two steps, then loomed over so closely that Ward needed to rotate onto his back to see the man's face. "There is not enough room in the trucks," Kang said. "One more will return in the morning to pick up remaining men. Then you will go north."

Ward wasn't certain, but he seemed to detect, there in the failing light, a hint of a smile on Kang's curled lips. The man was finally going to get his prey.

"OK," Ward whispered, acting neither concerned nor excited.

"We will move you to another hut with other patients. Take your things."

Against all instincts, Ward slowly rose and gathered up his blanket. For a fraught instant, he wasn't sure what to do. If he were forced to stay in a hut with all the other stragglers, escaping in the night would be nearly impossible. But what else was he going to do? He couldn't disobey Kang.

A few seconds later, the head medic appeared at the door again. "No, no, no," he said to Ward. "You stay here."

Kang fired back something in a burst of short words.

The two men argued for a moment, then the medic, who seemed to have won the exchange, pointed to Ward. "You stay here. No get other patients sick."

Kang spun away with a quick exhalation through his nose.

Ward lay back down. And, suddenly, he found himself alone in a hut with no guard. He could simply walk out into the night. Not now, he thought, not quite yet. But soon. After the medic made his final check, he would slip into the darkness.

CHAPTER 28

Barbara Millar was going crazy. She paced in front of her parents so much that her father had quipped, "You're going to wear a hole in the carpet."

In her hands, she had twisted a napkin from the dinner table so much that it now resembled a rope. She handed it to her mother. "Sorry." Outside, in the back, her multitude of siblings played with Adrian.

"What can we do?" her mother asked.

"I don't know," Barbara said. "I just . . . I just have to find a way to get my mind off this. All day long, it's all I think about. I go to Mass, I take care of Adrian, I help around here, I decorate the apartment, but . . . I can't breathe. I can't stop thinking about him."

"I know," her mother said. "It's hard." Her parents sat on the couch, watching her through their glasses. All her life, her father had been a model of rugged, practical, can-do toughness, but the look on his face now was simply one of concern.

"What if I gave you some more work?" he asked.

"No," Barbara said. "There's just too much around here to remind me of him." She pointed through the walls to the other house next door. "I mean, we lived right there for heaven's sake." She continued to pace. "I just . . . I don't know what to do. I have to get my mind off this, but, then . . ."

"What?" her mom said.

"Nothing," Barbara said. She couldn't say what she was thinking out loud. It would be too much.

"Tell us," her mom said. "It will help. I promise."

"I can't sleep, I can't breathe—I want to find a way to take my mind off it, but, then I feel guilty. Ward doesn't get to have a break. Wherever he is, he doesn't get to stop thinking about what he's going through. So why should I? I just feel like I'm being a bad wife if I stop thinking about him. And I don't want to stop thinking about him. I know he's alive, and I want him to know I'm always there with him."

Neither of her parents spoke.

"I don't want him to ever think I lost faith in him. Is that crazy?" Barbara asked.

"No," her mother said. "It's the sanest thing I've ever heard."

Barbara stopped pacing and finally took a seat across from her parents. All three sat in silence for a time, a rare occurrence in their house and so unusual that Barbara noticed it. "It's quiet," she said.

"Won't last," her father said with a chuckle. Then he added, "Perhaps there is another way you can think about this."

Barbara perked up to show she was listening.

"Have you considered what Ward would want you to do?" he asked.

Barbara hadn't really thought of that. Her mind felt dense, numb. "No," she said. She sat a few more minutes in silence and intense concentration and finally said, "I guess he'd want me to be strong. He'd want me to take care of Adrian and myself."

"Well," her mother chimed in. "You can't do that if you're not taking care of your mind. So maybe doing something to help with that is exactly what you should be doing. You can still pray for him and you can still get your apartment ready. But maybe you need more to occupy your thoughts."

She nodded. "I set up the radio last night." It was the first piece of furniture they had ever purchased together: a chartreuse cabinet, radio inlayed, turntable on top, drawers and cabinets inside to hold all sorts of things. Finally, an idea alighted on the wave of her thoughts like a flower petal on the surface of a choppy lake. "Maybe a different job," she said. "Away from here . . . No offense, Dad."

"None taken," her father said. "I think that's a swell idea. You go get a job, and when Ward gets back, you'll have that extra money to buy something other than a radio."

• • •

And suddenly he was free. Ward Millar, Captain, United States Air Force, Acting Squadron Operations Officer, who at one time soared over the skies at nearly the speed of sound, was able to move of his own accord, to cover great distances. Sort of.

He hobbled into the night, away. Clinging to his poles, he hobbled and kept on hobbling.

He maneuvered through a cornfield directly behind his hut. A swirling evening breeze rustled the corn, providing him some audible cover. Along the way, he took stock of the supplies he'd been able to collect: his G-suit, which he'd worn since day one; his flight suit over that; a blue scarf one of the other prisoners had given him; his deflated Mae West; his many-pocketed vest; the tin lid he was planning to use as a knife; a tin of meat; the rock salt; several small green apples the medics had given him a few days earlier; a small piece of soap; the rags and galoshes that allowed him to walk; his sticks; the two hundred won the trader back in Ho's village had given him for his pen and shirt; and all around him, corn, corn, corn.

It would have to be enough.

He scanned the corn for ripe ears he might be able to pick, but all were too young. He stayed in the cover of the cornfield until he reached the end of the village, then moved to a dirt road. His original logic still prevailed: the last place they would look was to the north. And roads seemed the safest option for travel. It was not his first instinct, but over time, he had come to realize that the Communists used these roads only rarely at night. The supply routes near the front were constantly busy and trafficked, but back in this area, the trucks traveled mostly during the day. Ward also had another concern: the hills and fields off to the side were simply too treacherous given the condition of his legs. The chances were too great that he would twist his ankle or break his leg. He couldn't risk it.

Once he was well out of the village, he halted. He listened to the night. Nothing but the breeze. What he didn't know was whether there were guards protecting the perimeter of the village. If there were, he would likely walk right into them.

As if responding to his worries, the clouds in the heavens broke and revealed a moon fuller and brighter than Ward ever remembered seeing. Its pale light increased visibility so much, it might as well have been the sun. Ward considered this, the miracle of it, this giant orb swinging around the earth like a stone at the end of a rope, affecting the tides and the waves, a pivotal key in the teeming life on earth, held there by the countervailing forces of gravity and speed. It was remarkable, and in that moment, it was a problem Ward could do nothing about.

It only got worse when he looked down at the mud behind him and realized a horror the moonlight had revealed. His galoshes—he recalled wondering where they came from—were leaving obvious tracks in the muddy road. And now he knew who had made them. Each track left a clear and distinct U.S. royal emblem in the mud, the one affiliated with the Marines.

Ward shook his head. It was too late to go back. Move on or die.

All he could hope for was something to wipe away the tracks, rain or a truck.

He continued his slow and steady gait. He had left the hut a little after midnight. He had time to put some distance between himself and the village. He passed several random huts. In front of one, two Korean children slept on blankets. He passed them quietly. They didn't stir.

A few minutes later, he stumbled upon something else. The image he had anticipated but hoped he wouldn't see. The glow of two cigarettes in the middle of the road. He froze. The perimeter guards. Each carried a rifle, slung over the shoulder. They mumbled to one another in Chinese. He could tell, from their nonchalance, they clearly hadn't seen or heard him.

He sidestepped off the road, into the cover of the trees.

What he found was an irrigation ditch. It was too narrow to traverse on his feet with the sticks, so he was back to crawling. He made it a few feet before climbing out of the ditch and into another cornfield that paralleled the road. He plunged into the corn until he was confident it gave him cover, then turned north again, circling the perimeter checkpoint. Along the way, he checked the cornstalks—they were far taller and more mature than the other field, but they had already been picked clean.

He panicked. His entire plan depended on being able to get his hands on corn in these fields. He suppressed the feeling. If he was going to die, he'd rather it be out here, trying to get back to Barbara, not in some camp in Siberia or at the hands of men like Kang.

The guards were oblivious to his presence, and soon he made his way back to the road.

There, fatigue set in like a weighted blanket draped over his muscles. Everything felt so heavy he could barely hold onto his sticks or move his feet forward. He came to a rest on the shoulder of the road and plopped into the dirt. He ate one of the apples, savoring its juices, then took a swig from his canteen.

Almost immediately an overwhelming desire to sleep possessed him. He glanced at the ground. It was inviting, with the same intensity as a cozy bed. He could lie down and rest, just for a few minutes. He wanted to press on, but his body had other plans. He berated himself for not sleeping more during the day. How foolish he'd been, although with all the excitement of the trucks, he doubted he would have gotten much shut-eye even if he'd tried.

As the ground pulled him closer, its arms enveloping him like a seductress, somewhere, in the deep recesses of his mind, another voice, his own perhaps, spoke to him: *You've only gone a mile, Millar. The Chinese will find you.*

Ward shook his head. *On. I need to push on.*

He tried to stand, but his legs had grown so stiff they would barely move. Only through an act of sheer dictatorial mind over matter did he stretch them, force them to bend, then support him as he climbed up his sticks to a standing position.

He was on the move again. A slow slog. Every rise and dip in the terrain might as well have been a mountain. He held the images of Barbara and Adrian before him in the moonlight, always just out of his grasp, always close enough that if he took a few more steps, he might be able to hold them. It kept him going. In the back of his mind, he said the Lord's Prayer again and again and again, as steadily cadenced as his own breathing.

A dip in the road, through a stream. The water was so cooling, a relaxing balm on his aching feet. Once again, sleep called him. Just lie down in the water; it's so refreshing. Just for a few minutes. He pushed the thoughts away and forced his legs forward.

Then he heard them. Voices. Behind him in the dark. He could barely make them out over the thrumming of his own pulse, as if his heart were actually in his ears. They were coming. And his galoshes tracks made for an easy trail to follow.

Ward lunged, directly perpendicular to the ox trail. There was a slope. He stumbled down it, his sticks and arms flailing until he lost control and collapsed onto his knees, then his face. He slid down a patch of damp grass until he came to rest at the bottom of the drop. Darkness was still on his side, even with the moon so bright. He forced himself to all fours and crawled until the last of his strength gave out and he found himself in a grassy field.

The voices edged closer and closer. Were those women's voices? No—the Chinese guards wouldn't bring women with them on a manhunt. You're hallucinating again, he thought. He rolled onto his side so he could see them coming. If he was going to die, he wanted to be facing his enemy.

What he saw next was almost as bizarre as the snake he'd seen during his first attempt.

No soldiers. No guns. It was almost ghostly: a group of Koreans, approximately a dozen, dressed in white, black shoes, many carrying large clay pots on their heads, chatting with each other as if out for a summer stroll. They passed right by Ward. And why wouldn't they? What reason did they have to search for some American along the side of the road? Most importantly, their own steps trampled down the trail, most likely, he hoped, erasing his own footsteps.

Ward waited until they were out of earshot. Lying in the grass, he could barely keep his eyes open. He tried to stand, but his arms and legs wouldn't obey. *We've got nothing left,* he imagined them saying.

Please! Just a little further.

No. We've taken you as far as we can.

It was a devastating moment. Ward felt he was far enough away, but he was exposed. He needed shelter.

Then, it was almost as if something else took control of him, as if he were watching himself from a distance, a marionette controlled by strings. He rose first to a sitting position. Soon, he was on his feet, then placing one foot in front of the other. He observed himself moving forward, first to the edge of the road, then to another cornfield, where he found some ripe ears. He cracked and yanked them from their stalks and shoved them into the pockets of his vest.

The Koreans stay out of the hills during the day, he heard a voice in his head say. It was Lester, the quiet man from Maine who almost never said anything. *They stick to the fields unless they're searching for firewood.*

Ward stumbled past the cornstalks, their leaves whipping against his shoulders as if to nudge him forward in encouragement. He reached a rising hill, and the force controlling him bent him over, placing him on his hands and knees. Then he was crawling. Ten feet. Twenty. Fifty. Sixty feet up. Until he found a thicket of bushes dense enough to hide him. He burrowed in like a rabbit, took a long pull on his canteen, and fell asleep.

CHAPTER 29

J ae Pil rolled into Na-Han-Li to what looked like panic.

In stark contrast to the day before, when the entire village seemed to be on a leisurely stroll, as if there weren't a war going on just a short distance to the south and the soul of Jae Pil's beloved homeland were not at stake, today looked like someone had lit a fire in the middle of every single hut. Soldiers sprinted from building to building. Three Chinese soldiers darted this way and that in the cornfield behind one of the huts, as if chasing a skittering rat. Villagers, those lucky enough not to have been forced into the army, scurried up and down the trail, their eyes fixed on the mud, obviously searching for . . .

"What are they looking for?" Pak asked.

"Don't know," Jae Pil said.

He engaged the air brakes. He and Pak stepped from the truck.

At the entrance to one of the huts stood a lieutenant. He wore a full blouse, the duck-billed cap, the red star. His hair poked out from under the cap almost to his ears. Young. He might have even been younger than Jae Pil. In a different time, in a different setting, that might have mattered and given Jae Pil a slight, unspoken upper hand in whatever exchange occurred between them. Here, however, Jae Pil had no choice but to salute.

Pak did as well, with his usual gusto. "What is this?" Jae Pil asked.

"We have lost a patient," the lieutenant said. "What is your name?"

"Kim . . . Seok Jin—Private," Jae Pil said, nearly forgetting his fake name.

"I am Lieutenant Kang. Did you drive the patients yesterday?"

"Yes, sir," Jae Pil said.

"When you arrived at your checkpoint, were they all there? The numbers were the same?"

"Yes, sir."

"Did you see the men unload from your truck?"

"Yes, sir."

"I assume there was not an American among them?"

"An American?"

"Yes! I mean what I say!"

"No, sir," Jae Pil said. "I mean. I would have seen one." He dared a look at Pak, who offered a slight, almost imperceptible shrug and shake of his head.

"There was an American here, sir?"

Lieutenant Kang nodded.

An American. Here. When Jae Pil had been ordered to pick up the patients and had driven into the village the day before, it had never occurred to him there might be a *miguk-saram* in one of the huts.

"He is missing," the lieutenant said.

"When?" Jae Pil asked.

"Some time in the night. If he didn't sneak and join in the convoy of trucks, he must be nearby. He must have left on foot."

"Could he have been flown out?" Jae Pil asked.

Lieutenant Kang waved this concern away. "No. There were no

planes or helicopters through here last night. And both his legs are broken. He couldn't have gotten far."

Suddenly there was shouting from some of the villagers. Near the last hut. They waved their arms and hopped up and down around a particular point on the ground, almost as if they were in the middle of a game of Yut Nori.

Lieutenant Kang marched toward them, blowing past Jae Pil and Pak as if they weren't even there.

The entire scene made sense now. The Chinese soldiers in the cornfield stopped their search and joined the lieutenant and the villagers on the trail. Jae Pil despised them, these interlopers from the North with their Russian rifles and ideas, infiltrating his country. By and large, the People's Army and the Chinese worked separately. Jae Pil was grateful for this. He was rarely forced to interact with the Chinese, except to drop off or pick up supplies. How dare they? How dare they come to his homeland and fight on his soil, the earth of his ancestors. In the early days of the war, the Americans had almost won it outright, and Jae Pil was certain the Communists would be defeated. In no time, his family would have been able to return to their worship, to their fields, to their church. But then the Chinese had swarmed over the Yalu River, pushing the Americans into retreat, and the war dragged on like a sickness, spreading over the peninsula and blighting every part of the land.

These soldiers from the North, Jae Pil thought. Without them, I would be home already.

Without them, Father, Mother, Sister, Grandfather, and I would be together.

Watching them now, their body language, the way they hovered next to Lieutenant Kang, an ominous presence, overseers, Jae Pil sensed that something was changing; the globe was changing. An overwhelming shift—gravitational, climatic—like the world being baptized anew into something altogether different. It was coming, and the only question, thought Jae Pil, was where he and his family would be standing when the seismic change was over. But these were concerns he would need to address another time, for Lieutenant Kang and the Chinese were now coming back toward him. Kang was barking orders, and in response, more and more soldiers appeared from the huts and the fields.

"We found a footprint," Lieutenant Kang said. "He followed the road north. We must find him." He looked at Jae Pil. "You drove from that direction. Did you see anything unusual?"

"No, sir," Jae Pil said.

The lieutenant shifted his gaze to Pak. "Nothing, sir!" the private roared.

"He could not have gotten far. As far as we know, he could barely walk, and he needed to use sticks. He will have little food and little water. Find him! He has been treated fairly and kindly under orders of the commanding officer and yet has chosen to escape and take our secrets with him. He is to be executed on sight."

Other than Jae Pil, the Koreans in the group, including the villagers and Pak (where he was headed, Jae Pil had no clue), bounced away.

The Chinese did not. "Those are not our orders," one of the soldiers said in Mandarin. He appeared to Jae Pil to be some sort of medical personnel, although Jae Pil wasn't certain. He had only a vague familiarity of the Chinese uniforms and ranks. Even the language was difficult to understand, but Jae Pil captured the idea.

"He will escape," Lieutenant Kang said in Mandarin.

"Our orders are to see to the evacuation of this camp. We will continue to engage in that until we receive different orders."

Lieutenant Kang considered this for a second. His eyes burned with protest, but he finally nodded. The Chinese walked away.

"Sir?" Jae Pil said.

Lieutenant Kang turned to him.

Jae Pil bowed. "We are under orders to drive the remaining patients north, sir. Are those still our orders?"

Lieutenant Kang chewed his bottom lip.

Pak returned, apparently realizing he had no clue where to even begin searching. Or perhaps because he saw Jae Pil talking with a superior and felt he might be missing an opportunity to do the same.

"Yes," Lieutenant Kang finally said. "But search everywhere you drive for him. He'll try to signal American planes. Look everywhere you can for any trace of him. Again, he is to be executed upon capture."

"Yes, sir!" Pak shouted.

Jae Pil saluted, then turned to his truck. His first and primary duty was to load injured soldiers.

CHAPTER 30

Lieutenant Kang stood in front of a map, examining the landscape all around the village.

Escaped into the night, he thought. Under my watch. What
punishment would he receive? What discipline would they inflict
upon him? How? How had Millar slipped away? He couldn't even
walk.

A trick? Perhaps? Millar may have fooled everyone. But Kang
didn't think so. He had seen Millar's legs. They were no thicker than
the bones within them, his muscles wasted away. He couldn't have
gone far.

Kang should have executed the man when he'd had the chance,
he thought. There might have been retribution from the Chinese,
but he doubted it. There would be far greater punishment from his
own army for letting an American escape. At best, it looked like in-
competence. At worst, neglect. In the new regime, when the smoke
and the bombs cleared and the South was captured and punished for
its rebellion, there would be a new order. Kang wanted to be at the
center of it. In the circle inside the circle inside the circle. One could
not achieve that by making mistakes.

His eyes scanned the map. The footprint in the ground suggested the American had ventured north. That seemed ridiculous. A

ruse? Perhaps he was trying to mislead them. Where would he go if he wanted to signal American planes? A hilltop, an open field? There were plenty of both in the area, and Kang didn't have the men at his disposal to scour them all. Most of the Korean units were near the front lines. Around here there were only Chinese.

Kang shook his head and let a whisper of air eke out his nostrils, releasing his breath slowly. The cursed Chinese army. They were a useful tool, a necessary force to push back the capitalists. They had done their jobs well, but now, because of them and their insistence that the American be treated well, Kang would suffer.

Before the war, he had been a student, a man of curiosity. He was one of the first students to attend the newly formed Seoul National University. He had been a student of economics at Gyeongseong Economics School, but the American military—invaders all, no better than the Japanese—had merged several schools into one.

They were insufferable.

Even as a student, Kang could sense it. They installed military law. They imposed their will upon the Korean people. They put an American as the new president of this new university they had opened. They forced their views of economics on Kang and all the students. The indoctrination came from everywhere: Can't you see? Can't you understand how much better our system is than what the Japanese forced upon you?

Sitting in those classes, all Kang could feel was skepticism. Wasn't anything better than what the Japanese had forced on them? Why not consider other possibilities?

In the evenings, he would sit in a basement lounge he and some friends had put together and talk about the issues. Some of them were learning from the communists. So they debated— something not allowed in the classrooms. There in that space—which was really nothing more than a square room with cinderblock walls and pillows for seats—Kang caught the vision. It was like seeing an expansive universe, previously hidden from him, unveiled. The way a city dweller might feel the very first time they reached the isolation of the country and took in the glory of the stars unobscured by urban lights. They could have it all: equality, no ruling class, the pursuit of knowledge over wealth, no scarcity for anyone, the means of production in the hands of the people. After that moment of clarity, he couldn't get enough of it.

The Americans had another vision, of course. They tried to push it on him and the other students. Freedom, free markets, property ownership—it all felt hollow to Kang. The risks were too great. The end result would be the same as it had always been: some would get rich, others would get poor. He could not abide that. Under the Japanese, his family had been relatively wealthy, for Korea. But Kang watched as his family enjoyed money and protection while others barely scraped by, by eating, literally, scraps.

Those days would be gone. If his fellow citizens were too selfish, too eager to hang onto their wealth, too unwilling to share it with those less fortunate, then the Party would take it from them. Some would resist. Some would likely die. But it was a necessity. The only way to deal with human narcissism at times was force. This was not a war of invasion; it was a war to take from the selfish and ensure equality for the citizenry.

Of course, the Americans did not agree. Faculty protested. Kang joined them. But the new governing power class would hear none of their arguments.

A huge faction of the old faculty left the new university in protest. Kang followed them. He left his family behind. They could hold onto their wealth. A new world was churning. It was being birthed right before his eyes. A revolution. A rebirth. A baptism, if that helped the Christians understand it. And he wanted to be on the front lines.

The hour is at hand, the communist leaders in Pyongyang had declared in a rally to Kang and other students. You will lead in a new era in human flourishing!

Kang liked that vision. And he wanted to be a part of it. Now, this one American would ruin everything.

Kang stepped close to the map. He needed to find him.

CHAPTER 31

Ward did not wake up so much as slowly materialize into a new world, disappearing bit by bit from an orange grove where he was standing with Barbara and reappearing in a state of pain and confusion. The citrus scent and dry warmth of California yielded to a patchy brightness he needed to blink away to keep at bay. His senses reassembled. Most of his body seemed incapable of movement. He was on his side, in the fetal position. Distant birds chirped at one another. A hint of burning wood moved over him and reminded him of the campfires of his youth.

He managed to lift his head.

Down below, snakes of smoke rose from huts that dotted the valley floor. In the fields, civilian Koreans were already working their corn and bean crops. Ward couldn't see the hospital village; the road he had traversed in the night wormed through trees and around a ridge until it vanished out of sight. What lay before him in the valley below was one of the most peaceful scenes he had ever seen. The Land of the Morning Calm. If there was a manhunt under way for him, they weren't searching in this direction.

He dropped his head to the dirt. He had made it.

Sleep found him again. When he woke the second time, it was midafternoon. Every muscle ached. He needed to get to higher ground. His plan was still intact: he was certain he was close to the coast. If he could only get high enough, he'd be able to see an inlet or bay, then it would just be a matter of walking there and flagging down a UN ship. Memories of Ho suggesting that they were much farther inland than Ward thought snuck into the closets of his mind, but he closed the doors. The kid was a young, illiterate country boy; Ward had flown over the country thirty times with a sky's view of the landscape. He knew where he was. In the distance, a knobby peak with a few pine trees stood like a lone sentinel over the terrain. It would be the perfect place to get his bearings. *I'm coming, Barbara.*

But first he inspected his feet. They were, he realized, in the precise condition he should have expected. Blisters had formed on his heel and on several of his toes. Some had already torn open. The insteps of both feet had been rubbed raw. If the rest of him didn't already hurt so much, he supposed he would feel the pain from this even more. Still, he couldn't let it get worse, or even moving was going to become impossible.

He stared at his feet for a long time, the same way he used to look at the engine of his and Barbara's old Hudson—*what a piece of junk*—when trying to fix its latest problem. While considering how to solve the puzzle of his feet, he pulled the corn from his vest. He unwrapped the leaves and silk from the first ear, then peeled away some more. And some more. By the time he was finished, he held an ear of corn so small it might as well have been a baby carrot. The kernels were barely formed. He popped the entire thing in his mouth, cob and all. It was small and starchy, but it was nourishment.

The answer presented itself. The piles of corn silk on the ground. Ward stripped the rest of his corn sticks and popped them in his mouth. Then he wrapped his feet in the tassels of silk and stuffed the rest into the empty spaces, filling out the galoshes. Not socks, but it would get the job done.

The going was arduous. He stayed on the hillside. The trees and bushes gave him enough cover to stay hidden, and he figured no villagers would be hiking up this high in the heat of the day. He would need to descend eventually, into another cornfield, then up to the top of the peak. At his current pace, he figured it would take him at least a full day, maybe two. But once he reached the peak, he'd know precisely how far he would need to go to get to the ocean. Traipsing through the bush, he released his prayers to God. Under his breath, he alternated between saying the Hail Mary and the Lord's Prayer. They focused his thoughts, and he asked that God create a path for him to reach the ocean. The right bay—a place where boats might see him, or where he might float far enough out into the ocean for an American pilot to spy him and send help.

The afternoon yielded to evening. Under cover of darkness, he descended into a cornfield. Maneuvering downhill was far more difficult than going up. At every step, he nearly tripped or caught his walking sticks in the underbrush. Whether ascending or descending, it seemed gravity was his enemy.

When he finally reached the field, he picked more ears and stuffed them into his pockets. Throughout the night, he hobbled across the valley floor and to the bottom of the ascent that would take him to the peak he wanted.

Crossing yet another oxcart trail, he finally reached it . . . and realized it was much steeper than he had guessed. All his strength had dissipated, like water evaporating. He couldn't go on, not in the night. His original plan had been to move after sundown, using the darkness as protection, so he could follow the easily navigable roads. But now, after a day of evasion, he realized he needed to adjust his thinking. First, the roads didn't cut directly west; they twisted all over the Korean landscape, usually in a north-south orientation, so they were little help to him. Second, it appeared that as long as he remained on the hillsides under cover of the trees, few people would search for him up there. So, he would need to travel in the day, where he could see where he was stepping, and sleep at night.

Since he lacked the stamina to keep moving anyway, he decided this would be his plan going forward. Well off the trail, up the hillside, he found an ancient Korean gravesite, a large mound with a stone placed next to it. Ancient writings Ward could never hope to understand were etched into the rock. His tongue felt thick and heavy. His limbs seemed to carry the weight of a thousand stones. He dropped to his knees and in the cool grass next to the grave, he offered his prayers again, begging, hoping, pleading, that when he reached the mountaintop, his path would be made clear.

• • •

The following morning, in the predawn gray, Ward stared at the hill before him the way he imagined David must have stared at Goliath. How could he possibly climb this thing? And even if he could, how would he survive the journey? He felt his canteen. It was full, but it held only a quart of water. In this heat, after he climbed away from the valley floor and its many streams, he would soon have nothing and no way to get more.

Nearby, the trickle of water sounded both like a solution and a mirage. It meant nothing if he couldn't carry it. He pondered the problem for what seemed like far too long. Time relentless; time dripping away like blood from a wound. The longer he sat here, the more likely he would be found, but moving forward without a means for survival was pointless. Finally, when he reached into his vest for an ear of corn, the idea hit him like a hammer.

His G-suit.

He patted his legs. The G-suit!

In the early years of jet flying, several pilots had crashed and died because the g-forces of flying at high speeds caused them to black out. Scientists soon realized that high rates of acceleration caused blood to stall in the lower parts of the body, rather than run its normal course back to the head. Once the brain no longer received the blood it needed, pilots' vision would blur, then tunnel, until they finally lost consciousness altogether. Researchers learned throughout the great wars that if tubes were inserted into the pilots' suits to put pressure on the lower extremities, the effects of gravitational forces would lessen on them. The suits were known as anti-gravity suits, anti-g suits, or just G-suits. In the cockpit, the tubes in the suit attached to a valve that filled them with air and put tremendous pressure on Ward's legs and lower body.

Now he was going to use them for something else.

He pulled out his tin can lid-knife and carefully cut open the seams of his G-suit. From between the fabric, he pulled out the tubes, and cut them free. They lay in his lap like pet snakes. He tied one end of them together, then shuffled over to the stream. He filled the tubes, letting them expand until they looked like bulging rubber bladders. After he tied the two together so they wouldn't leak, he hung them around his neck.

Between them and his canteen, he could carry a gallon of water at any one time. It would weigh him down, but he could survive.

Now to tackle the mountain.

With his feet bent so awkwardly, he had no idea how he could make his way up. The only way forward was to try.

He dug his sticks into the ground to support his weight, brought his right foot forward, and then leaned on the sticks so he could drag his left foot to match his right. He then pushed on the sticks until his weight was over his body's fulcrum. He yanked the sticks forward and planted them into the dirt to keep from slamming his face into the slope. Once he found his foundation, he started the process all over. Foot by foot, he progressed up the mountain, the sting of blisters forming on his hands. His fingers gripped his poles so tight he couldn't extend them to let go even if he'd tried. The sun burned his back and neck, each drop of sweat trickling away the last of his energy.

Still, he pushed.

Each grunt brought him closer to his goal.

He passed an abandoned slate quarry, and a short time after that, a spot where lightning had blasted a web of trenches into the earth outward from a blackened center.

Every few hundred yards, he stopped to take a swig from his canteen or bladders and pinched in some of his salt with the water to keep his body's saline levels high.

By evening, he had made it only halfway up the slope. He could keep going, but, suddenly, he became aware of every pain his body was capable of generating. The worst of it came from his ankles. He collapsed to his knees, then flopped to his side. Once he regained enough energy, he slipped off his galoshes and the thrashed corn silk. The flesh around his lower legs had swollen so much he wondered if he had rebroken them.

Halfway up the peak, the sun now below the skyline, he wondered if he would ever make this climb. Even if he did, how on earth would he then reach the ocean? It wasn't far, he told himself. Probably just on the other side of the peak. A painful descent, but then: beaches, ocean, and an inviting rescue ship, followed by Barbara and little Adrian.

The image sparked some motivation inside him. But he couldn't move forward with his ankles like this. One time, many years before, when he'd lived in Oregon, he had sprained his ankle, and the doctors had advised him to elevate it to reduce the swelling. Since nightfall was approaching, he figured he might as well do that again. He pivoted in the grass so his feet were uphill; he set his bladders and canteen by his side and made a pillow of his vest and scarf, then lay back. Almost immediately, he could feel them: the lice. They sprung out of the ground as if waiting for an idiot like Ward to lie down, like they'd been tracking him as surely as Lieutenant Kang was. He spent the night picking them out of his hair, from his beard, off his chest, everywhere.

He also pulled out his cross. Holding it between his thumb and forefinger, he prayed that he was on the right path, that the path would lead to the ocean, that it would lead him back to his family.

• • •

Beams of sunlight kissed the mountaintops: dawn. Ward woke to find that once he had fallen asleep, the lice had partied all over his body, and he had continued to rub his cross so much it had created a blister on his thumb.

He checked his ankles. The swelling had decreased.

He downed more ears of corn, swigged some of his water, and felt his strength return. In that moment, he felt God's presence. Whatever God was, He was with Ward. It seemed certain. Too much had gone right to allow him to escape for that not to be the case.

He repacked his galoshes, gripped his sticks once again, then pushed toward the peak. The sun journeyed across the sky, reached its zenith, then began its descent.

Ward struggled forward all the while. Finally, he reached the rocky outcropping at the summit. His timing was perfect, he knew. With the sun setting, he would see the most glorious of sights: the descending fiery orb dipping into the sea, casting long and inviting shadows across the Korean landscape, revealing to him the path he would need to follow to salvation. It would be, he knew, a moment of almost spiritual exaltation. He crawled to a rock and eased onto it, then swung his legs to hang off the side.

Ho was right. The little boy was right.

Ward let out an exasperated breath; suddenly the weight of gravity pulled down on him like heavy chains. He couldn't believe it. His back slumped. Before him, for miles and miles and miles—he guessed he could see at least thirty or forty—was nothing but ridge after ridge after ridge, interrupted by the dark shadows of the many valleys that separated them. How could he have been so wrong?

A familiar white noise. Distant, quiet, but expanding to fill the entire sky. Ward scanned the heavens to see three jets rip through the air above him. They circled the area. Two ridges over, they dropped their payloads, and a series of powerful booms shock waved to Ward's position. On their return, they soared directly over Ward.

He waved, knowing full well they would never even notice him. A chance to escape, so close he almost felt he could touch them. But they might as well have been a thousand miles away.

Once again, Ward felt familiar emotions trying to break free. He sealed them away. They were like shadows, a darkness inside him that, if let loose, would consume him completely.

He felt like a fool. Why hadn't he listened to Ho? He would have come up with a different plan, some other way of making it south, if he had just believed the little boy. Now he'd wasted valuable time, energy, and resources and perhaps reinjured himself climbing a forsaken mountain for No. Reason. Whatsoever. He slid off the rock like mud and collapsed onto the ground. He pulled his cross from his vest and stared at it. It was nothing but two twigs he had manufactured for himself. Lifeless.

Worthless.

He flicked it into the nearby wild grass where it belonged.

CHAPTER 32

After Adrian was asleep and she was alone in her apartment, Barbara Millar felt impressed to write a letter. She laid out a piece of paper and a pen and began to scratch out the feelings of her heart.

August 21, 1951

My Dearest Ward,

I just know we'll see each other again and that you will be returned to me. Others doubt; time will prove them wrong. First, let me tell you about little Adrian. She is walking and stumbling over everything. She doesn't like to eat anything but beans right now, but I keep trying to get her to eat other things. She's as strong-willed as you are!

I visited both your parents. They are doing well. My parents thought I was a little crazy, but they let me go anyway. The Mercury is still running strong! Best decision we ever made!

Every day, I go to Mass and pray for you. I just know we'll see each other again. I'll give you the biggest hug and we'll talk and talk and talk. The way only we can. I pray for that moment every day.

I'm sure, wherever you are, you must be very low right now. I know you won't read this until you're free, but maybe it will get to you. Or maybe it will be of some comfort to you if you read it even after you're back to me. Either way, I was thinking the other day of your old roommate Sig Mathison. We had the best times together in Portland. Remember his story? When he was shot down over Cologne and broke his ankle when he crashed, he crawled out of the burning wreckage and the Nazis immediately captured him. They took him to some hospital and he was burned and broken. They had him there for seven months, and he nearly died. He said other prisoners, injured way less than he was, actually did die. He was convinced that what kept him alive was that he avoided self-pity. He decided to focus on serving his fellow patients and never on his own problems. And he was convinced that was what kept him alive. The others died because they gave up hope; he refused. He was stubborn and wanted to live.

I'm praying for you, my darling. I'm praying that you will never give up hope. That in your darkest moments, you will remember that I am here for you. That St. Francis is watching out for you. That as you walk through the valley of the shadow of death, you will not fear, but God will comfort you.

I am, faithfully and always, yours.

Love,
Barbara

CHAPTER 33

Ward felt detached from the world. Raindrops, as large as bullets, began to pelt him.

Splashing onto his clothes and hands, they spread across everything. They saturated the ground, his G-suit, his very soul. He could see it in his mind. He would become one more skeleton in a land full of them. The weight of it crushed him, so much so that he felt he might as well have been under this mountain rather than sitting atop it. He felt it deep inside: the sting of defeat.

Rivulets of water began to form around him, snaking away from the peak. Mustering the energy to move even one muscle seemed impossible. If he were going to die, this seemed like a good place. A testament to his efforts.

He lost track of how long he sat there. Then, a memory. It came to him like a voice on the wind: an old roommate of his who survived a crash in World War II, who returned and testified that what kept him alive was the avoidance of self-pity. He had refused to surrender to despair, so he had lived when others died. Ward considered this for seconds, minutes, hours, while water trickled off his hair and around his face.

He could move, or he could die. The decision was that simple.

He wrapped his fingers around his sticks, forced himself to his feet, and soaked in the challenge before him. He took his first step, then paused. On the ground, nearly buried in mud, was the cross he had fashioned. It seemed so pointless now. Still, he bent and picked it up from its grave. For reasons he couldn't explain, he stuffed it into his vest pocket next to his letter to Barbara, planted his sticks in the ground, and took his first descending step.

· · ·

They were in the mountains now, far north of the front lines. All conceivable paths to an escape had disappeared, erased like tracks in blowing snow. He should have been able to come up with a solution, but all he saw was the same mountain ridges they'd been driving around for days. They had dropped off the last few patients at hospitals far in the north, then received a multitude of other mundane orders. It was all so pointless. The journey seemed to have no meaning other than its own, intrinsic, go here, go there, go somewhere else. It was as if the army merely wanted Jae Pil to keep moving, as long as that movement kept him away from escape.

The American escapee? He seemed to have vanished into the mountains like a ghost. Jae Pil had never been ordered to search for him, only to keep an eye out. He and Pak did, although Pak did it with much more gusto. They saw nothing, no tracks, no campsites, no hints of men on the mountaintops trying to signal passing jets. Did he make it south? That would be the ultimate insult, an injured American finding his way to freedom before Jae Pil. It seemed that was the way of the world: a constant mockery. No matter how much Jae Pil prayed, no matter how righteous his desires, God allowed him to achieve less than a crawling American who likely couldn't move faster than a snail.

"Private Kim Seok Jin," his commanding officer snapped at him. Another man whose name Jae Pil didn't bother to remember. Just another officer who enjoyed shouting orders and who followed the regime blindly.

"Yes, sir!" Jae Pil said.

"You have served admirably," the man said.

Jae Pil did not respond, but looked straight forward, as expected. "You are hereby promoted to corporal." The man handed Jae Pil a new shoulder strap, blue with a yellow stripe, which he could attach to his uniform.

Jae Pil accepted it with both hands, then bowed. It wasn't humanly possible for him to care less about this, but he pretended to be gratified. Next to him, he noticed Private Pak grimace slightly, the way a small child might when he sees a friend getting the bigger piece of rice cake.

"You have new orders," the man said. "You are to lead these men." He waved to a group of a half dozen privates standing by a nearby hut.

"Yes, sir," Jae Pil said.

The man then handed Jae Pil something different.

Jae Pil looked at it. It appeared to be a package of cloth. He unfolded it to reveal a pair of large, blue overalls. "Sir?"

• • •

He hadn't made it more than four miles. Ward's body simply wasn't capable of generating the energy he needed, not on a diet of corn and water anyway. He'd eaten the small can of meat one of the medics had given him, but it had provided only a temporary boost. Now, after two days of falling asleep and not waking for nearly fourteen hours, it became clear to him that he needed another solution. The only one that came to mind seemed more suicidal than helpful: he needed to ask the local villagers for help. They couldn't all be sympathetic to the Communists, he figured. Of course, some most certainly were, so every encounter would be a roll of the dice—literal Russian roulette.

But desperate times and all that. He descended from a hill, his clothes still soaked and his hands blistered and sore from trying to navigate through underbrush and mud with sticks so slippery it had become nearly impossible to maintain his grip. In the distance, along a path that divided a bean field, he saw a man walking with his hands behind his back.

Ward scanned the area. The path led over a rise and into what looked like a small village.

All Ward could see were the tops of several of the structures, one with a string of smoke rising from it. The rest of the field was empty. Just the man, dressed in white. The setting seemed perfect: a solitary figure, no one else around. If he was hostile, it would take him time to sound the alarm to soldiers in the village, if there were any. If he was friendly, he could assist Ward without drawing any attention to himself.

Ward emerged from the evergreens.

The man shuffled along, his head down, as if there wasn't a war going on all around him.

"Annyeong!" Ward called out. He knew the expression was some sort of greeting in Korean.

The man turned.

Ward raised his arm and a stick and waved both.

The man looked for a moment, then swiveled back to his path, seemingly unimpressed. He continued on his way, slowly, methodically.

Ward yelled again.

This time, the man paused, then squatted, appearing to wait for Ward.

Shuffling and tottering, Ward made his way down the path.

When he reached the man, he said, "Chingu," patting his chest. The man didn't respond. He was looking at the dirt.

Ward waited. Crucial seconds passed. He glanced up at the village, hoping no one would come.

Finally, the man raised his head. Ward jumped back, nearly tripping over himself.

The man's face—it certainly was a face, with all the usual features: eyes, ears, mouth, nose—looked more animalistic than human. His eyes seemed almost unseeing, as if they were made of wood, and the skin around his mouth was so tightly drawn, his lips seemed to not even exist.

"Chingu?" Ward said again.

The face remained expressionless. Suddenly, the man leaped to his feet. His arms gesticulated wildly, and he grunted and moaned—emanating a series of sounds Ward had never heard in his life. He sounded more like a wild beast than a person, and Ward was certain that whatever was coming out of his mouth, it was not intelligible language.

"Your jip?" Ward asked, trying to keep his voice quiet, not sure if the man would understand a single thing he said. "Your house?"

The man nodded, pointing to the village over the rise. "Soldiers?" Ward asked, pointing his stick like a gun. Another nod. Then a hand signal: many soldiers.

Ward needed to move. Even if this person were friendly, Ward couldn't trust him to sneak into the village and steal food for him; he seemed too mentally unstable.

Ward spun back to the mountains and forced his legs to move along the path. When he glanced back, he saw the villager shuffling back to the village, this time with much more speed than before, his arms swinging at his sides. How long did he have before the man said something about him to the soldiers? One minute? Maybe two?

He pushed forward and plunged into the trees, then climbed

as fast as his sticks and legs would carry him. When he was high enough and found a thicket of brush that would conceal him, he dared a look back at the village. Sure enough, he saw the man talking to two soldiers.

They appeared Chinese, but they could have been North Korean—Ward couldn't quite tell. This was it. The manhunt would begin. His sojourn was about to come to a crashing halt.

Then the unexpected, even the unfortunate: the soldiers pushed the poor man into the mud, brushing him off the way they might a pesky fly. He stumbled and landed on his backside in the muck. Then the soldiers walked away, laughing, back to the village and out of Ward's sight. For a time, the villager just sat there, his lower half covered in filth. Eventually, he rose and shuffled into the closest hut, his head down.

Ward collapsed into the bushes, his heart raging against his rib cage. His own stupidity made him want to vomit. How could he have been so careless? He could survive on his own. He didn't need help. With shaking hands, he pulled on his sticks and rose. He needed to put as much distance between himself and the village as possible.

• • •

Jae Pil had reached a new low. Literally and figuratively. He was standing in a tunnel, dressed in overalls, wondering how God had led him here. Yes, he'd been promoted, but his unit's orders were to drive even further from the front lines and then dig out tunnels in the mountainsides for the parking of trucks so American jets could not see them to bomb them. If he had cared about progressing in the People's Army, as Private Pak so obviously did, the assignment would have been humiliating. Manual labor was the least respectful work one could receive, even with a promotion. But more discouraging was the fact that God seemed uninterested in answering his prayers.

"It doesn't need to be especially deep," he said to one of the men working for him. "Just enough to hide the trucks during an attack." He pointed to some of the evergreen trees towering nearby. "These will provide plenty of cover as well, so if the trucks can fit halfway in, we should be fine. The Americans won't see them."

"Yes, sir," the man said.

Why on earth would he care if they did? Jae Pil thought. This was the last place on earth they would bomb at this point, so far from the front lines. How many times had he prayed? How many days? Asking for help, only to be led to a place so devoid of interest and possibility it might as well have been the bottom of the ocean.

Jae Pil exited the tunnel. A few meters away, Private Pak leaned against a tree, staring into the distance. He had refused to don the blue overalls, claiming they were for menial workers, not for soldiers. And he was a soldier.

Jae Pil had wanted to argue with him, even point out that the overalls kept their uniforms from becoming soiled, but he just didn't care that much. If Pak wanted to cover his uniform in dirt and grime in the name of wearing it proudly, so be it. Jae Pil had bigger problems. It seemed clear to him now that the only way he would ever "escape" the Communists was if the Americans won the war outright. But all the scuttlebutt claimed the two sides were negotiating their way to a ceasefire. If that happened, he would be stuck here in the North, with no way to ever practice his faith again. His men were digging out three truck shelters along this particular mountainside. Jae Pil navigated around the rear of one of the trucks and took in the progress of a tractor digging out the opening for the second tunnel.

It was as if the tractor were digging Jae Pil's tomb.

• • •

The binoculars hit the wall of the hut with a gratifying thunk. The rumors of some monster roaming the countryside were the final nudge to push him over the edge. This had to end immediately.

Lieutenant Kang turned to one of his men. "They say there is a monster in the mountains?"

"Yes, sir."

"Did it ever occur to them it might be the American? The one we told them they might see?" He swore; sometimes these villagers could be as stupid as dirt. No wonder some were naïve enough to want American capitalism.

The private next to him didn't answer the question, which, Kang had to admit, was probably the right move. Finally, someone with some common sense. "Where did they see him last?"

"No one with a right mind has seen him, sir," the private said. "Just rumors. Farmers claiming their corn has been stolen, in the fields near Sibyon-ni. One imbecile in the same area claims he spoke to an American, but the Chinese soldiers do not believe him."

The Chinese. Kang shook his head and exhausted his anger through his nose. Those idiots had cost him dearly. "Where was he?"

"Just a farmer's village," he said. "A few huts, nothing more. The man was born with some kind of deformity. His mind doesn't work."

"Prepare a jeep. We'll head there. There is always some truth behind rumors. The American is out there. His legs are broken. He can't go far."

• • •

Ward stumbled. The very small part of his mind that was still conscious of his surroundings knew that he had slipped into a sort of dreamlike delirium. That part of him was surprised when he stepped around a copse of trees and nearly bumped into a mother and her son.

He jerked to a halt. Nowhere to hide. No way to undo what had just been done. He was seen. The woman was older, wrinkles reflecting years of hard labor in harsh conditions, with a large gourd on her head. She paused and gulped in a sharp breath. Her white skirt flapped about her ankles in the breeze.

The boy—ten perhaps?—leaped away from both her and Ward. He paused a few yards away, ready to bolt if Ward did anything even slightly threatening.

"Chingu," Ward said, puffing the words out with great effort.

The woman stared for a second that felt like hours, then she raised both hands to the gourd and lowered it from her head. She carefully set it on the ground at her feet and squatted in front of it. It was covered in cloth, which she gently peeled away, revealing a mound of rice.

Ward's mouth involuntarily soaked itself with saliva. He fumbled into his vest and pulled out the two hundred won the trader had given him. He extended it toward the woman. "Please," he said. "Please." He also fumbled into another pocket and pulled out the empty meat can. The woman pointed to the can and took it from Ward. She scooped a heaping mound of the rice into it. From her pocket, she pulled some sort of leaf Ward didn't recognize, which she used to cover the rice. Gently, like a mother with a baby, she tucked the leaf over the rice, then handed the package back to Ward.

He bowed slightly, smiling. She returned the gesture.

He held out his hand with the Korean money, but she waved it away. Ward bit his lip to fight back tears pushing to the surface.

The woman merely smiled, then reached out to her son, took him by the hand, and continued on her way.

• • •

After that, his spirits and energy buoyed, Ward decided he had no choice but to risk encounters with Koreans; they might capture him, but they might also lead him to salvation. His chances of survival, he figured, were zero if he tried to keep moving on his own, so any chance that other Koreans might assist him increased his odds of making it to the sea.

Over the next several days, he encountered a number of Koreans, some who openly increased his odds of success, and others who didn't: an angry, frothing woman whose house had been burned to nothing by UN aircraft; an old man who tried to report Ward to nearby soldiers but who, shockingly, moved even slower than Ward did, giving him time to escape; an old man in a hut who seemed to want to capture Ward but who quickly gave up the search after Ward disappeared into the hillside; two young women, one with a baby strapped to her back, who seemed so terrified at the sight of Ward that he just let them be; a boy who wrapped rice in two lettuce leaves for Ward but who then immediately started screaming to anyone in the nearby fields who would listen; a dozen boys who seemed to be hunting frogs or other animals along a stream; a half-dozen men and women building a dam along the same creek.

Ward did not engage the latter two groups, but one thing was clear, more and more Koreans knew an American was loose in the countryside. It would be only a matter of time before word reached Kang or whoever else was on the hunt for the escaped American. Still, Ward couldn't help himself. He needed assistance, and because of the food he'd been given, he was making better time.

Finally, he stumbled upon the oddest of sights: a middle-aged man naked in a pool of water. The man noticed Ward immediately. That he was naked didn't seem to bother him in the least. As far as Ward could tell, the man was taking a bath.

It felt like a basic-training exam question put to some new soldier as a joke: you're on a trail in hostile territory behind enemy lines and you come across a naked man who may or may not be an ally. Do you engage or try to escape?

For Ward, the answer was easy, he put his head down and pushed on, hoping the man would just leave him be.

It didn't work.

Almost immediately, from behind, there was frantic shouting and splashing.

Ward glanced back. The man was lunging through the water, not bothering to cover himself. He closed the distance between himself and Ward impossibly fast and latched onto Ward's arm.

Ward froze, unsure of what to do. Was this a capture? Should he try to escape, beat the man away with one of his sticks? The man released his grip. A few steps away, his clothes lay in a jumbled heap along a rock. He grabbed his trousers and slid them on.

Ward watched, deciding he could never escape. The man looked to be in his forties, fit, nimble. If he wanted to catch Ward, he would.

"E Syng Man?" the bather finally said, pointing to Ward.

The Korean leader in the South. Ward and his fellow Americans called him Syngman Rhee. Ward nodded.

The man thought for a moment. Finally, he pointed to the southwest. Ward followed his finger. The rooftops of several mud huts jutted up over a distant hill. Beyond them was another ridge and a multitude of evergreen trees.

The Korean held his arms as if holding a rifle. *There are soldiers there.*

Ward nodded, offering a half smile. *I understand. Thank you.*

The man made a series of other gestures and points. Amazingly, his directions seemed clear: *hide in the cornfields until the sun goes down.*

Again, Ward offered thanks.

As he turned to the field, another Korean appeared, a younger man, in his teens most likely, dressed like a field worker but probably just on the cusp of joining the army. His eyes widened. He stumbled back from Ward like someone does a venomous snake.

Ward stretched forth his hand. "Chingu," he said. The boy turned and bound toward the huts.

With a speed Ward wouldn't have suspected was possible, the bather sprung away from his pool and bolted after the boy. "Ya!" he screamed. He latched onto the boy's shoulder and spun him around. In hushed, desperate whispers, they argued with one another. Ward decided he wasn't going to hang around to find out how the argument ended.

He plunged through the stream and forced himself up the hillside. Sticks, legs, sticks, feet—he moved faster than he had in months, over the hillside, down a rocky ravine, back up a scrub-covered slope. Sweat flowed down his face as intensely as the rain from days before. He climbed higher and higher. His heart seemed to beat throughout his entire body all at once, scraping against his ears, thumping in his skull, bursting from his palms. Soon, whatever energy he had regained thanks to the generous Koreans vanished.

A gunshot. A rifle blast? Maybe a pistol?

Ward thrust his stick into the earth and dared a look back. Snot filled his nose. Breaths came as if through a damp cloth: difficult, strained. No one had crested the rocky ravine yet. Who was shooting? What was their target? Had they killed the man bathing in the pond for helping him? He couldn't go any farther. If they were hunting him, they would spy him lumbering through the brush. The few evergreens on the slope wouldn't provide any cover.

More important, his stamina was near zero. For days he'd been envisioning a line graph in his mind. It was simple: his energy levels ran along the y-axis, and time (measured in days) ran along the x-axis. Now ten days out from his initial escape, the resulting line was near zero. He had wasted himself and had nothing left to give.

His only hope was to hide before soldiers crested the ravine and saw him. Nearby, a thick bush looked to be his best option. He crawled to it, slithering and burrowing as close to its base as possible.

CHAPTER 34

The first bunker was complete, the second coming along. Jae Pil signaled for some of his men to move their equipment.

"Who is that?" Private Pak asked.

Jae Pil looked first to Pak, then followed his eyes to the short rise leading toward some cornfields. "I don't know. What's he saying?" Someone was running toward them, his arms gesticulating wildly. He was shouting something but was still too far away for Jae Pil to make out what it was.

"That boy from the village," Pak said. Jae Pil nodded.

Behind the boy, one of the farmers trailed, his shirt off. What was going on?

Finally, like the volume being turned up on a radio, the boy's shouts became audible: "An American! American!"

Jae Pil and Pak looked at each other and then sprung into action. Pak sprinted to the tree where he'd been resting earlier and snatched up his submachine gun. Jae Pil darted to the cab of his truck and yanked his pistol from under the seat.

The other soldiers had paused their work and were watching quizzically. Jae Pil pointed at one of them, a bushy-haired man with a paunch who, based on his slovenly dress, looked as if he wanted to be in the Grand Leader's army even less than Jae Pil did. "Grab your rifle and come with me," Jae Pil ordered. He looked at another man, wearing the same blue work overalls and holding a shovel. "You come too. The rest of you stay here! Be ready!"

When Jae Pil turned, the teenage boy nearly collided with him. Trying to steady his breathing, he said, "An American . . . there . . . by the stream."

"Did you talk with him?" Jae Pil asked.

"No," the boy said. "He did."

At that moment, the shirtless farmer had arrived, skidding to a stop behind the boy.

"What is he doing? What did he say?" Jae Pil asked the farmer.

"He wanted to help him," the boy said.

The farmer raised both his hands as if trying to tame a wild animal. "No," he said. "I was trying to stall him so we could tell you he was here."

"Is he armed?" Jae Pil asked.

"No," the farmer said. "He carried two sticks. That was all."

"Let's find him," Jae Pil said.

He led the charge up the trail. The two soldiers he had ordered to come followed, as did the boy and the shirtless farmer. Pak fell in line as well. Jae Pil glanced at him sideways, considered ordering him to stay behind, but let it go. One more weapon and a soldier who knew how to use it might be helpful, especially if the American was a threat.

They crested the rise and took in the cornfields. Nothing. "Where did he go?" Jae Pil asked.

"He started to go up the hill," the boy said.

Jae Pil steered the group through the field. When they reached the end of it, near the stream, the farmer collected his shirt from off the ground near a pool and slipped it over his torso. He also picked up a scythe and gripped it in two hands like a sword.

Just then, Pak fired his weapon, a single shot. "Do not fire!" Jae Pil ordered.

"I thought I saw him!" Pak hissed, refusing to take his eyes off the hillside.

"Do not fire unless I order you to do so," Jae Pil said. He stepped to Pak. "Did you hit him?"

"No," Pak said. Then, after a delay, he added, "Sir, I thought I saw him, but it was just that bush."

"What was he wearing?" Jae Pil asked the farmer.

"Rags. Looked like American clothes. Torn up. Long beard. Skinny. Two sticks he was using to walk."

"Do not shoot unless ordered," Jae Pil said. "Fan out. Let's go."

They crossed the stream above the farmer's pool and then navigated up the slope behind it. Pak sidestepped close to Jae Pil. "Did Lieutenant Kang change his orders?" he asked.

He was right, of course. Their orders were clear: execute the American on sight. "We must ensure this is the same man," Jae Pil said. "There are many prisoners of war." He didn't want any further argument. "Stop talking. Keep your eyes focused."

Jae Pil held his pistol in front, staring down the barrel, as he peaked the hill and then dropped into a ravine. There were few trees here, but the bushes were thick. What if the man had already escaped? What if they couldn't find him? Jae Pil could only imagine the punishment he would face if his superiors knew he'd tried and failed when he'd been so close. Beneath his feet, the surface was unstable, packed with mud and small rocks. He slid, forcing his eyes to stay up, looking for any movement at all.

He signaled to each of his men and the two civilians that they were to remain silent.

• • •

Ward lay in the bush for some time. Twigs poked into his back and thighs, but he didn't dare move. Since he'd heard the gunshot, he hadn't seen any other indication that he was being followed. Had he really lost them? Perhaps they had never pursued him at all? By instinct, Ward pulled his cross from his vest and rubbed it with his fingers. As soon as he became cognizant of what he was doing, he stopped. What was the point? All the prayers, all the begging, all the hope that something in the vast universe actually cared about him alongside the billions of other lifeforms—it was all so naïve.

He opted to hold onto the cross, not because he believed anything would help him, but because it reminded him of Barbara. If he was going to die right now, at least he would have that connection to her.

• • •

He'd disappeared. How could he have disappeared?

Last they knew, the man had been hobbling over these hills with two sticks. If he was the same man Lieutenant Kang wanted them to execute, his legs were broken, or at least still healing and extremely weak. How fast could he possibly move? There didn't even seem to be a trail. It just made no sense.

Not seeing any point in sprinting farther up a mountainside with no obvious trail, Jae Pil stood still. He scanned the terrain, asking himself where he would go if he were in this man's shoes. The farmer and boy trudged on up ahead of him. Private Pak stayed close, which was probably a good thing—the man was so eager to kill Americans he posed more of a problem than a help. To Jae Pil's left, the third soldier (he realized then that he should probably have learned the man's name) seemed to be wandering with the same aimlessness with which he'd gotten dressed that morning. Jae Pil didn't care about this army or its goals, but he could at least pretend he did. This man seemed unmotivated to do even that.

Just as Jae Pil was considering turning back, the farmer jumped, leaping away from a bush as if it had attacked him. "What is it?" Jae Pil asked.

"There he is!" the boy screamed, pointing into the bush.

The farmer was wielding his scythe like he was ready to start hacking at the bush.

Jae Pil fired two shots from his pistol: one into the air, the other into the ground near the bush. That forced the farmer to pause.

Then he was sprinting with Pak and the other soldier on his heels. They pushed past the farmer and boy. His pistol in front of him, Jae Pil plunged into the bush, snapping branches out of the way.

They were right. An American. Or at least a European. Jae Pil felt Pak and the other soldier crowd in behind him, nearly causing him to lose his balance. Now the crucial question: could he keep them from killing this man long enough to figure out what was going on?

"American?" Jae Pil asked in Korean.

The man, if you could call him that—he was more of a creature, really: gaunt, scraggly beard, sunken eyes, more bone than flesh, filthy clothes, and stench—nodded.

An American. A real American. Until now, the soldiers from the United States had been more of a myth than a reality for Jae Pil. Like stars: he knew they were there, could see them from a distance, but had never experienced one up close.

"How did you get here?" Jae Pil asked.

Squinting in the light, the American didn't seem to understand. Jae Pil motioned with his hands, asking the question again.

This time, the American seemed to understand the question. With hand signals and a few Chinese and Korean words, he seemed to say that he'd been in a hospital that had been bombed and had been left behind in the confusion. He'd been wandering the countryside ever since.

"Nonsense," Pak said. "This is the man."

"We don't know that yet," Jae Pil said.

"We are to execute him immediately," Pak said.

"Quiet, private!" Jae Pil hissed. "We will deal with him as I see fit. We have orders to execute only one American, and I will not execute this man until I know he is the same one."

Pak took a step back, although he did not lower his weapon.

Jae Pil thought for a moment, his pistol still sited on the American's forehead. In the recesses of his mind, images of the execution he had witnessed, of the deserter, continued to rise to his consciousness. They were horrible echoes: the man on his knees, his hands tied behind his back, his clothes ripped from his body, the commanding officer placing his pistol against the man's skull.

Jae Pil could not do that to a fellow human being. Especially one as pathetic as this poor American. The more Jae Pil looked upon him, the sadder he felt. The man had clearly suffered. He was depleted, a walking skeleton.

Jae Pil holstered his pistol. He reached into the bush and pulled the American into an upright position, then guided him from the bush into some open space. There, he patted him down, looking for weapons. He found nothing.

The American was wearing a vest and clothes with plenty of pockets. He could conceal anything in there.

Jae Pil ordered him to empty all of them onto the ground.

Various items spilled forth—a tin can, its lid, small bits of soap, a piece of folded paper, a bottle with some sort of pills in it—but Jae Pil's eyes had locked on something else. As the American had begun to empty his pockets, he had started his pile with something already in his hand: a wooden cross.

Jae Pil squatted and picked it up, turning it over in his fingers. He stood. "Christian?" he asked.

The American nodded.

"Jesus and Mary?" he said in English. Again, the American nodded.

"What are you talking about?" Pak asked.

"Quiet," Jae Pil said over his shoulder. Jae Pil pointed at the cross, then at the American. *You made this?*

The American nodded, then seemed to sign the words *I have been praying much.*

Just then both Pak and the other soldier stepped closer. "We should take him back to the village and follow our orders," Pak said.

"I agree," the other soldier said. He had leveled his rifle at the American.

The pair had obviously been communicating with each other behind Jae Pil's back.

Jae Pil turned from the American and looked at both of them. "This man claims he was in a hospital bombed by the enemy and was left behind in the confusion. If he is not our escaped American, we will be executing someone without orders."

"We have orders," Pak said.

The slovenly soldier seemed to have exhausted whatever willingness he had to question Jae Pil's authority, because his eyes had already dropped to the ground, his head bowed slightly. Under normal circumstances, Pak likely would have done the same, but he and Jae Pil were so close in rank, and were, for all intents and purposes, equals until only a few days ago, he had forgotten his place.

"Our orders," Jae Pil said with steel in his voice, "are to capture and execute the American who escaped from Na-Han-Li. If we execute this man, and it turns out he is not the same man, we will face severe repercussions. In truth, for all we know, this man may have important intelligence that could help us win this war. I will not report back to my superiors that I killed an important resource until I am certain with what I am dealing." Jae Pil reached up and placed his palms on the barrels of both the rifle and Pak's semiautomatic. He then pushed them both down until they were facing the dirt.

Pak did not challenge Jae Pil except for in his eyes. The man seemed to know, seemed to sense that Jae Pil was bluffing. Or was that just Jae Pil's own paranoia? He couldn't tell, but it didn't matter at the moment.

As for the other soldier, years of training in not challenging authority had cowed him into obedience. He would no longer be a problem.

"Each of you back away," Jae Pil said.

The two civilians and the sloppy soldier did so immediately. Pak followed, a little less enthusiastically.

Jae Pil turned back to the American, who stood on shaking, bony legs. Jae Pil pointed at his ankles.

The American eased to the ground and sat in the dirt. He pulled large rubber boot covers from his feet, then peeled off half-rotting corn silk and leaves.

Jae Pil grimaced. The man was mostly bone, but the flesh around his ankles was bloated and blue. The stench that arose from them forced Jae Pil to turn his head. This was clearly the man who had escaped from Lieutenant Kang. Pak knew it. So did Jae Pil, for that matter. But what was he to do? Especially knowing this man was a fellow Christian. And what possibilities did this American present? Jae Pil did not have a mathematical or scientific brain—he had never received any training in either field—but he wondered what the odds were of him running into this American in this spot at this precise moment, and it seemed impossible that it had happened by chance. How long he could keep Pak at bay, he didn't know, but he needed more time to see what walking through this door would bring him.

Can you walk? Jae Pil signed.

The American pointed to two long sticks in the bushes and indicated he used them to walk. He scooted toward them, but Jae Pil waved him off. He didn't have time to wait for this broken man to shuffle his way back to the village.

"Grab his belongings," he said to the boy, who was looking at the American with fearful eyes. He then motioned for the pilot to climb onto his back. "We will take him back to the village."

• • •

Ward had no clue what was happening. He clung to the back of the short, stocky Korean for dear life. One of the civilians was carrying all his belongings. The two other soldiers still looked like they wanted to shoot him, and both held their weapons in a way that suggested they might do just that if he even looked at them wrong. But most intriguing: this Korean seemed very interested in Ward's cross. He had spoken the words "Jesus and Mary" with perfect pronunciation, which made Ward think he might be dealing with someone who had met Christian missionaries before.

It was possible. For most of his time in Korea, in both the South and as a prisoner, he had met very few Koreans who understood the story of Christ, who knew the names. But he also knew there were plenty out there; their presence drew attention to themselves because they were so unique. Korea, unlike Japan before the war, had been more receptive to Christian missionaries than many countries in Asia. It had something to do with the Koreans' own creation story, which involved a heavenly son coming to earth to create Korean civilization. Ward didn't know all the details. All he knew was that it wasn't out of the realm of possibility that he could meet a Christian Korean in the North.

The implications of that? He had no idea. This man carrying him was clearly strong. He bound over rocks, sidestepped holes, and sprung across the stream with ease. The other soldiers and the two civilians needed to jog to keep up.

Ward knew that, in reality, he should be falling into an abyss of depression and emotional darkness. After all, he was a prisoner again. But there was something about this man carrying him—a warmth and reassurance—that put Ward at ease. Part of it was just his sheer exhaustion. The idea that he no longer needed to take another step on his own was enough to make him weep.

Soon, they entered a small village, similar to all the others Ward had seen. Ward's carrier paused in front of one porch hut and squatted so Ward could slide off, which he did, resting his back against two bags of rice.

Almost immediately, people seemed to materialize from the various huts and fields: older men, women, children. They gathered around Ward in fascination. They stood in the beating Korean sun. Their faces were a mixture of dispassionate fatigue and excitement. As they enfolded Ward, he had a sense of being slowly swallowed. Children rubbed his hair, only to be pulled away by their mothers. One older child tugged on his beard. Through the sea of faces, Ward could no longer see the soldier in the blue overalls who had brought him here.

For a moment, he started to panic. What if some of these people decided to kill him?

Then, one middle-aged woman emerged, cupping in her hands a tray with several small bowls of rice, potatoes, cabbage, and sesame seeds.

The soldier who had carried him stood behind her, and she seemed to be acting on his orders.

Ward accepted the tray with both hands but was unsure of what to do next. He was ravenous, but scarfing down all of the food with so many people watching him didn't feel right. He held the tray for a moment. He resisted the compulsion to shovel the food into his mouth until there was nothing left. Instead, he looked up to the woman; she nodded for him to eat and, behind her, the soldier did the same.

Ward could wait no longer. At their encouragement, he scooped the rice into his mouth. Then the potatoes. More rice. Then cabbage.

More potatoes. He shoveled more into his mouth than he could hold. Breathing heavily through his nose, he ignored the whispers and snorts of laughter that stemmed from the crowd.

The moment he finished, the Korean soldier stepped forward and signaled that Ward should go into the hut. He offered his arm for support.

Ward grabbed it, rose to his feet, then hobbled into the house. To the side, he noted one thing of importance: none of the soldiers looked happy, particularly the one with the submachine gun.

But in the hut they were alone. The room was what Ward had come to expect. Mud walls, thatch roof, one window, several pots, a lantern.

The soldier mostly carried Ward to the wall. Ward slid down it, resting on his backside.

Outside, the crowd had gushed a steady stream of whispers, but no one had followed them in.

Ward stared at his savior, who indicated Ward should lie down and get some sleep. But Ward couldn't just let this go. Who was this man? Why was he being so generous? "Chingu?" Ward asked.

The soldier looked to the door, then back to Ward. He squatted. "Chingu," he said, and for just a moment, Ward thought he saw the man's eyes begin to water.

"Kim Jae Pil," the soldier said, patting his chest.

"Ward Millar."

CHAPTER 35

The friendly introduction didn't last.

Before either man could say another word, Jae Pil heard a commotion outside the hut. He motioned for the American—this Ward Millar—to stay put and then bounded to the door.

What he was saw was simultaneously shocking and unsurprising.

Private Pak stood in the middle of the dirt road, just beyond the gawking onlookers, talking with three members of the Korean Security Forces. The Communist Secret Police—intelligence gatherers and secret enforcers for the Party. They wore their usual uniforms: tan pants and shirts with green shoulder straps. All three men seemed especially anxious, waving their arms wildly and shouting at Pak with such intensity he seemed to cower in front of them.

They must have been in the area, already in the village. It would have been easy for Pak to go notify them.

Jae Pil shook his head, masked his frustration, and marched from the porch. "What is this?" he asked.

"You have an American escapee in the house?" one of the three said, an older man with a commanding air. "We demand you give him to us immediately."

Jae Pil cast Pak an icy glare, but what he received in return was a look of defiance, albeit a subtle one.

"He is a prisoner of the army," Jae Pil said. "He is therefore under my command and is my concern. I will not turn him over until I feel it appropriate."

"No," the leader said. "We will want to interrogate him on behalf of the People. He may well have intelligence that will be helpful to us."

"I agree he may have intelligence, which is why the army will want to keep him under our control."

"In the name of the Great Leader, I order you to give him to us," the man said, even going so far as to pivot toward Jae Pil. A threat.

Jae Pil refused to back down. "The military has strict divisions," he said. "I must answer to my superiors, the officers in the army. You are security forces. You may have sway over these people in these villages, but your jurisdiction ends with that."

"Our jurisdiction begins with any people or situation that will promote the Workers' Party among the populace. That includes rooting out any threats to the Party."

"This American is no threat to the Party," Jae Pil said. "He is injured. He cannot walk. We have orders to execute him if he is an escapee. If he is not, he may well have important intelligence for the war effort. I will not go back to my commanding officers and tell them I let an American prisoner into your hands when we could have been interrogating him regarding crucial strategic information."

It was a bluff. Jae Pil had no idea if this man carried any information whatsoever. He was also almost entirely sure Ward Millar was the man he'd been ordered to execute, and Private Pak knew it. But he needed time, and if acting far more confident than he was would buy him that time, so be it.

The three men stood their ground, seemingly thinking about

their next move, Jae Pil refused to budge or show any sign of weakness.

"We will protest this," the man said.

"Do so," Jae Pil said. "If we receive orders from our superiors to transfer him into your custody, so be it. In the meantime, we will take him to our officers for questioning." The security officer considered this. Then, without a word, he spun and marched away, the two others following him.

• • •

Two days. Maybe three.

That was how much time Jae Pil figured he had before Lieutenant Kang found them. Or before the security forces returned, demanding the American. Then Millar would be executed and, most likely, Jae Pil along with him. Pak was forced by protocol to defer to Jae Pil, but when an officer appeared, he would not keep his mouth shut. It would all flow out: that Jae Pil was keeping the American alive, that he was treating him with kindness, that he seemed unusually interested in him. Even if Jae Pil could talk his way out of his own execution, there was nothing he would be able to do for the American.

It was time to act.

Waiting until everyone else fell asleep, Jae Pil threw off his blanket. He was in a hut separate from the American. Next to him, Pak and several other soldiers snored rhythmically. He picked up his pistol and holstered it, then slipped into the night.

• • •

Ward had been drifting in and out of strange, half-formed dreams, when he heard footsteps in his hut. Jae Pil had stepped into the room, no longer wearing his overalls, but dressed in the same uniform as all the other North Korean soldiers. In his right hand, he held an unlit flashlight. His firearm was holstered on his hip.

On the floor, two soldiers assigned as guards had drifted off to sleep.

Jae Pil placed his finger to his lips, then motioned for Ward to get up and follow him. Ward tried, but after just a few steps, keeping his balance without his walking sticks proved impossible. He nearly toppled into the sleeping guards.

Jae Pil caught him, then spun so Ward could crawl onto his back.

Within seconds, they were bounding away from the huts, along a narrow trail leading into the mountains. Beneath Ward, this man felt like a ball of pure muscle, pent up, endless energy. Then they were in total darkness.

Jae Pil huffed along the path, seemingly knowing where to step without light. Occasional branches whipped in Ward's face or brushed against his arms. He had no idea where he was being taken. For just a moment, it occurred to him he should be frightened. For all he knew, this was his execution. But there was something about the Korean—a general spirit he carried—that put Ward at ease. The man seemed both confident and unworried.

They emerged into a clearing. Two huts. One with a lantern clearly burning inside.

Jae Pil eased Ward onto the porch. From the door, an old man emerged, shirtless, appearing ghostly and haggard, a mere shadow with the lamplight behind him.

A string of words, sounding mostly slurred, slid from the man's mouth. He was talking to Ward.

"I don't . . . understand," Ward said, shaking his head at Jae Pil.

Jae Pil said something to the old man, who merely grunted, then wandered away from the hut, vanishing into the darkness.

"Oksusu," Jae Pil said. Ward shook his head. *Corn.*

"Do you speak English?" Ward said.

"No," and then, "jogeum." Jae Pil squinted, pinching his thumb and index finger close to each other: *just a little.*

But it was surprisingly easy to communicate. Through the Chinese and Korean vocabulary Ward had picked up, the English words Jae Pil knew, sign language, and drawing in the dirt, they started to get their ideas across.

The old man, Jae Pil said, was very sad. He had been married twice but had never had any sons, so there was no one to help him care for his farm or fields. Then the Communists had confiscated much of his land anyway, so he was left with very little. He would help them.

He did. As they spoke, signed, and drew their way through each of their stories, the old man returned with several ears of corn. He cooked them on a small grill on his porch.

Ward took in Jae Pil's story with amazement, and then shared his own. The longer they communicated, the more comfortable Ward felt with this North Korean, but the more uncomfortable he felt with the fact that someone might find him missing. He still wasn't sure if he should reveal the complete truth of who he was and how he had come to be in the North Korean countryside.

He signed to Jae Pil that perhaps they should get back. Jae Pil nodded but did nothing to make it happen.

The old farmer handed both men an ear of corn. Cooked and warm, its flavors exploded in Ward's mouth in ways he hadn't thought possible. He nodded his appreciation, to which the farmer, squatting on the porch and munching on his own ear, merely said, "Nae, nae." *Yes, yes.*

Jae Pil was still talking, explaining how badly many of the Chinese had treated the Korean villagers who were not in the military. He was not happy about it.

Ward nodded and tried to sign that he agreed.

We are ordered to execute you, Jae Pil signed. This came as a surprise to Ward. He realized he felt more shock than made sense. Of course their orders were to kill him. He had proven his usefulness. There was nothing left to get from him in terms of helpful intelligence. His legs had healed, which meant the Chinese who had been protecting him had fulfilled their obligations. And Lieutenant Kang's thirst for American blood had never abated.

All the more reason to get back to the huts before anyone found him gone.

Jae Pil must have perceived the worry in Ward's face. He tapped Ward's arm. I can protect you for now, he seemed to say.

He then turned pensive, staring at his now cleaned ear of corn. Ward wondered: could he trust this man? Would he help him escape?

Then, Jae Pil hopped off the porch, stepped into the darkness, and returned a moment later with a stick. He seemed to be reading Ward's mind. In the dirt, he drew a map of the peninsula and placed a dot where they were. Then he drew a long, squiggly line.

"Imjin," he said. "Ribber."

"The Imjin River?"

Jae Pil offered a thumb's up. His next message, coming through signs and partial words and phrases, wasn't clear at first. It manifested to Ward the way a landscape might as a fog thinned. Eventually, though, the ideas of Jae Pil's message caused Ward to feel an exhilaration he hadn't felt in weeks: *I want to go South.*

Ward sat straight up and urged him to keep going.

Jae Pil's plan was straightforward: he and Ward should hike through the mountains to the Imjin, he would swim across and tell the Americans on the other side about Ward, and they would come across and save Ward. They would need to leave right away. Ward immediately protested. Through their own crude language, he explained the problem: my feet aren't good enough to hike that far, and it's possible the Americans might kill you or refuse to believe you.

Jae Pil nodded and then rubbed his eyes. For the first time, he looked tired.

Ward tapped his shoulder to get his attention. What if we steal the truck? Then drive to the coast for a boat?

Jae Pil shook his head. There are too many people watching. They will kill us. And there are no longer any U.S. boats on those shores. The Communists have commandeered all civilian boats on the coasts and would see them.

They sat in silence for a long moment, both considering their options.

Ward glanced back into the darkness. How could this man not be worried about getting caught? They had been out here too long.

Finally, Jae Pil's eyes grew wide. Another five minutes of back and forth, and Ward understood what his new friend wanted to do: signal American aircraft.

It'll never work, Ward communicated back. There are no downed pilots here. They won't be looking for any signals, so the only possibility is that they fire on us.

Jae Pil sucked in a deep, frustrated breath. He pointed at the map again to indicate they would move forward with his original plan.

Ward waved his arms. It won't work! I can't hike fast enough!

Jae Pil stood, placed his hands on Ward's shoulder, and gave him a simple look: Trust me.

CHAPTER 36

Jae Pil was on his back in the darkness of his hut. His midnight
venture to the village with the American had been worthwhile
but ultimately unproductive. Ward hadn't seemed to think any of
Jae Pil's ideas for escape would work. And Jae Pil was now doubtful
as well. He now had precisely zero viable ideas for how to escape
with his prisoner.

The security forces would return, likely with commands from
someone that would override anything Jae Pil could make up.
And Private Pak was probably already trying to send messages to
Lieutenant Kang. For all Jae Pil knew, the lieutenant may have already heard the news of the airman's recapture and been on his way,
bouncing in some jeep across the countryside with his finger on the
trigger of his Russian Tokarev.

Outside, a soft breeze was blowing. It carried with it just a hint
of the coming fall. It was 0345 hours. Outside, the stars poised
above him like the tips of nails ready to fall.

Jae Pil was contemplating this, finally drifting off to sleep, when
the idea jolted him awake.

● ● ●

"There is only one way to resolve this," Jae Pil said. He was facing the leader of the security forces. "We must take the prisoner to our commanding officers so they can decide what they would like to do with him."

"A POW camp?"

"Possibly," Jae Pil said. "We have orders from at least one lieutenant regarding an American escapee who has already been interrogated and is to be executed. If this is that man, they can confirm, and he will be dealt with properly. If this is not him, then he may still prove useful."

The older man considered this for a moment. His shoulder straps indicated he was a master sergeant, quite high in the ranks, even if he had no direct command over Jae Pil. "Fine," he finally said. "But we will come with you."

No! Jae Pil thought. *Please, no*—his plea was silent, and it wasn't to them, but to heaven.

On the surface, he maintained a stoic expression. "I have room for only two of you," he said. "We are also hauling a great deal of equipment." Then he leveled his eyes at the master sergeant. "And you remember the rules. What I say governs when we are en route. It is my truck, and it is under my command."

The master sergeant hesitated and seemed like he wanted to argue, but instead bit his lip. "Fine."

• • •

Where was Ward Millar?

Nobody had seen him for ten days. Rumors. Whispers of a mysterious monster lurking in the fields. But nothing more. One minute he was here, seemingly unable to walk. The next he had vanished into the countryside.

Lieutenant Kang Dae Hyun's first true failure. It would be a blemish on his record he could never correct. A crack like that would widen. Every opportunity in the Workers' Party that was set to come his way would fall into it, and he would waste his days as a pariah. Where could Millar hope to get to? They were in the middle of North Korean territory, with nothing but ridges and fields and valleys for miles in every direction. The only way he could be rescued was with an American helicopter, because the jets couldn't land. So where was he going?

The days since the escape had passed in futility. His initial assumption was that the American would head straight south, but then they found the print on the road going north. A ruse? Perhaps there was a rendezvous point north? In the end, the print wasn't helpful.

They then assumed that, perhaps, he might try to reach a river, which he could float down until he reached an American checkpoint. But this far north, all of the rivers were far too shallow to float.

He must be hiding, one of Kang's men had told him. Hiding! Just find him then! It's not as though he blends in!

Kang was spending more and more of his time staring at his map, whole ridges and valleys exed out with a piece of charcoal. It was the middle of the day once again. How many nights had it been since he'd really slept? The last stretch of uninterrupted sleep felt like nothing more than a memory. No sooner would he drift into a dream than he would jerk awake, his throat so tight he could barely suck in a gasp of air. A recurring nightmare invaded his thoughts: he was strapped to an execution pole, and the Great Leader himself stood before him holding a rifle.

From in front of his map, he was simply at a loss as to how this American could have vanished. Could he walk faster than Kang gave him credit for? Was he getting help? Had he already escaped to the South?

"Sir!" a private entered the room, saluting with a bit more enthusiasm than Kang felt like reciprocating.

"Yes?"

"Rumors of an American captured near Pak-Chan-Ni."

"Millar?"

"No other information, sir."

"Who told you?"

"It came over the signals along the roads, sir. No radio."

Kang folded his map. "Find a jeep. And send word back that he is to be guarded closely until I arrive."

• • •

An entire day had passed. An entire day! They still hadn't moved.

Ward lay awake on the floor of his hut in the middle of the night. Next to him slept a man with a gun who had moved in to guard him. He wasn't an ordinary army man but seemed to be part of the North Korean secret police, sent to replace the two other rank-and-file soldiers who had been there before—apparently their leader had grown skeptical of how Jae Pil was handling the situation and wanted to keep a closer eye on this American from nowhere.

As far as Ward could tell, his situation had gone from bad to worse. Jae Pil had indicated he had everything under control, but nothing had happened. All throughout the day after their nighttime meeting with the old farmer, Ward had been expecting his new friend to sneak in and tell him about their plans for this night. But then he never saw him. It was as if they had never had the conversation about escaping.

Now, Ward guessed, it was one o'clock in the morning, and still just silence. It was time to take matters into his own hands.

One factor was in his favor: the North Korean and Chinese armies didn't have the best radio communication, certainly nothing near as robust as what the Americans enjoyed. Often their best way of communicating was to send a series of signals by bugle, clicks, or whistles along the shipping routes. It was crude, but it got the job done. Word was able to spread relatively quickly. It was not as fast as a radio signal, but fast enough to get word to Lieutenant Kang that Ward had been recaptured. It was possible, of course, that no one in this village would send word to anyone, but something told Ward that just couldn't be true. Call it a sixth sense or a gut feeling, but a small whisper, an instinct deep in his consciousness, told him that Kang was coming.

Ward couldn't wait any longer. Come hell or high water, it was time to get out of here. He sat up. The secret police guard lay right next to him. When the man had fallen asleep earlier, Ward had noted that he'd used his holstered pistol and his shirt as a pillow.

Given how those items were situated under the guard's head, Ward was confident that, with a lot of care and a little luck, he could get the pistol out. He reached over to the man's head and felt the pistol in its holster. Two decorative leather tassels locked the pistol in place, but if Ward could release those, he could slip the pistol from the holster.

He tugged on the first. It came free. The guard's breathing paused. He swallowed. Ward fell back onto his sleeping space. When the guard's breathing returned to its normal rhythm, Ward slunk back to him. He started on the second tassel. It released with ease. The guard didn't stir. Ward pinched the pistol grip with his thumb and index finger and tugged. It moved a fraction of an inch.

Minutes passed. Then hours, it seemed. Any time the man's breathing changed, Ward flopped back to pretend sleep. But millimeter by millimeter, tug by tug, he finally freed the pistol. Once it was clear, he hopped to his feet and moved for the door. In the back of his mind, he knew this was a suicide escape. He had little food. His walking sticks had been taken. Jae Pil was a useful ally, and Ward was, essentially, abandoning him. But what choice did he have? There could be little doubt that Kang was on his way. If his chances of survival were one percent on his own, they were close to zero if he stayed. It was a tragedy, but Jae Pil was simply not as resourceful as Ward had hoped.

Ward slid off the hut's porch. All around him, the night was silent. He gripped the pistol in his right hand and then rose to his feet. With the food he'd been given over the last day and half, he felt stronger than he had in weeks. Walking would be precarious, but he was confident he could cover some distance. Along the way, he'd hunt for sticks among the trees.

He took a step. Then another. A third.

Just as he passed the next hut over, a shadow emerged in the door.

Ward raised the pistol, but the man was too fast. He closed the distance between the two of them before Ward could even threaten to protect himself.

CHAPTER 37

Ward nearly let out a yelp, but a powerful arm wrapped around his back and a hand covered his mouth. "Shhh," the shadow said.

The next thing Ward knew, he was being dragged away from the village, toward the latrines. When they reached them, he was released. He tried to stand, but his legs couldn't hold his weight, and he fell to his knees.

His captor flicked on a flashlight. It was Jae Pil. Ward knew immediately: his friend was furious.

Mostly through signs, Jae Pil's message was clear: *What are you doing!?*

Ward tried to convey his own angry message. *We can't wait! They are going to kill me!*

I have a plan! Jae Pil said, jabbing his finger into his chest. *Wait! Just wait!*

Ward bit his lip and heard his own breath rushing from his nostrils. *I can't wait.* He signed again about his pending execution.

It took them a few minutes, but Jae Pil signaled to Ward that he had come up with a plan that was better than Ward trying to make it on his own.

Ward was open to considering it, so he motioned for Jae Pil

to try to explain it. And he had to admit, once Jae Pil was done, it did sound like a better option than what Ward had come up with. Jae Pil had convinced the secret police and the other soldiers that they needed to take Ward to a POW camp. They had spent the day loading equipment into one of the trucks, and he had convinced the other men that they could not take a direct route to the camp because the road was too rough to follow while hauling the valuable equipment. Instead, they would need to follow a more circuitous road that was gentler, but that dipped far further south, close to the port city of Haeju. If they could stop there, the two of them could then escape to the ocean and hopefully find a friendly ship. Jae Pil would likely need to swim out into the ocean and hope he could find a UN ship where he could tell them about Ward.

What about all the ships being under the Communist guard? Ward asked.

Jae Pil shrugged. *I didn't say it was a perfect plan.* Then he pointed at Ward's ankles. *But it's better than you running on those.*

Ward nodded. The man was right.

Jae Pil held up a finger. *One more thing.* Again, it took Ward some time to understand what Jae Pil was telling him, but eventually, he figured it out. Jae Pil had spent the night siphoning gas from the truck's tank, enough so that, as he figured it, the truck would run out of gas somewhere very close to Haeju. They would be forced to stop. It would take a significant amount of time to get more fuel, and during that window, they would find a way to escape.

It wasn't perfect, it had holes aplenty, but it was better than Ward's half-cocked, pistol-stealing, hobbling-into-the-night plan. Ward caught Jae Pil's attention. *I'm sorry.*

Jae Pil waved it away, then signaled that Ward needed to get back to his hut and return the gun.

Ward did. It took him another two hours, slipping the gun in place without waking his guard, but he did it. He flopped onto his back less than an hour before sunrise. How the guard hadn't woken up either time was beyond him, but he hadn't. Ward didn't have time to revel in that fact . . . once again, his life was in the hands of this Korean man he barely knew, who, Ward marveled, was infinitely more resourceful and thoughtful than Ward had given him credit for.

• • •

Jae Pil ensured everyone was in the truck immediately after sunrise. They needed to get moving, before any orders to stay put arrived, or even worse, Lieutenant Kang himself. Word traveled slowly back here, but it did travel. They couldn't take any chances.

In his mind, Jae Pil did a quick assessment of his assets and liabilities.

The liabilities were clear: Private Pak was still assigned to him, and it would have looked too strange to order the man to stay behind—he was, after all, his codriver in training. And the two security officers were still planning on traveling with them, both of whom were intent on keeping a careful watch on their prisoner.

His biggest asset was that only he knew how to drive the truck, and army rules mandated that he maintain total control over their route and who traveled with him. The American, Ward, with his ankles and his ill-advised escape attempt the night before, deserved to be on the liability list. Still, Jae Pil needed him, as he was the reason that he could get closer to the south, and the only person who could vouch that Jae Pil wanted to defect. One of Jae Pil's biggest worries surrounding his hoped-for escape had always been the Americans. Would they believe him? If there was no one who could testify to his genuineness, the Americans might shoot him or put him in prison as a potential spy. Either outcome would be disastrous.

The truck growled out of the village before the sun had even peaked the nearby ridges. Ward sat in the cab with Jae Pil, Pak to his right against the window.

Pak had been furious about the seating, insisting the prisoner should be in the back with the equipment, but Jae Pil had refused to budge. He didn't give Pak a reason, but the reality was he didn't want Ward back there with the security officers. Too much could go wrong.

The drive, by and large, was uneventful. If anyone questioned Jae Pil's choice of road, they didn't raise their concerns vocally. His mind, meanwhile, was on anything other than the road. What if the truck ran out of gas too soon? Too late? What if they were bombed en route? How would he manage to sneak himself and Ward away from Pak and the security forces? What if Lieutenant Kang caught up with them before he could escape? How would he find a UN ship in the harbor? How would he respond if a Communist ship snagged him from the water first?

Should he take Ward with him when he first swam out? If he did find a UN ship somewhere, would they kill him on sight? How far would he need to swim to find a UN ship? How far could he swim?

The questions bounced around his head like bullets off metal. So much could go wrong, he was starting to think the entire plan was a fool's errand. But what choice did he have?

Behind him lay death for the American and severe punishment for him.

For the first time in days, he turned to something he had given up on. He asked God for a miracle.

• • •

Sometime midafternoon, the truck sputtered.

The younger man to Ward's right said something. Jae Pil responded, shaking his head.

Ward kept his head down. They both knew exactly what was

happening. A few minutes later, the truck did it again. It gasped and seemed to snort.

Jae Pil threw up his hands, a look of disbelief across his face. He said something to Pak, and Ward could only assume he was letting the soldier know they were out of gas.

Then the engine died altogether. Jae Pil maneuvered to the side of the road, allowing the truck to coast down a hill until they creaked to a stop at a stream and under some trees. He hopped from the cab and waved for Ward to follow.

Outside, the other Koreans had leaped from the back, obviously upset. The older man, his face red and eyes angry, shouted at Jae Pil, who shrugged and continued to feign disbelief. Overhead, several American jets roared past. That seemed to change the trajectory of the conversation, for Jae Pil signaled to the others that they needed to cover the truck.

Ward stood for a while but eventually collapsed to the ground next to one of the vehicle's massive tires.

While camouflaging the roof of the truck with branches, weeds, grass, and leaves they collected from the ground, the four Koreans engaged in a heated exchange. Ward couldn't understand any of the specific words, but the gist of it seemed straightforward enough. The two security officers, insistent and in short, choppy language, were demanding that Jae Pil and the other, younger truck driver go find the gas while they guarded Ward.

The entire plan was about to blow up in their faces, and Ward couldn't do a single thing to help. There, in the dirt, he scanned the ground for anything he might use. Nothing. He scoured his own mind, trying to think of some excuse, some illness, a different injury perhaps, that would give Jae Pil an excuse for staying with him. Still, nothing.

Above, more airplanes roared past the area. Must be a bombing mission.

It was a strange feeling to Ward Millar. This total, abject help-lessness. Even during all that time as a prisoner in the hospital, he had felt he could do little things to prepare for his escape. He always felt he had some control over his situation. Now, with these two men pressuring Jae Pil, he dug into his own bag of tricks and found it wanting.

His only option, he realized, was to pray. He hadn't done it since that day on the mountain, when he'd realized he had no chance of escape, when he'd felt that God had failed him. Now, he returned to it with all the energy of his heart.

Ward didn't know how he did it, but Jae Pil refused to back down. It was admirable. The man had an air about him to take command of a situation. The talking, talking, talking seemed to last forever, but by the end of it, Jae Pil was in control of what was to happen. One of the security officers would go in search of gas. Jae Pil, Pak, and the other security officer would guard Ward.

It was something. With Jae Pil's genius, Ward's guards had been reduced from three to two.

• • •

Kang leapt from the jeep before it even stopped. This was the place.

He barreled into the first open door he saw, only to find the house empty. When he exited, he called to a young boy walking by on the road. "Where is the American?"

The boy shrugged. Infuriating. Didn't he know he was talking to an officer in the People's Army? "I said, where is he?"

For just a moment, the boy registered a semblance of proper respect. The respect Kang deserved. "Army has him."

From a different building, another soldier emerged. No, not a soldier. Security forces. There was a time when Kang had aspired to be in their ranks. The Party's secret police. He could have done great things among them, but he had instead received orders to join the army as an officer. Now, he found these men mostly worthless.

"You are looking for the American?"

"Yes," Kang said.

"They left this morning."

"This morning?" Kang stepped from the porch and marched closer to the man. "I sent specific instructions that he was to be guarded until I arrived."

"We never received that message," the man said. "One of your men, an army truck driver, said they would take him to a POW camp and then army officers would sort out what to do with him there. Two of our men went with them to ensure he is properly interrogated if he has any intelligence."

"He has already been interrogated," Kang said. "At length!"

"We didn't know," the man said.

"Did you ask him?"

"Your army man would not let us get close to him. Besides, how could we trust the American? We would still want to interrogate him."

"He is to be executed," Kang said.

"How do you know it is the same man?"

"Do you know of other Americans with broken legs wandering the countryside?"

The security officer shrugged. "No," he finally said.

Kang shook his head. Imbecile. If the man were in the army, he would be punished severely for his nonchalance alone.

Kang marched to his jeep, the private driving him still sitting behind the wheel. "Where did they go?"

"They drove south, toward the POW camp," the security officer called. "They didn't go directly because the road was too rough; they took the smooth road near Haeju. It will be dark soon. You should wait until morning."

"I don't have time to wait until morning," Kang said. If they were going to a POW camp, he might lose all control over Ward Millar. Every officer there would want a piece of the American, and they would all take credit for having captured him. For his own sake, for his future's sake and the reputation of his name and family, he could not let that happen. With a flick of his finger, he indicated for his driver to follow the road to Haeju.

CHAPTER 38

I start on Monday," Barbara said to her parents.

"That's wonderful, sweetheart," her mom said. Her dad smiled but offered nothing.

They sat on the back porch of her parents' house, each in a separate wood chair. The first glimpses of fall were already whispering in the air. It would be another cool night. The chill in the breeze suggested every night from here on out would be colder than the last—imperceptible changes at first, but then, like a thief in the night, winter would be upon them.

"What's wrong?" her mother asked.

"I don't want him to think I've forgotten about him," Barbara said. "By getting this job, I mean."

"He won't," her mother said. "He'll be proud of you for not just lying around doing nothing. You're a strong woman, and he knows it."

Barbara nodded, even offering her mom a glance and a thankful smile. "I went to the library the other day and looked up the weather in Korea. It gets cold there. Like New York. Winter's coming."

"The reports say it was brutal on our guys last year," her dad said.

Barbara let an involuntary groan seep from her lips and caught her mom throwing a deadly stare at her dad.

"Sorry," her father said.

Barbara swallowed hard, which had the effect of burying any inclination her body had to cry. "It's okay, Dad," she said. "I just worry about him. I want him to know I'm thinking about him, even if I'm working. I want him to know I love him. I want him to know I'm praying about him."

"He knows," her mom said.

"I hope so."

They sat in silence then, the three of them. Finally, Barbara admitted something out loud, something she'd kept to herself for fear that stating it openly might make it all too real. "He's going to be different when he comes back, isn't he?"

"Probably," her father said. "A lot of guys were after the big war. It changed 'em."

"But not our Ward," her mother said. "He's so smart. So tough. I think he'll come through just fine."

"All the better that he has you. Someone he can always rely on," her father said, offering that soft, subtle smile of his. "War throws a lot at people. They see things no one should ever have to see. They lose people they should never have to lose. Seems like the only thing they can plan on is that they can't plan on anything."

CHAPTER 39

Jae Pil, in the woods, carried Ward until he was certain they were out of earshot of the security officer.

He had convinced Pak and the security officer that Ward needed to be carried to where he could relieve himself, since his dysentery was still quite awful. The security officer had waved them off, but other than that, he was vigilant. As was Pak—always predictable. Jae Pil wasn't sure how they were going to simply disappear into the night. Both men were obsessed with guarding Ward, as if their honor and that of all their ancestors hinged on it.

Jae Pil lowered Ward to a fallen log.

What do we do? The American signed.

Wait at the truck, Jae Pil told him. *I will be back.*

Where are you going?

Jae Pil signed that there was a small village nearby. They couldn't go anywhere until dark anyway, so he would go see if any of the villagers might be able to help them, give them supplies, intelligence, anything.

More sign language, some pictures in the dirt. Ward wanted to know how much time they had before the other man returned with the gas.

Maybe until tomorrow only. Ward nodded.

Just as he was bending to pick up Ward again to take him back to the truck, the American tapped his back.

Jae Pil looked back. *What is it?*

Ward actually did have to relieve himself.

• • •

Back at the truck, Jae Pil lowered the American to the ground. "I will go to the village over the rise to see what intelligence I can find out. Guard him."

"Yes, yes," the security officer said. Private Pak stood near the truck, watching intently.

"He is not to be harmed," Jae Pil said, casting both the security officer and Pak a hard glare.

"Yes, yes." A flippant wave of the hand. Pak nodded.

With that, Jae Pil lunged up the path. It didn't take him long until he'd found a smattering of homes. It was midday. Most of these people were probably out working in their fields. He wandered from house to house until he found an old man standing ankle deep in muck in a rice field that looked recently flooded. "Grandfather," Jae Pil called.

The old man looked up from underneath his hat, then offered a grunt in return. He seemed wholly unimpressed that a soldier had just appeared on his land.

"How far are we from Haeju port?" Jae Pil asked.

"Close," the old man said. "Half a day's walk that way."

Jae Pil felt a flush of excitement. Half a day. His timing with the gas had been right. And half a day for this old man would be considerably less for Jae Pil, even if he was carrying the American. He could do that in a night. He bowed and turned away.

"Why didn't you come through with the others?" the old man asked.

Jae Pil paused. "What others?"

"Three convoys came through here this morning. Many troops. All headed to Haeju."

"Three?"

The man grunted a yes.

Three. In Haeju. "How many troops were there?"

The man shrugged. "I don't know. Many. I didn't count."

Jae Pil felt his excitement vanish like ice in the sun. Not only did he have all the problems of finding an American ship, assuming one was even out there, but he'd have to do it with the entire area swarming with troops. He suddenly felt tired, heavy. How could he have fooled himself into thinking this would work? He felt close, but the reality was that he was no closer now than he'd been months ago. He'd be caught, and the army would execute him as a traitor without hesitation or remorse. It was that simple.

He stepped to the man's porch and plopped onto it, then rested his forehead in his hands.

He knew the old man was probably watching him, but he didn't care. The weight of all of this finally hit him. He had failed; his family was gone, scattered to the winds. His mother was far to the north, trapped. For some time now, he had known, but had not wanted to admit to himself, that he would not see her again. Just as he knew he would not see his father and sister and grandfather. They, like he, would become myths, stories of bygone peoples forgotten by future generations, resurrected only by the stories of the few who would remember them. If he couldn't make it south, even those stories might not last.

He wanted to scream at the heavens, even cast his gaze up to the clouds traversing the sky, but he knew the old man was there. Who knew where his loyalties lay? If he saw Jae Pil praying, he might report him.

Jae Pil entertained the thought for only a moment.

Then another replaced it: What did it matter? He was beaten.

God, for whatever reason, didn't want to help him escape. Best to just submit now. He leaned back and looked to the skies. "Why?" he asked. "Why?" It was a scream this time. It seemed to come from a place foreign to him, as if an animal inside him were erupting forth, and Jae Pil could do nothing to stop it. The images of his life came with it: his grandfather, their ancestors' graves, his sister, the church they had always wanted to build, his father, the countless hours he had spent praying to a sky that seemed devoid of any answers in return.

He rubbed his eyes.

To his right, he heard the tinkle of water and then the shuffle of feet across dirt. Soon the old man stood before him. He paused only for a second and then moaned into a position next to Jae Pil on the porch. "Are you here to search the wreckage?" he asked.

Jae Pil considered this for a long time. It was the way of older people to sometimes say things that didn't make sense at first. But the more he considered the question, the more he realized he had no idea what the grandfather was saying. "I'm sorry," he finally said. "I don't know what you mean."

"The wreckage," the grandfather said. "Since you aren't with the other convoys, I assume you're here for the crash."

"That was just our truck," Jae Pil said. "We ran out of gas."

The grandfather guffawed. "Now it is my turn to confess I don't know what you mean."

Jae Pil gave him a quizzical glare.

"I was talking about the airplane," the man said.

"What airplane?"

"Over the hill," the man said, pointing. "An American jet crashed over the hill there yesterday."

"An American . . ." Jae Pil started. "Where is the pilot?"

"I don't think he survived," the old man said. "American jets and planes were searching for him, but they didn't seem to find anything."

• • •

Ward was beginning to worry.

It had been some time since Jae Pil had left. The kid with the submachine gun was looking more and more anxious. He had shown an immediate disliking to Ward from the moment the group had captured him. Ward had no idea how well North Koreans adhered to the chain of command, but he had the unsettling feeling that, at any moment, this man might haul off and shoot him.

The other security officer, however, hadn't been all bad. He was actually somewhat talkative. Ward still didn't know his name, but he was lanky, tall for a Korean, and seemed to be in excellent shape. To Ward's surprise, he even knew a few words of English and had, he claimed, traveled to the United States for some sort of sporting event when he was young. It occurred to Ward that it was possible this man might be an ally as well.

Just as he was pondering that, Jae Pil returned. He was sweaty and seemed unusually excited. He exchanged a few words with the other men, then paced in front of Ward for several minutes.

Ward watched, curious. Jae Pil seemed to be thinking about something.

Several times, the Korean made eye contact with Ward, as if he wanted to tell him something. Finally, Ward couldn't take it anymore. He waved his arms again and pointed to his rear, suggesting another bout of dysentery was rearing its ugly head.

As soon as he did, Jae Pil sauntered over to him, feigning an annoying look of disgust.

Minutes later, they were back in the woods where they could communicate. Almost immediately, Jae Pil was gesticulating wildly. Ward watched and realized that, once again, the man wanted to flag down American jets.

No! No! No! Ward said, waving the idea away with his hands. He had already told Jae Pil what would happen.

Jae Pil slapped Ward's hands aside. He snagged a nearby branch and motioned for Ward to look at the dirt. In it, he drew a plane, then indicated it had crashed.

"A plane crash?" Ward asked. Jae Pil nodded, seeming satisfied.

"Here?" Ward said, pointing to the ground.

Jae Pil smiled and nodded. Then he pointed to the sky and motioned with his hands. *They will be searching for the pilot.*

Ward considered this for a second. A tingle slithered from his neck and down his arms. His captor was right. This explained the jets and planes he'd been hearing since they stopped. Any jets flying in this area might well be looking for a signal. If they saw one, they might send a rescue helicopter. "Wait, wait, wait," Ward said, waving his hands in front of his face. He looked back over his shoulder to ensure the other two North Koreans hadn't wandered this way out of curiosity for the lapse of time. *Did the other pilot live?* He asked through hand gestures and in the dirt.

Jae Pil shook his head. *He was killed in the crash.*

Still, no one on the American side would know that. They would continue to search as though the pilot were alive. He clapped the Korean on the back and soon they were headed back to the truck.

CHAPTER 40

They still had an hour or two before the sun would dip below the horizon. Time enough to signal a jet if it came by.

The American had told him that they needed a mirror, so Jae Pil had set off to find one, claiming he was returning to the village to get some food. Miraculously enough, a mirror lay in the old man's house. It was large enough for Jae Pil to see his entire face in it, and the grandfather had willingly handed it to him.

When Jae Pil returned to the truck, he announced to Pak and the other officer that the villagers had no food; he would take the American in search of apples.

"Apples?" Pak asked.

"Yes, apples," Jae Pil said. "They will help with his dysentery. One of the farmers says there are wild apples over that ridge. We will bring more back if we find them."

"Why do we care about helping with his dysentery? They bomb our homes, kill our people, try to force their way of life on us. Let him bleed."

"I am tired of carrying him into the trees," Jae Pil said.

"You are spending too much time with him," the security officer said. "Leave him here."

"You are welcome to carry him next time and watch his blood and feces spill into the weeds."

The man offered nothing in response.

"Until then," Jae Pil said. "We will hunt for apples, and I will make him do the work of picking them so I can rest like both of you." He turned and waved for Ward to get to his feet, then feigned offering him only meager help as they made their way up the hillside. They reached the summit of the ridge with an hour of sun left. There, they found a perfect place to hide—a small, bowl-shaped pit in the earth, almost as if someone had dug it out years before and left it just for them to find that day. They crawled into it.

Ward signaled for Jae Pil to hand him the mirror. For just a second he looked into it at his own face. It must have been the first time he'd seen his reflection since being captured, because he cast Jae Pil a grimace.

Jae Pil smiled and shrugged.

The American then worked until he had the mirror casting a spot of light on the rim of the bowl. Then he signaled the plan: they would reflect the sunbeam onto the bowl until they had a plane in sight. As soon as the plane lined up with the light, they would flash the beam up out of the bowl, hoping it hit the pilot. It was their only hope.

Jae Pil gave a thumbs up. "Good," he said. It was one of the few English words he knew. Then he signaled for Ward to control the mirror while he stood watch on the trail. They didn't want to be caught by surprise if Pak decided to come snooping.

For the first fifteen minutes, nothing.

Another fifteen passed. Not a single plane had even come close to their location.

Ward lay in the bowl, picking lice from his clothes and hair. Jae Pil paced, his eyes both scanning the trail below and the skies all around them.

Finally, another eighteen minutes in, a group of planes appeared as spots in the distance. Jae Pil clapped, getting Ward's attention, then pointed.

Ward sprung to the ready, positioning his mirror so he could get a bead on the planes. At just the right moment, he tipped the mirror skyward. Nothing. The planes propelled past without even a single indication they had seen either man.

Jae Pil turned to the sun. It was deserting them, merciless in its drop to the horizon. Soon, its useful light would be gone.

Another ten minutes.

Then, the rush of a jet. Ward heard it before Jae Pil and was already positioning himself.

When it raced by, he hit it with the mirror, the sun's reflection clearly hitting the cockpit.

The plane reacted, dipping its wing.

This is it! Jae Pil thought. He rushed over to join Ward as the F-80 made a wide, arcing turn. Ward tried to stand and waved his arms frantically.

Jae Pil joined him.

But his excitement did not last long. Whatever the pilot thought he saw, he didn't react in a way one might if he were going to rescue someone. The plane leveled off, continued on its flight, and vanished into the distance. Jae Pil watched until it was nothing more than a pinprick against the gray sky.

• • •

The pilot returned, three friends in tow.

Ward couldn't believe it. Had it worked? By then, he and Jae Pil had already returned to the truck. They were resting in the fading twilight when the whine of the jet engines forced them all to their feet.

Ward monitored the skies. Four jets. A rescue mission. They

turned sharply, then peeled off in formation. The realization hit Ward instantly: this wasn't a rescue; it was an attack. He looked at his three captors. They had no clue. "Cover!" Ward yelled. He dove for the truck and pulled Jae Pil by the arm as he went under. They curled up under the engine. Ward hugged the tire and closed his eyes. He'd been one of these pilots. He knew the payloads they carried. If they had seen the truck and dropped napalm, everyone single one of them would be burned to a crisp.

On the first pass, the jets fired all over the area. The ground around the truck seemed to come alive as if exploding from underneath, the bullets popping up the ground and blasting dirt and rocks into Ward's legs.

He knew they weren't finished. He motioned for Jae Pil to stay put. Where the other soldiers were, he had no clue. If any of them got hit, they would take their wrath out on Ward.

On the next pass, Ward prayed for no napalm. He heard the thunder of the machine guns, felt the tremble of the ground as the bullets pelted the earth, but the heat of fire never came.

After the second pass, the whine of the jets dissipated.

Ward crawled out from under the truck and scanned the area. Both of the other soldiers were fine.

Jae Pil was right behind him. He stood and tapped Ward's shoulder, then made a signal that he was going to check on the farmers living nearby. He said something to the Koreans, presumably the same.

Ward lay on his stomach for a time, trying to calm his breathing. On the ground, right next to his face, a bullet had carved out a pockmark the size of his palm.

· · ·

Kang's driver slammed on the brakes. The jeep skidded to a stop under an evergreen. He immediately cut the lights. In the distance,

American fighter jets were attacking. It seemed farther up the road, but close enough that if they saw a jeep with its lights on, they wouldn't hesitate to bank this direction.

They sat in the dark, listening to the attack. The peace talks were supposedly still on-going, but until they resulted in an actual treaty and ceasefire, both sides would keep up their assaults. Kang was not happy about the prospect, not if it meant leaving half the country in the hands of the Americans. They would ruin it. The North would prosper, and his countrymen in the South would suffer. He couldn't tolerate that. Yet he wasn't in a place to make commands.

Still, he took comfort. Time would prove him right. The passing of the eons would show the world whose system better served society.

The attack seemed to have come to an end. Kang listened as the jets' engines appeared to grow faint. "As soon as we can no longer hear them," he said to the driver, "move forward. Go slow. Stop occasionally to listen for more incoming."

• • •

Ward lay with his back against the tire of the truck. He was half asleep, half trying to fight off the sneaking suspicion that, one way or another, someone was going to kill him in the next twenty-four hours. Either the Koreans or an American pilot.

Someone shook his arm. He blinked open his eyes, and although he couldn't really see him, he knew his awakener was Jae Pil. He motioned for Ward to get to his feet. It was easy enough to obey. Ward couldn't see the other men, but he assumed they were asleep.

Jae Pil held something out for Ward to carry.

It was a headlight. From the truck. What on earth? Jae Pil offered his elbow. Ward latched onto it, carrying the headlight in his other hand. Together, they maneuvered up the mountainside.

• • •

A short time later, they were back in their hole.

Jae Pil's plan was now obvious to Ward. His Korean friend had taken the battery and one of the headlights from the truck. They could use both to send signals to passing jets. The man was a genius. Except that last time the jets had tried to kill them.

When Ward tried to raise that point to Jae Pil, the Korean suggested that Ward use Morse code.

Ward couldn't disagree. He did know Morse code. He could flash S-O-S, and if they captured any plane's attention, he could then flash his name, rank, and serial number. A properly trained pilot would return to his base, check the "missing in action" lists, and, hopefully, return with the entire air force. Although, at this point, Ward would have settled for just one helicopter.

The last thing Jae Pil pulled from his pocket was some wire.

Ward took it and used it to connect the headlight to the battery poles. He left one wire free, so he could tap against the node like a telegraph key.

The moment they tested the headlight, it emitted a light so bright it would have sent a signal to every Korean on the peninsula. It also had the double effect of temporarily blinding Ward.

Jae Pil slapped Ward's hand away, casting them both into darkness.

Ward had instinctively covered his eyes and was now trying to blink away the after-images of the bright light. Jae Pil climbed from the hole, was gone for a few minutes, and then slid back in. *No one's coming*, he signed. In his hand, he held a piece of heavy paper, which he handed to Ward and indicated he should cover the light with it. They cut a small hole in the paper, then sliced it larger until it let out the amount of light they needed.

What time is it? Ward asked Jae Pil.

1:30. We will need to return at around 4 a.m.

They sat in silence. More than once, squadrons entered their air space. Ward flashed his signals.

S-O-S.

S-O-S.

S-O-S.

In between flights, he practiced signaling his name and other information. It had been so long since he'd used Morse, he was afraid he might not be able to tap it out fast enough if they did catch a pilot's attention. For a long stretch, he stripped off his flight suit and ripped out some of the white fabric lining from the interior. He wasn't sure, but he figured a white flag might come in useful at some point, especially after the attack earlier.

More time passed. And then some more.

Finally, the last plane, a solo, soared overhead. Ward tapped the battery again and again. If the plane saw it, it appeared that the pilot didn't care.

At 4:15 a.m., Jae Pil tapped Ward's shoulder. *We have to go. I need time to put these back.*

Ward was reluctant, but he knew Jae Pil was right. Together, they hiked back down the mountain.

CHAPTER 41

K ang welcomed the dawn.

All night, the going had been slow. The road was smoother than most and quite passable, but they had pulled over often: at the sound of jets in the distance, to listen for the sound of jets in the distance, when they finally needed some sleep. But now, with the soft, featureless light of dawn, they felt comfortable moving at full pace.

"Faster," Kang snarled. His own voice sounded like a bark to him, like he was a dog on the hunt. These past days, hunting the American, had been exhilarating. He realized, more than ever before, that he loved it. More than the fighting, more than establishing a system for the people that would ensure equality among the masses. The pursuit—that was where his joy was. He had a knack for it. Bouncing along the road, he considered there must be some way to make this a part of his life once the war was over: chasing criminals, enemies of the People.

For now, however, his mind was focusing on something else. A part of him, deep down, call it instinct, was whispering to him. Its message was clear: his prey was close.

• • •

Jae Pil tapped Ward's shoulder.

They had returned with enough time for Jae Pil to reinstall the battery and headlight and even get some sleep. Now the sun was rising, and, if they held any hope of escaping, they needed to signal a plane soon, that morning if possible. The security officer would be back with the gas that day. Once he arrived, Jae Pil would be out of excuses.

He tapped Ward's shoulder again. The American stirred awake. Whatever grogginess would normally weigh a man down seemed to vanish almost instantly. The man blinked twice and was ready to move. By Jae Pil's guess, he was feeling just as anxious and excited as Jae Pil.

Jae Pil helped his friend to his feet.

"Where are you going?" It was Private Pak, behind them.

Jae Pil barely looked over his shoulder. "The American must relieve himself again. I will take him."

"You didn't find any apples yesterday?" Pak said.

Jae Pil helped Ward wrap his arm around Jae Pil's neck. "None," he said. "We must have looked in the wrong place."

"I can take him," Pak said. "You can stay and rest."

"It's alright," Jae Pil said, taking a few steps with Ward.

"Perhaps I should come with you," Pak said. "We could search for food, and I can help you carry it if we find it."

Jae Pil paused. *Oh, God,* he thought, *give me the wisdom to know what to do.* "Stay here," he finally said. "He will relieve himself. If we happen to see anything, I will call for you. In the meantime, look out for the gas. When it arrives, ensure to immediately fill up the truck so we can keep moving. Understood?"

In his side vision, he noted Pak give a terse bow.

Beginning his ascent up the hillside, he silently offered thanks that the security officer wasn't nearly as skeptical as Private Pak. Jae

Pil bore no authority over him. If he decided he wanted to come, there was nothing Jae Pil could do to stop him.

• • •

At the top of the ridge, Ward motioned to Jae Pil. *I will be back. I want to find a place where a helicopter can land if one comes.*

Jae Pil seemed to get the message. Neither man was in the hole. Jae Pil seemed especially nervous about his comrades and was watching the trail back to the truck.

Ward considered asking him about this but decided to let it go. There was nothing he could do about it anyway. Hobbling, nearly falling several times, he wandered along the ridgeline until he found a clearing that might be suitable for a chopper. They didn't need much, but a little clearing with no large trees to hit the blades was crucial. After ten minutes, Ward found it.

He limped back to the bowl.

Jae Pil had found a seat on a rock and was staring downhill, his pistol in his lap. From this vantage point, the truck was out of sight—hidden behind trees and the natural curvature of the hill. The dawn turned toward morning. At times, the peaceful silence was the most frustrating sound Ward had ever heard.

With nothing to do but wait, he eased to the ground, then lay on his back, feeling the early morning sun on his face. He reached into his pocket and fingered the cross there.

• • •

Private Pak Byung Ho was tired of waiting.

It seemed that all he'd been asked to do in this battle for the destiny of his country was wait. Wait to drive equipment and food behind the front lines. Wait to rise in the ranks. Wait while his superiors wasted their days negotiating with the capitalists. What were they negotiating? You couldn't negotiate with men whose sole goal was to rape your lives for their own profit and gain. Such men could not be reasoned with or placated. If the Workers' Party failed to end this war, they would be condemning every single person in the South to a life of servitude to American taskmasters. It was immoral.

Off to the side, the security officer yawned. He is wasting his life, Pak thought. What a tragedy. Here this man is in a position of power. Unlike Pak, he could stay with the American. He might even be able to execute the man. Sure, the army controlled him for now, but really, what would the consequences have been if the security officers had simply decided to take matters into their own hands. Instead, they sleep. They get gas. Pak shook his head. It was ridiculous.

Then there was Corporal Kim, his newly minted superior. The most taunting slap from a universe that seemed especially derisive as of late. Just what was his interest in the American? Pak wanted to argue with him, but that wasn't their way. Kim was Pak's superior, in both age and rank. Unless he knew Kim was deliberately engaging in acts hostile to the army, Pak would just need to keep his mouth shut. Once again he felt the infuriating tick-tock of the waiting clock.

"I am going to check on the villagers," he announced.

The security officer acknowledged this with a lazy wave of his hand.

Pak picked his way up the path, his submachine gun at the ready. For what, he couldn't say, but that was their training: always have it at the ready. He didn't care that everyone else seemed to ignore that directive.

After a few minutes, he happened upon three houses. He stopped at the first, which was empty, then wandered over to the second. Inside, an old man sat on his mat, a bowl of rice and corn cupped in front of him.

"Did you find anything?" the old man asked.

"What?" Pak said.

"Oh," the old man said. "I thought you were the other soldier. He was going to hunt in the wreckage for supplies."

"What wreckage?"

"An American jet crashed nearby a day ago," the old man said.

"Ah," Pak said. "No, they are hunting for apples."

"Apples?" the old man said. "There are no apples here."

"Across the ridge," Pak said. "My superior said that someone here told him there were apples there."

Through a mouthful of rice, the old man nodded. "I don't think so. I told one soldier about the crash. I am the only one here. I didn't say anything about apples. I have lived in this valley my entire life. The only time I have ever seen apples is when traders have brought them to us."

No apples . . . Pak let this discovery linger in his mind for some time. Then what were Kim and the American doing?

CHAPTER 42

It materialized, seemingly, out of nowhere. An F-80, blasting over them at about five hundred feet.

Ward wasn't even able to move to the mirror. His legs simply did not respond to the urgency in his mind. Their window was narrow, perhaps five seconds or less. Then the jet would roar past, and they would be just another ridgetop among hundreds of them.

Jae Pil was clearly not going to let that happen. He sprung off his rock like a pouncing cat. Diving into the bowl, he snatched up the mirror. It took him less than a second to establish his beam of light, which he lined up in the lip of the pit, then flashed toward the plane.

For an excruciating second, Ward couldn't tell if Jae Pil had done it or not. Then the jet banked, flipping onto its side. It circled.

To Ward's amazement, Jae Pil was able to keep the light from the mirror directly on it. The question was would this jet attack, or would the pilot perceive what was actually happening? Ward ripped off his over jacket to reveal his bright, yellow Mae West. If anything would identify him as a pilot, that would. From his pant's pocket he yanked out the white flag he had crafted the night before. Back and forth, back and forth, he waved it above his head. More than once, he nearly toppled.

"Keep the mirror on him," Ward screamed. "Keep it on him."

After several circles, the pilot dropped in altitude. He was either going to fire or he was taking a closer look. "Keep the mirror on him!" Ward bellowed. He waved his cotton fabric even more vigorously. The pilot thundered over them so closely that Ward had to duck and cover his ears. After one more circle, the jet started to gain altitude. It was climbing, higher and higher.

In the hole, Jae Pil had finally stopped shining the mirror. He said something to Ward, a question. *Is he leaving?*

For the first time, Ward let himself believe they'd been seen, truly seen, and no one would abandon him now. He shook his head. "I don't think so," he said. "He's getting up high enough so he can radio for help." Ward tried his best to signal that message to Jae Pil. Then he pointed to the truck below. Ward had no illusions: the other soldiers would have seen the jet, may have even suspected that Ward and Jae Pil had signaled it. If they weren't already on their way, they would be soon.

Jae Pil saluted and then leaped from the pit. He twisted and slunk his way into a strategic position among some bushes and out-cropped rocks. He must have been thinking exactly as Ward, because he aimed his pistol down the hill, toward any possible attackers.

• • •

Kang happened upon the truck midmorning, parked and abandoned along the side of the road near a stream.

"Stop," he said.

His driver obeyed.

The moment Kang stepped from his vehicle, a rustling motion caught his attention in the trees. Two men suddenly appeared. One, whom Kang had never seen before, wore the uniform of the security forces. The other, a private, looked familiar.

"Sir!" the private said, skidding to a halt and offering a quick salute. "American jet."

"Attacking?" Kang asked.

"No, sir! We think they hailed it."

"Who hailed it?"

"The American and Corporal Kim Seok Jin."

Kang was not a man of passion. In fact, for so much of his life, he considered his ability to control his emotions to be one of his primary assets. He was analytical, calm, rational. These were traits, he told himself, that allowed him to reach logical and balanced conclusions even as the world around him seemed to be in a constant state of chaos. So it surprised him when he felt a sudden burst of blood flush to his face. And when one word erupted from his lips—"Traitor!"—it seemed to come from somewhere else, a different person even.

Without thinking, he yanked his pistol from its holster. "Where?" he yelled.

"Up the ridge, sir!" the private said.

"Follow me."

• • •

The first shots didn't hit anywhere near them. Jae Pil couldn't even see who had fired them. So he held his hand, his finger tickling the trigger. Ready.

Fifty paces away, the American stood in the clearing where he was hopeful the helicopter would land. How much time had passed? How had Pak known they were trying to escape? Were they even firing up here? It was entirely possible the shooting had nothing to do with them.

The next bullet ricocheted off a rock between Jae Pil and Ward. Now Jae Pil was certain: they had been caught. Their fates were cast. Either they escaped, or they died.

• • •

Ward saw the F-80 returning. Alongside him, sun spangles danced in the sky. Other jets.

Ward waved his flag, hoping they would see him.

From below, another shot fired, hitting the rocks behind him. Ward ducked, trying to stay out of the line of fire but still waving his cloth so the pilots would be able to find them again. The minutes had an annoying ability to elongate themselves. Ward knew, from all his flights and all his mathematical training, that the jets should reach them in less than two minutes. But the time felt like hours. He scanned back, looking for Jae Pil. As far as Ward could tell, the man had yet to fire his pistol, which meant he didn't have a bead on the men firing at them.

Another rifle retorted somewhere. Ward hugged the earth.

Then the jets were upon them, circling. Five in total. Ward continued to wave his flag. He crawled back to his and Jae Pil's hideout and slid in, then grabbed the mirror. He flashed it up toward the jets, knowing how easy it would be for them to accidentally lose sight of their position.

More fire from below.

Jae Pil fired two rounds from his own gun.

Where was the blasted helicopter? His friend couldn't keep those men at bay for long.

In the sky, the first jet started to peel away. Ward knew why: out of fuel. As he turned south, the pilot wiggled his wings. The other jets continued to circle.

In the distance, another speck came onto the horizon. "The chopper!" Ward screamed at Jae Pil, but immediately regretted it. It was just more airplanes. This time, four Marine Corps Corsairs, propeller aircraft. When they arrived, the jets peeled away.

Ward cursed under his breath, but at least he knew, for certain, the rescue was under full swing. The Joint Operations Center knew he was here. They were scrambling planes. A helicopter couldn't be far behind. The only question was whether he and Jae Pil could last.

• • •

Jae Pil fired twice into the trees below. He could see them now. Three men. The security officer and Pak. The third: Lieutenant Kang. "Traitor!" the officer screamed. "Traitor to your people!"

For only a second, Jae Pil considered the accusation. From a man whose army had attacked its own people, it felt hollow. It passed through Jae Pil's consciousness like a train at night. It came. It left.

His more immediate worry was that he wouldn't be able to hold all three of them at bay. His pistol held only a few shots. After that, death would come quickly. What had the American screamed? He seemed excited about something. Above, new American planes had arrived, while the others had banked away.

Pak fired from his hiding place behind a rock below.

Jae Pil returned the shot. But they had nowhere to go. How many rounds did he have left?

Four? Maybe five?

A sudden eruption forced Jae Pil to drop his gun and clap his hands over his ears. The new American planes had unleashed their firepower on the ground below. The slope below Jae Pil seemed to spit dirt as machine gun fire bore into it. Even further away, the Americans launched rockets into the trees. The blasts shook the entire mountain.

Amidst the din of the planes' motors, Lieutenant Kang's shrill accusation still echoed in Jae Pil's mind, "Traitor! . . . Traitor!"

• • •

Jae Pil collapsed into the pit next to Ward. One sign was all it took for his message to hit Ward like a bomb. *I'm out of bullets.*

Ward looked to the sky. The Marine flights were peeling away. Ward could only guess, but they were also likely out of fuel. A different set of F-51s had arrived to replace them, but what was the hold up? Too much time had passed since the first jet had seen them. There was no explanation for the delay. And with Jae Pil out of ammo, how long would it be before their attackers were upon them?

Again and again, the new planes strafed the ground between the ridgetop and the enemies below.

Ward lay on his back, his palms cupping his ears. Then it dawned on him, as he looked upon Jae Pil, a horrible, sinking realization: perhaps JOC had vetoed the mission. Perhaps they had vetoed the helicopter, thinking all of this was just some elaborate Communist trap. Jae Pil was, after all, still wearing his North Korean uniform.

Just as the thought began to fester, Ward heard it. The nonstop, repeating flop of blades churning against the wind.

He crawled to the edge of their bowl. There it was, two ridges away. The helicopter.

The earth next to his head exploded as a bullet blast into it. He pulled away and signed to Jae Pil that the chopper was coming.

The landing spot Ward had found was about seventy-five yards from their location. Ward again edged to the side of the pit and pointed both arms toward the site.

Inside the bubble of the chopper, the pilot nodded. From the open side door, an enlisted man squatted, ready. The helicopter turned sideways, then sunk its landing skids into the clearing's wild grass. Dirt and weeds skidded across the landscape. Jae Pil moved as fast as Ward could think, motioning for Ward to get on his back. Then they were out of the hole. Between the chopper and the planes circling overhead, Ward could no longer tell if and when the men below were firing at them. He clung to Jae Pil's neck as if it were the only thing in the entire universe worth holding.

A rock in front of them shattered, a bullet careening off it. Jae Pil bounded from rock to rock, over a fallen log, across gravel. Ward gasped against the bounces.

Finally, they hit the clearing. The path flattened. Jae Pil lowered his head and sprinted, no longer watching where he was going. They approached the chopper, and Ward realized they were about to spring headlong right into the spinning rear rotor blade. He latched onto Kim's head with one hand and twisted, steering him almost like a jockey would a horse. They missed it by a few inches.

Then they were at the door.

The enlisted man, a medic, pulled back, his face contorted in confusion.

"It's okay!" Ward screamed so the man could hear. "I'm a downed USAF pilot. This man is a friend!"

After a moment's pause, the medic nodded, then helped both men aboard. Next to him, was a rock the size of a basketball. Ward knew it was there as a ballast. He sidled up next to it and helped the medic push it over the side.

Ward and Jae Pil scrambled back into the center of the chopper.

The pilot gave the chopper the gun, and they rose out of the field. Ward lay on his back, looking at the grass fluttering in the gusts.

• • •

Jae Pil was in the helicopter and lay on his back, panting.

When he came to his senses, he scooted until his back leaned against a bulwark and he could see out the side door. The helicopter's fight with gravity churned his stomach, and more than once he felt he might retch all over himself. The only thing that prevented it was the scene unfolding below him. From the trees, both Private Pak and Lieutenant Kang had emerged. Pak was still firing his rifle, but the lieutenant had lowered his firearm.

On Kang's face was a look of absolute, resolute rage. The grass around him fluttered and flittered, in contrast to his statuesque stance. His arms were rigid at his side, and his eyes were so sharp, Jae Pil was certain they would be firing missiles at the helicopter if they could.

Traitor! Jae Pil knew that was Kang's primary thought.

The word revisited Jae Pil's consciousness.

Below him, Kang was growing smaller and smaller, but it seemed to Jae Pil that their eyes had locked. Kang was watching him. What was he thinking? His face seemed to convey a simple message, *This war is not over, and I will kill you.*

But Jae Pil experienced a different sensation. He knew he would never set foot on this land again, at least not as long as men like Lieutenant Kang governed it. The only question in his mind, as he watched the ridge and Kang and Pak recede into the distance, was whether any of his family would make their own escape. As his enemies shrunk away, that query filled the gaps they left behind.

He pivoted back to his current situation.

Ward seemed lost in thought, staring down at the landscape as Jae Pil had been. The other American eyed Jae Pil warily. Jae Pil smiled, then reached for the pistol in his holster.

• • •

Ward watched North Korea vanish beneath him. If he was correct about the date, he'd been rescued almost ninety days from when he had first crashed.

Questions filled his mind, a multitude, some serious and grandiose, others as silly as a toddler's. How would those ninety days affect him? He'd been locking his emotions away for so long, what would happen when he finally let them free? How could he explain all that he had experienced? Who was right—him or Lieutenant Kang—about which system would be better? Where was Barbara right then? When would she learn of his rescue? What if they got shot down on the way back? Would he want to eat normal food after all this? Why did he get rescued and live, while the other pilot in the area had died? When would he see Barbara again? Would he ever walk normally again? Would little Adrian remember him, or would she shy away from him like a stranger?

What on earth was his North Korean savior doing? That question shoved out all the others when Jae Pil reached for the gun at his side.

The medic stirred, but Ward waved for him to stay calm.

Jae Pil pulled the pistol from his holster, flipped it around, then stretched it out, grip first, to Ward. *I am your prisoner now,* the gesture seemed to say.

Ward smiled and took the gun. He handed it to the medic for safekeeping.

The chopper banked, plunging his gut into his body, making him feel as if he were in a dream. On this day of miracles, why not? he thought. He watched his new friend, eyes locked on his own, and realized the improbability of their meeting, the impossibility of it all: the perfectly blue sky, the downed plane in the area, the timing of where they'd stopped their truck. It might as well have been a dream, a figment of his imagination, a rescue he had fantasized about for so many hours and so many nights he had lost track of reality.

Except it was not a dream.

He was here. Jae Pil lay before him. As their eyes met and held, the visage of Jae Pil shimmered in Ward's mind. This was no longer an enemy he saw, or a friend dressed in enemy's garb, but himself. How long they held that gaze, Ward couldn't guess.

Around them, the air, the wind, the world, the clouds swirled. Soon this moment would end. They would touch down. Interrogations of a different sort would ensue, for both Jae Pil and Ward.

Not yet.

Ward pressed his lips together with a slight nod of respect. Jae Pil returned the gesture.

CHAPTER 43

September 11, 1951. Summer in its final throes. Barbara sat down at her workstation. The chair was uncomfortable, but what office chair wasn't? She looked around the room. Her job would be simple: helping administer the office of a small insurance company, basically the same work she'd been doing for her dad for years. It was her first day. Her boss had given her a stack of letters and other mail to sort. The mound lay in front of her.

She hoped it would take her mind off Ward. Nothing else could. The notion struck her like a two-edged sword. It seemed she couldn't find a winning solution. On one side, she couldn't take the constant worry and anxiety that came from knowing her husband was a prisoner and might die. It was just too much, so she welcomed any distraction she could find. But every time she did, the other side of the sword cut into her. She didn't want to forget Ward. She didn't want Ward to ever think she had forgotten him. No matter how long it took him to come home, she knew he was still out there. And she would keep writing him letters, no matter how busy this job kept her.

She sighed. So this was her life: let the anxiety of worrying about him shred her to her core, or let the guilt of not thinking about him eat away at her nibble by painful nibble.

And who knew how long it would last?

"Barb?" her boss said from behind her. *My name is Barbara,* she wanted to say, but she bit it back. Not on the first day.

"Yes, sir?"

"Will you get started on that mail?"

"Yes, sir." She gripped the metal letter opener in her closed fist and sliced open the first letter. She had to admit: there was something gratifying in that motion.

The office phone rang. One of the new rotary ones. It rang again.

"Can you get that, Barb?" her new boss said. "That will be one of your responsibilities."

"Yes," Barbara said. She jumped from her seat. In two steps, she held the phone in her hand. "Peace of Mind Insurance of Portland. This is Barbara. How can I help you?"

"Barbara," her mom said, then released into the phone what sounded like something between a laugh and a cry.

"What?" Barbara said. "What is it?"

Her mom was still making strange noises.

"What? Mom? What?"

"You were right, sweetheart." Her dad had taken over the call. "They found him. He's rescued."

"Oh," Barbara said, covering her mouth. "Oh! I'll be right there."

Her dad started to say something else, but she slammed the phone into the receiver. "I have to go!" she said. Her hands were shaking.

"It's your first day!" her boss said. "You can't leave."

Barbara didn't listen. She snatched up her purse. Then she was running, sprinting, pushing through the office door. She was on the sidewalk, waving her hands wildly for a cab. Passersby cast her strange looks. Behind her, she was certain her boss was looking on, incredulous. Maybe even angry.

It was her first day. She also knew it would be her last.

• • •

Barbara burst through her parents' front door. Her mom was already standing there, a wide smile under tear-swollen eyes. She held the telegraph in her hands. Neither she nor Barbara needed to say a word. She simply handed her daughter the paper:

> *WESTERN UNION*
> *=MRS WARD MILLAR=*
> *=YOUR HUSBAND CAPT WARD M MILLAR*
> *A076614 HAS BEEN RETURNED TO FRIENDLY*
> *FORCES ON TENTH SEPTEMBER. HE IS WELL*
> *AND WRITING DETAILS.*

Barbara held the brown paper with trembling hands, reading the bright blue words again and again and again. It was a paper of wonder, like an ancient scroll or long-lost historical text. She felt like she was holding something sacred, something too profound and deep for one mind to bear. In the room, her parents looking on, there was a quiet stillness, infinite almost, the universe kneeling in acknowledgment of the moment. It was broken only when little Adrian toddled into the room, too young to form the words but with her face bearing a simple question: *What's going on?*

After one look at that face, Barbara Millar did the only thing possible. She knelt down next to her little girl and wept.

• • •

Ward shifted his head slightly when he sensed someone at the door.

He was in a hospital in Tokyo, lying in a bed that, even after several weeks, still felt as comfortable as a cloud from heaven. The previous weeks had been more of a blur than his crash: treatment, hospitals, flights, trying to keep Jae Pil safe, intelligence gatherings, questions, his first meal (something he had fantasized about for weeks: bacon and eggs, toast and coffee—heaping mounds he inhaled from a tray while sitting on the side of his bed), reading the letters from Barbara that had been waiting for him.

"Captain Millar, you called for me?" It was the chaplain.

"Yes, sir," Ward said. "Please, come in."

The man entered the room. He was kindly looking, as most chaplains were. Balding, but still young. Catholic.

"Thank you for seeing me, Father," Ward said.

"Of course. You've had quite the ordeal."

Ward nodded. "So you've heard my story?"

"Just the thirty-thousand foot view."

In Ward's lap lay a letter he was writing to Barbara on paper provided to him by the American National Red Cross. He had just finished an important sentence. *Until we can be together again, I don't dare release the pent-up emotions that are repressed under terrific pressure as a result of these past three months. So my letters to you will seem flat, colorless chronicles that will show nothing of my great and abiding love. I can't afford to let my emotions release now, or I will never be able to stop the tears . . .*

Shifting his mind from his wife and Adrian to the chaplain, he said, "Father, I need to tell you about my experiences."

"OK," the man said, pulling a chair up next to Ward's bed.

When Ward was done telling his story, he said, "I've had a change, Father. I don't know why some men live and others die, why I was spared and others were not, but I just can't look at everything that happened and tell myself that it was all coincidence. I am convinced now that there is a God and that He must hear our prayers."

The chaplain nodded thoughtfully.

"I also think the Catholic Church is where I can find the best expression of my faith."

"I see," the chaplain said. He crossed his legs thoughtfully and placed his hands, fingers interlocked, in his lap. After a long silence, he said, "Would you excuse me a moment? I'd like to get you something."

"Of course," Ward said.

The man left and returned a few minutes later, a book in his hands. "This is a Bible, Captain Millar. I'd like you to have it. I encourage you to study it."

Ward accepted the present and turned it over in his hands. It was a book, he had to confess, he hadn't spent much time considering.

"Men experience many things during war. I am glad you have found faith, as I have, and I am glad you have come to know that God is real and truly cares for each of us, but do not rush into conversion. Give yourself time to process everything that has happened and look back on it with proper perspective. We see often that some, when they come to faith through extraordinary circumstances, tend to be too overzealous in matters of religion. That can lead to great works, but it can also lead to tragedy, if their faith ever falters, or if they force their new beliefs on others. Don't be overzealous. Know that God works in subtle ways, in times of great stress but in the quiet moments of our lives as well."

"Thank you, Father," Ward said, offering the priest his hand and looking him straight in the eyes, sending the message. *I hear and understand you.* "Thank you. I wonder if you might do something for me?"

"Anything," the chaplain said.

"Actually two things," Ward said.

"Don't push your luck."

"Do you know what has happened to Kim Jae Pil? I haven't heard where he is. I need to know he's safe. Can you check on him?"

"I'm sure he is," the chaplain said.

"He was, when I left. I saw him almost every day, but I'm worried people are going to lose track of him or mistake him for someone else. Last I heard, he was being transferred over to the South Korean military. Can you just look into it?"

"I'll see what I can do," the chaplain said with a nod. "The other favor?"

On his bedside table, Ward's letter to Barbara, which he never did get to mail, lay under the cross he had fashioned. He slid the letter out and handed it over. "Would you mind throwing that in the garbage for me on the way out?"

CHAPTER 44

Barbara Millar stood on the tarmac at Travis Air Force Base.

She had been waiting for six weeks. Six weeks! It was incomprehensible. She still didn't understand it. In her view, once Ward had been rescued they should have put her on a flight to see him. She'd heard of that happening with other wives. Why not her? She swore, most days it seemed the military was run by a cabal of imbeciles.

Across the way, a plane touched down. Ward's plane.

She stepped toward it, as if she'd be allowed to run up and hug its nose, then paused. She could wait a few more minutes, she told herself. The air was cool, perfect. The sky was clear.

Only a light fall breeze disrupted the placidity of the moment. She was also alone. She'd been adamant about that. She wanted to meet Ward alone, just the two of them, at least for one day. So her parents had stayed in Portland, his at their homes. A cousin and his wife were watching Adrian.

The plane was taxiing now, turning toward her. It rolled to a stop and the door opened.

Two airmen pushed long, metallic steps up to the belly of the beast. And there he was. He appeared out of the dark interior like a figure out of a movie poster. He was in his officer's uniform, his clothes sharp, his hat dapper.

She waited. They had told her to wait, but every cell in her body wanted to break through that invisible barrier.

He was hobbling, clinging to the rail to make it down the steps, using a cane to steady himself. When he finally hit the ground, he limped, his face bright with a smile. He leaned heavily on his cane, but with his free hand, he waved. Barbara could wait no longer. She stepped first. Then again. A walk, then a jog, then a sprint. She ran until that thread between them, that invisible connection through time and space, shrunk to the point of invisibility.

Ward cast aside his cane. And the two of them, at long last, embraced.

• • •

In the backseat of the taxi, Ward sighed as Barbara leaned her head against his shoulder and wrapped her arm around his chest. For Ward, it was a sensation of strange warmth. Was he here? Was she holding him? They hadn't said a word, except that she told him she had arranged for a taxi and a hotel room. In silence, her touch was enough. Her smell. The tickle of her hair against his throat. Time and space seemed meaningless in that moment—a construction of humanity that limited others, but not them, not then.

They glided over the Bay Bridge. Its expanse was beyond comprehension. At another time, Ward would have paused to take in the marvel, the light, the views of the San Francisco Bay and the water all around him. But not now. Only one thing mattered, and he held her so tight he feared he might break her.

"Where are we going?" he finally asked.

"Oh, you'll see," she said.

"You're not going to tell me?"

She didn't answer. On they drove. Ward felt a contentment he hadn't felt in . . . years? Ever? Barbara continued to snuggle into his shoulder, shifting her head this way and that as if she couldn't get close enough. Just the feel of her made his heart pound.

Eventually, as if no time had passed at all, the taxi squealed to a stop. Barbara jumped out first, guiding Ward by the hand, refusing to let him go. Within minutes, they were checked in. It was the fanciest hotel Ward had ever seen. They reached their room and flung open the door.

Before they crossed the threshold, Ward wrapped his arm around Barbara's waist. He looked in her eyes, and she didn't even blink. "What is it?" she said.

Ward distanced himself from her, just a touch, not too much, enough to reach into his pocket and pull out his handmade cross. He lifted Barbara's hand, set it in her palm, then closed her fingers around it.

She looked up, quizzically.

For the first time in as long as he could remember, he let tears flood his eyes. "I have so much to tell you," he said.

Barbara guided Ward into the room. He let her.

She cupped his chin, gently rubbing his cheek. "We're the only ones here," she said, closing the door.

CHAPTER 45

Many months later, Ward received a letter. He had been trying for weeks to determine the fate of his friend. The fog of war was thick, confusing. At times, it seemed so random. The two American men he had been in a pit with—Thomas Ward and Lester McPherson—had actually been released. They didn't even have to escape. Ward had learned about them after news broke of his miraculous escape, and they'd read his story in the papers. Each of them, separately, had reached out to tell him how happy they were he had survived.

But Jae Pil. He seemed to have vanished; it was as if he had never even existed. What Ward had discovered was that Jae Pil had been transferred to a South Korean unit, out of United States control. From there, his trail had turned cold. It was unacceptable. The man deserved a medal, a reward. Ward had been working ever since to make that happen. But at every turn, all he found were Americans who had never heard of the man.

Finally, some news. Ward tore open the letter and read.

> *Dear Captain Millar:*
>   *Enclosed herewith is a copy of the statement made by*
> *Jae Pil Kim, as transcribed by personnel of my headquarters.*

Please read the attached statement and advise of the truth and accuracy of his story. I would appreciate your preparing an affidavit concerning the veracity of Kim's statements as related herein and returning the affidavit to me as soon as possible. If Kim's story is true, it is my desire to help him in any way in recognition of his services and assistance to a downed American pilot.

Sincerely,
S. E. Anderson
Lieutenant General, USAF Commander

Ward set the letter aside. He allowed the smallest tear to escape before he wiped it away. Within seconds, he was preparing the affidavit.

• • •

Jae Pil stood before an empty plot of land in Seoul. It was here his spirit had seemed to rest. It was here he would honor his family.

The last many months had been a sort of personal journey through the underworld for him. The Americans had treated him well, but his fellow countrymen, the South Korean army, became convinced he was a spy. They had sent him to the Geoje Island POW camp, run by the United Nations. That would have been fine except that the UN lacked proper control of the facility. Except for major security issues, the camp was essentially run by Koreans. There were two groups: the Communist sympathizer prisoners and the South Korean guards.

Neither group accepted Jae Pil. The Communists had accused him of treason and treachery. On more than one occasion, they had cornered and beaten him. The guards were no better—they didn't believe his story. Far too many Communists had pretended to be defectors only to turn out to be spies. They had beaten him as well.

For months he had endured this. Still, now, looking at the plot of land, he felt the wounds, the aches in his arms and back. He figured they would probably never leave him entirely. Such was the world: *And ye shall hear of wars and rumours of wars: see that ye be not troubled: for all these things must come to pass, but the end is not yet. For nation shall rise against nation, and kingdom against kingdom: and there shall be famines, and pestilences, and earthquakes, in divers places. All these are the beginning of sorrows.*

The beginning of sorrows, Jae Pil thought, his mind on his lost family. But the beginning of friendships as well. For it was his friend that had finally delivered him. The Americans had come looking. At first, they didn't believe his story, but Captain Millar had verified it. Every word. The good American, now back in his homeland, had been urging the United States to give Jae Pil a reward for some time.

Jae Pil had resisted. He didn't deserve a reward for simply trying to escape, even if he helped an American along the way. But Ward Millar was persuasive. The gift had come: a combination house and store in Seoul and a sizeable amount of money.

Jae Pil had taken some of the money and purchased gifts for Ward and his family. He had mailed those and was on his way back to his house.

Then his thoughts had turned to his family. He still hadn't found them. He didn't expect he ever would. The war was ending, both sides stalemated, staring at each across the same line the North had crossed in the first instance. It all seemed so pointless. Jae Pil took comfort that he wasn't alone. His was the fate of millions of Korean families—the last casualties of the great world war. If they had to wait for reunification, at least they could wait together.

Many nights, while in prison, he had considered how he might honor his family. Now, looking at this plot of land, he knew. It was carpeted with a grass so lustrous it looked like a piece of fine cloth. When he had happened upon it, the ground had practically spoken to him. A breeze had developed; the sun warmed patches of the grass in an almost playful pattern. He walked forward, hesitantly. It was almost as if he didn't belong here, that he was profaning a place of sacred quietude, but the moment his feet touched the soft blades, they seemed to embrace him, welcoming him.

Here, he would use the money to construct a church. It would be the building he had started so long ago with his grandfather, father, mother, and sister. He would build his church, their church. And he would wait for them.

AFTERWORD

W ard and Barbara Millar built a successful life together. They had four more children, three daughters and a son. Ward took a position at the Pentagon in intelligence and thrived in his career. His experience changed him, although perhaps only Barbara noticed the subtle differences; he was a bit more reserved, pensive. But he never treated her any differently. He would often tell his children: "There is meaning in everything." He and Barbara remained happily married until his death in 1999.

Ward Millar enjoying his first meal after escape

Ward, Barbara, and Adrian Millar shortly after his return

Kim Jae Pil continued to build his church in South Korea and remained dedicated to it and his family. He eventually married and raised a family of his own. His faith never wavered. As for his mother, father, sister, and grandfather, he never saw them again. That was the plight of millions of Koreans after the North's invasion. To this day, many families look forward to reunification.

Kim Jae Pil receiving award

Kim Jae Pil, his wife, and baby

AUTHOR'S NOTE

Over two decades ago, after I had spent time living in Korea, I returned home with a desire to tell a story about the country, its people, and its unique culture. In doing research, I found myself in the lowest level of a university library, where I found, amidst dozens of other books about Korea, a long-out of-print memoir about a pilot who had crash-landed during the Korean War, broken both his ankles, then escaped alongside a North Korean Christian.

The story was obscure, unknown to far too many people. For twenty years, I've longed to bring it to life.

When the opportunity finally arose, I sought out both families. Although Ward Millar and Kim Jae Pil had both passed away, their widows and children were still alive and provided valuable information. I'm grateful to them. They have shared details I couldn't have otherwise found.

As for this book itself, I faced a dilemma: keep it purely nonfiction or make it a novel based on the true story. I opted for the latter, which allowed me a bit more control over narrative pace and the number of characters to manage. The vast majority of what I have written, however, is true. In some places, I consolidated multiple people into one character. Lieutenant Kang, for example, is a composite of many people Ward dealt with during his captivity. In other places, I needed to skip some events or conversations, just to keep the story moving. Finally, I added dialogue to flesh out characters or issues, but never in a way that strayed from the research.

Aside from those minor deviations, I was able to follow the actual events as they occurred. A good rule of thumb for the reader is this: the more unbelievable the detail or anecdote, the more likely it is actually true. Ward did indeed crash and break both of his ankles upon ejection; Kim Jae Pil did get drafted, escape, and was redrafted. Barbara Millar was in fact as determined as I've portrayed her. Jae Pil and Ward met on a hillside exactly as I've described, and their escape was just as miraculous as I've detailed it. I'm grateful to both of them and their families.

ACKNOWLEDGMENTS

First and foremost, my wife and children deserve more gratitude than I can give. Any time I write a book, my mind becomes consumed by the content and the deadlines. Even when I'm not actively drafting, I'm a bit more stressed than I should be. They are always supportive, quick to give advice or to pick up the slack around the house. Quite literally, this book would not be a reality without them. And, Jerusha, when I write of love and connection, you are my inspiration. I need only think of us for the words to flow.

Many of the details of this book would not have been possible without the tremendous assistance of Barbara Millar and Adrian Shelton. In her mid-nineties, enjoying the fruits of a life well-spent, Barbara is as feisty and sharp as ever. She didn't need to meet with me, but she agreed to sit down for hours of conversations over two days, for which I'm grateful. For her part, Adrian opened up her home and her mother to me, trusting me with material that was precious to the family. I know how difficult that can be, and I hope I've lived up to the trust they've shown me. She also endured multiple follow-up calls, texts, and emails, and then provided an invaluable review of the manuscript.

Adrian's brother Rand provided a similar review of the manuscript, leading to many important changes. I'm thankful to him.

As for connecting with Kim Jae Pil's family, I could never have done it without the help of my dear friend Jeemin Chung. When I first reached out to her to see if she might help me track down the family of a relatively unknown man in Korea, I figured the chances of finding anything were close to zero. She responded in less than a day with a goldmine, then helped me with interviews, manuscript review, cover design feedback, and general cultural advice. She is a genius. More importantly, she is a wonderful human being, mother, spouse, and friend. I'm also appreciative to film director Jung Sueun, who proved to be an invaluable bridge to the family of Kim Jae Pil and who selflessly provided me a great deal of information about Jae Pil, his story, his survival, and his family. I'm also thankful to Jae Pil's family for trusting an American with their story.

My research assistant, James Sutherland, found details about North Korea that proved crucial to understanding the conditions Jae Pil faced and the persecution inflicted by North Korea.

No book would be complete without beta readers. To Taani Secrist, Tonya Wendell, Sandra Garcia, and Jennifer Sutherland: thank you for the feedback. It is more valuable than you know.

Finally, I'm grateful for Chris Schoebinger, Lisa Mangum, Leslie Stitt, Janna DeVore, Troy Butcher, and the entire Shadow Mountain team. Your professionalism, promotion, editorial advice, thoughtfulness, and support are beyond compare. I'm grateful I get to work with you.